A King Production presents…

A NOVEL

JOY DEJA KING
AND *Michelle Monay*

This novel is a work of fiction. Any references to real people, events, establishments, or locales are intended only to give the fiction a sense of reality and authenticity. Other names, characters, and incidents occurring in the work are either the product of the author's imagination or are used fictitiously, as those fictionalized events and incidents that involve real persons. Any character that happens to share the name of a person who is an acquaintance of the author, past or present, is purely coincidental and is in no way intended to be an actual account involving that person.

ISBN 13: 978-0984332588
ISBN 10: 0984332588
Cover concept by Joy Deja King & www.MarionDesigns.com
Cover layout and graphic design by www.MarionDesigns.com
Cover Model: Shanel Nelson
Typesetting: Keith Saunders
Editors: Joy Deja King and Linda Williams

Library of Congress Cataloging-in-Publication Data;
A King Production
Mafia Princess/by Joy Deja King & Michelle Monay
For complete Library of Congress Copyright info visit;
www.joydejaking.com

A KING PRODUCTION

A King Production
P.O. Box 912, Collierville, TN 38027

A King Production and the above portrayal log are trademarks of
A King Production LLC

Dedication

This Book is Dedicated To My:
Family, Readers and Supporters.
I LOVE you guys so much. Please believe that!!
—Joy Deja King

   This book is dedicated to everyone from the struggle that is determined to make it to the top. Know that all things are possible if you just stay on your grind and work hard!!!!!! Also, to my wonderful mother Tonya Cole, great job on raising me to be a determined and respected young lady. Mommy we have seen the bottom so there is only one other way to go!! Thanks for everything!!

   —Michelle Monay

A KING PRODUCTION

MAFIA
Princess

A NOVEL

JOY DEJA KING
AND *Michelle Monay*

Prologue

THE SETUP

In the ghetto there are two kinds of street chicks: slut chicks and gutta chicks. If labeled the latter that meant you were on your A-game in the 'hood, fitting Semaj's guise naturally. As she lay snuggled in Gabe's strong arms on the king-sized bed, Semaj smiled inwardly. Gabe was knocked out from the pussy she'd put on him. She glanced at the digital clock atop the nightstand. For the last hour she'd slyly observed the red illuminating numbers change on the dial in anticipation of what was to come.

Just as midnight turned into the one 'o clock hour the sounds of "*CLICK-CLACK*" startled the light sleeper and for dramatic effect, Semaj screamed fearfully.

Instinctively, Gabe went underneath his pillow, and frantically began to search for his weapon. It was an empty space, which he found rather odd. He always slept with his ratchet within reach, but he had realized that he'd left it inside the dresser drawer due to Semaj's persistent request.

"You already know what time it is, fam! Where?" the intruder said calmly as he pointed the barrel of the AK-47 in between the two.

"Where what, man?" Gabe's eyes bugged wide in shock.

"Don't play with me, son. Fuck is the cash at, my man?"

"I don't keep nothing here, B. Shit's at another spot."

"Now this nigga playing games. It's at another spot, huh?" Murder Mitch said disbelievingly. "So you gon' keep playin' wit'me, nigga?"

"On some real shit, I don't keep shit here." Gabe shrugged his shoulders. "There's nothing in the house."

Murder Mitch's patience was running thin and he was not there to play games. Abruptly the sound of a gun's blast erupted. Murder Mitch had sent a bullet an inch above Gabe's head, causing the wood to splinter down the middle. "Don't think you wanna keep playin' around with me, playboy. Take me to the stash." Murder Mitch pressed the hot barrel to Gabe's chest.

Semaj's body shuddered violently as if she was desperately afraid, but the moment she noticed a silhouette in her peripheral view her fright became a serious fear. The moving shadow was approaching with a pistol in hand, and at that instant, Semaj locked eyes with the foreigner. She had to warn her father. "Who is that?" she asked, her heart galloping in uncertainty. Before words could be exchanged, Murder Mitch swiftly shifted his aim. The guy never saw it coming and a slug had been introduced to his head, sending mucus and brain splatter spraying throughout the hallway.

"What the fuck?" Gabe roared in devastation. He knew that he was in deep shit.

Murder Mitch had had enough of the bullshit and sliced the side of Gabe's face with the knife on the AK-47, causing it to instantly swell up and bleed. Gabe grunted and winced in excruciating pain. "Now, I know I ain't gotta ask again, my man." Murder Mitch said calmly. The insane glare in his eyes was indication that he was itching to let bullets pierce the flesh.

"Shoebox in that closet!" Gabe said, willing to give up his money in trade for Semaj's safety. If Semaj weren't involved he would have spit in his face, not giving the stick-up kid the satisfaction of robbing him; he would have died for his no doubt. But more was at stake…Semaj.

"You grab the money for me," Murder Mitch said coldly as he held Gabe at gunpoint and tossed his daughter a knapsack. As instructed, Semaj scuffled over to the closet. She retrieved the money from the Timberland shoebox and a brick of coke that was wrapped in tubes, resembling small fingers. She stuffed the dope and the money into the knapsack. Semaj handed her father the bagful of goods as he backpedaled out of the room, continuing to have the weapon trained on Gabe.

Something told Murder Mitch to put a hot one in him, but it was as if Semaj were speaking through her eyes and nixed the notion. Easing out of the room, he said threateningly. "Don't move for sixty seconds." He stepped over the fresh corpse as if it was litter on a city street and exited the house.

The daughter and father had accomplished another street robbery, but for some reason an eerie feeling passed over Semaj. Something in her bones felt wrong, and she wanted nothing more than to get out of there. *Damn! We were supposed to play this shit smart not reckless*, she thought. *I ain't know nobody else was even here.*

Gabe wasn't willing to helplessly watch as the stick-up kid got away without an attempt to take his life. Instantly, he popped up and grabbed his .357 chrome Magnum. Semaj held the solemn expression that crossed her face as Gabe left out of the room enraged. He stepped onto the porch, but it was too late. The car was long gone.

Ten minutes later

Gabe hopelessly paced back and forth inside the living room as the human waste was becoming unbearable. The stench had come from the empty bowels from the dead body and the blood mixture. It wasn't the excessive stink that bothered him though. It was the body, the missing drugs and the money. To owe Gio was to start making funeral arrangements for yourself. Not to mention a dead relative. What looked to be a good come-up turned into a bad situation.

The man had been sent by the notorious Dominican drug boss to deliver him a brick of cocaine via his bowels. The plane had landed that night and he was supposed to do the job, stay overnight and then head back home. Nobody knew that he would no longer be returning. Gabe was hesitant to dial the number he'd been given in case of an emergency. But he knew Gio would find out one way or another, so he manned up and dialed the headman.

"What's the problem, Gabe?" a voice with a thick Dominican accent said.

"Your nephew is dead. Some nigga ran into my spot, but—"

Gio cut him off mid-sentence. "You know I told my family that I could trust you. I vouched for you. Now you are telling me that my family is dead?"

"It's fucked up." Gabe wanted to be apologetic, but with a man like Gio, an apology was no good. He had sent his nephew down out of trust. When that line was broken so was their business relationship and things would only turn deadly.

"You know I have to bury my nephew into the dirt while you remain on earth, Gabe," Gio said as his voice became more aggressive and assertive with each word. "We will meet again, my friend." He hung up.

A piercing scream followed and Gabe's phone collided with the flat screen plasma TV, causing it to split down the center. Gabe threw things around the room violently and fought himself. He frantically grabbed his head and paced the room, fuming. "Word to my mutha, I'm gonna murder everybody that's associated to the people that set me up! I'ma find out who was behind this shit, son!"

Semaj felt her body temperature rise as her heart began to beat erratically. The sounds of shouting and rattling blared loudly in her ears, sending a twinge up her spine. Her chest became tight as she fidgeted nervously. *I hope I don't look like a suspect,* she thought as her breathing became deep—very deep—panicked.

Finally after his rage subsided, Gabe scuttled into the bedroom. "We gotta get the fuck out of Dodge! Ain't no tellin' when them slick hair muthafuckas gon' come gunning for my head!" He grabbed as much as he could before they fled from the apartment.

Chapter 1

The club filled quickly as New York's street prestige walked through the door prepared to celebrate the grand opening of Big Pat's strip joint. Everybody who was anybody came out to bring in New Year's Eve with Big Pat and his entourage. A big time hustler, everyone knew who he was. Big Pat and his team were stationed in the glass-skybox that overlooked the club on the third level. Bottles of champagne flowed freely at their table and butt naked strippers danced for the 'hood's elite. The VIP area was full of New York's finest and the only people allowed up were the privileged. Big Pat smirked as he sipped his bubbly and stood amongst his circle. In New York, Big Pat was like a celebrity. It was his town. Everything about him rang old money too. Dope Money…Dirty Money…Blood Money.

Observing as people poured in, Big Pat focused his attention on the brown-skinned beauty and admired her from afar.

Semaj turned heads as she walked through the crowd and he loved how she had instantly stolen his attention. Her red Prada dress looked as if it were painted on her five feet seven frame, showing off her thick thighs and long legs, and the ostrich thigh high boots made her shine like a rock star in a crowd full of duds. Her hair was pulled up high, in a loose ponytail, and her soft baby hair rested flawlessly around her edges. Everything from her eyebrows to her French-pedicured toes was on point and the attention she was getting let her know she had put herself together right.

Envious glares were trained on Semaj as she and Tala made their way up to the bi-level VIP longue. They found a table by the rails, overlooking the live crowd. Semaj could feel the intense stares too, but she wasn't tripping. She was one breed that women loved to hate. But one thing about Semaj, she knew it and understood why. *If these bitches only knew, I'm not here to try to get their nigga. If anything, I'ma hit that stash and send that nigga right back to ya ass,* she laughed inwardly.

"Let me get a glass of Moscato and a bottle of Louie Xlll, the 50 milliliter bottle." Semaj said to the waitress. She ordered the glass just to be extra. Her robbery money was consistent, so she was good and she showed out wherever she went. "It's for all the thirsty bitches lookin' like they wanna fuck a bitch or somethin'." She and Tala shared in laughter.

"Think you mean you'll have a glass of the Louie too. Because the bottle is five hundred plus," the waitress replied with an attitude.

Semaj wasn't the type of woman that bickered. She simply reached inside her designer clutch and pulled out one thousand dollars. Peeling off six hundred dollars, all Grants, she said with a cute smirk, "No, I mean bottle, but thanks for clarifying. Now can you get the Louie and my glass of Moscato?" The waitress didn't even bother to respond and stomped off.

"Why do bitches always seem to be mad? Gotdamn!" Tala exclaimed.

"They ain't comfortable in their own skin. It's just in their damn nature to be angry with the next broad. That's the only explanation I can give for these ratchet ass hoes, auntie." Semaj flung her ponytail. "But I'ma enjoy my birthday. Feel me?" She waited patiently and watched as everyone in VIP got their drink and smoke on.

"Here's *your* glass of Moscato and bottle of Louie," the rude waitress said after finally returning with Semaj's order. She removed an ice-filled bucket from the tray along with her request and placed everything on the table. "That will be $594.00, even," Ms. Attitude said holding her hand out, as if the money wasn't already in front of her.

Semaj snickered, finding the chick comical. She simply picked up the small stack of bills from the table and then smacked the money inside of her sweaty palm. While the waitress counted the money, Semaj popped the cork off the bottle and passed it to Tala.

"And… umm, Big Pat said come up to VIP. He wanna holla at you," Ms. Attitude spat as her nostrils flared wider with each word spoken.

"Who is Big Pat and what he want with me?" Semaj asked as she wrinkled her brow in confusion.

"Girl, you know exactly who Big Pat is. Don't act like you don't. Please!" she said in annoyance. "Everybody and they momma know that nigga. Don't be cute."

"Sorry, but I'm not everybody and their momma," Semaj retorted.

"I'll make sure to let him know you're uninterested."

"Yeah, you do that," Semaj said as Ms. Attitude turned to walk off. "Ay, but sweetie," she called out behind the waitress.

She spun around before responding and thought to herself, *groupie bitch knew she was happy I mentioned Big Pat from jump. Acting all snobbish and shit.* "What's up?"

"You forgot my change!" Semaj smiled, holding her hand out.

She stared at Semaj long faced as though she was speaking a foreign language. Tala looked at the waitress, and then back at her niece and burst into a fit of laughter. The shit was too funny. "Bitch, you are fuckin' petty."

"What? No, I'm not. This broad wanna twist and pop her neck every which way. She ain't gettin' shit from me but what I owe her which don't include a tip."

Digging inside the apron, Ms. Attitude pulled out six crumpled dollar bills. She put them on the table, rolled her eyes and walked off pissed.

"Damn I know she hot. That's what her ass get though. But did she say that Big Pat wanted you?"

"Sure did. I wonder what that's about." Semaj said, scanning the club. She knew that the girl was right about her knowing exactly who Big Pat was. Who didn't? He had the streets on lock and ran a very lucrative drug business.

"You know his old, fat ass probably try'na take you home tonight. You know how they say he do."

"Nigga surely don't want me to be the choice of the night. He won't have a home to come to fuckin' around with me," Semaj joked, but was serious.

"We came out to enjoy ourselves, not searching for potential victims. Damn girl! Take a night off. Ain't you chillin' tonight," Tala stated seriously.

"You know I ain't passing up an opportunity. Feel me?"

"Already know." Tala was too familiar with her niece's intentions and deceitful tactics.

"But watch how I work this stunt though. School's in session, so take some notes. You just might learn something from the G!" They both cracked up laughing and then Semaj smiled cunningly. She wondered how the game would play itself out tonight.

The girls sat modestly as they watched the crowd grow thicker and they partied like socialites. It was just a little after midnight and unsurprisingly the club had reached its capacity. At that moment, Semaj noticed her father cashing security out for admission. "Mitch's ass always lurking," Tala said as she spotted Murder Mitch easing his way into a booth in the corner. He was so far back that he was almost hidden by the shadows of the abandoned section of the club. All of the other partygoers were crowded around the stage while Murder Mitch was scoping out the scene, trying to be as inconspicuous as possible.

Just then a tall dark skinned guy approached them. "You in the red, my boy said come holla at him up in the VIP."

"If you want my attention, then say excuse me. But if your boy wanna holla at me," she pointed her forefinger at herself and then at him, "Why is he sending you to do his job? What you his spokesman or some shit?"

"Nah," he sucked his teeth. "It ain't shit like that. He just up in VIP. He ain't try'na get tackled coming down here and shit. It's Big Pat. You know how that shit be. We move different from the average nigga."

"Knows nothing about that, my man. But this what you can do for me. Tell your boy if he try'na get at me, he know where I am. There's no need to send other niggas. We all grown here. I'll be here for a li'l while longer though," she faked a huge smile.

"Dammmmn! You just cut like that huh? I see you got ya swag thang going," he laughed, finding her rare response amusing. "But I'ma be sure to tell the nigga what's up."

"You do that," Semaj said as he turned to walk off.

"Nigga just don't know he walkin' his self into a fuckin' fucked-up trap. Stupid niggas a holla at anybody with a pretty face." Tala shook her head. She'd seen it all one too many times.

"Don't hate," Semaj laughed. "This my shit right here, Tala." She stood up with the bottle in her hand. She graciously moved back and forth to the hip-hop tunes. It was cute how Semaj was so gorgeous as if she stepped out of *Elle* magazine, but was bopping to Gucci Mane as though she was nothing but street, and street she was.

"Kick a door nigga… kick a door nigga… everybody… everybody on the floor nigga!" she chuckled, chanting along to the lyrics. *"On the low dawg… I'm cutthroat, nigga…"* She hoodishly but femininely grooved to the beat.

"Damn, I really had to travel all the way down here huh?" a male voice behind her said.

Already knowing it had to be the infamous Big Pat, she decided to immediately put her plan into motion. Playing a role, Semaj quickly glanced back at him and replied, "I mean it was your choice." She stepped a foot forward as if she was uninterested. Semaj knew trying to play the hard-to-get role was chancy, but she didn't care because in most cases it was the payoff.

Big Pat chuckled, knowing she couldn't know who he was. "A man like me never has to come to anybody, everybody comes to me," he whispered in her ear smugly. "Want you come and chill with me and my peoples in VIP? It's exclusively for us. It's my birthday, so we doin' it real big up top."

"How ironic. It's my birthday also," Semaj continued to slowly sway her mid-section as she overlooked the crowd.

"How old you turn?" he asked with a charming smile.

"I'm twenty-two," she responded.

"That's what's up! Come up and kick it with me and my entourage. It's a celebration"

"Thanks for the offer, but I'm no groupie. I'm good." Semaj still was throwing shade and had barely given him any face. She was half-glancing him to death and placed her attention back to the animated crowd below her.

"I can tell that. And that's what I like about you. So can I get a name?"

"And why do you want my name? Big Pat is it?" she questioned, her Brooklyn accent rolling off thick. "You can get at any girl in here I'm sure. Being that you have spokespeople, I assume you are the man around here."

He laughed at her as he rubbed his goatee. "I see you an ol' comedian or something. You got jokes."

"Seriously. You got people coming down here like I was 'pose to know you. Who are you really?" Semaj questioned, glancing back at him.

"Patrick is my name. Yours?" He gently grabbed her arm and turned her around to face him.

"Now that's much better." It was now game time. Time to seem interested. "Nice to meet you Patrick. My name is Ashley." Semaj decided to go with her gut instinct and gave him a fake name. "Now what is it that you want with me?"

"Everything," he replied.

"Everything?"

"Come chill with me up top. We can discuss more up there."

"Nah, me and my girl was finna bounce in a few minutes. I gotta go to work in the morning," she lied, but it was all a part of her plan.

"What somebody as fine as you doing working?" Big Pat asked. "See, if you was with a nigga like me you wouldn't know what it felt like to work."

"That's corny bum shit," she shot with a smirk. "And for the record, I'm independent. I make my own paper, baby."

"I respect that shit," Big Pat grinned, finding this woman to be a piece of work. Running the streets he had dealt with all sorts of women but it was just something different about this one right here, something intriguing. "Why don't you leave with me tonight? I'll make up for your paycheck."

"Sorry. Not a one-night stander or none of that, babes. I'm not into going to hotels, traps, or none of that desperate shit. For a guy of your suppose caliber," Semaj said sarcastically. "You just pick random girls up at the club frequently?"

"I see you just gon' give me a hard time."

"No doubt. What you thought I was going to be easy?"

"Nah. Fo'real, I done already deciphered your persona. You rare, I can admit that. So going to the hotel and one-nighting you ain't happening. Where I lay my head comfortably is where you'll be. Trust. So you leavin' with me?" he asked confidently.

"Sorry, but I don't leave the club with dudes that I don't know. That's not my persona either," she stated as she shifted all her weight on one leg, giving her hips an enticing shape. Semaj was a professional in the area of sizing a nigga up, and knew she had dude right where she wanted him to be. If the streets required a degree, she'd already graduated summa cum laude. "I'll give you my number though. Maybe when I get off work tomorrow we can go out somewhere. That's if that's cool with you, you know."

Big Pat stared at her intensely. He was astounded.

Semaj was really holding her own. Her behavior was of a woman that had respect for herself, the type of female you would consider courting. She appeared harmless, lovable, innocent, but in actuality, all Semaj knew was harm and she had lost her innocence as a child. It was a shame what the world had turned her into. She was a con artist and a very manipulative woman. She was untrustworthy and had been for a very long time.

"No doubt, ma. I'm feelin' that." He pulled out his BlackBerry and handed it to her. She stored her number and handed the phone back to him. "I'ma get up wit' you tomorrow evening some time."

Semaj graciously nodded her head as she said, "C'mon, Tala." She purposely set the half of bottle of Louie atop the table. She walked out of the VIP lounge and down the wraparound stairs. Big Pat watched from the railing as she left the building, just as she knew he would. *I got him,* she thought silently as she exited the club all the while texting her father their next potential victim.

Chapter 2

"*Damn, Semaj you really throwing nigga shade when shit get fucked up and a nigga lockdown. But before it was all good. You was lovin' everything about me, huh? That's fucked up on some real shit. I showed you love and now you can't return the love. It's cool 'cause you ain't gotta let me borrow the bond money and I'ma still bounce back quick.*

Mu'fuckas tellin' me you had that Big Pat nigga all up in ya ear last night. Since my money ain't long no more and I'm out of sight, I'm out of mind too, huh? You going to the next baller huh? That's why I don't fuck wit' you bougie 'hood bitches. Fuck you, cause you ain't shit!. Try'na not answer my muthafuckin' calls," Gabe said on her voicemail as she listened to the message for the second time and hung up.

"Tala, tell me if I'm trippin' and this just ain't no clown shit this nigga on, ma," Semaj chuckled, finding the voice message ridiculously silly. She walked up to the mirror that sat above her mantelpiece and began fixing her hair.

"Girl, that's his ass on there, pissed as shit that you cut his ass off and leaving him in there."

"I don't know why he mad at me. Nigga need to be mad at his muthafuckin' self. I ain't no gotdamn charity. Like seriously, dude betta go on 'head wit' all that bull. Can you believe that nigga though?"

"Hell yeah! Bitch you're the reason he broke and can't bond out. And I heard money on that nigga and his family's head."

Looking over at Tala, Semaj scrunched her face into a scowl. "I see you got jokes, bitch. Funny!" she turned around hastily, faking a smile full of sarcasm and resumed back to pulling her hair into a high ponytail. "He don't know that shit. He'll never think that it was me that had my daddy run up into his crib. Fuck it!" she hunched her shoulders. "It ain't my fault the nigga only had thirty grand to his name and a brick and went to jail a week later. Hell, all the talkin' and splurgin' he used to do, you would've thought he was that nigga 'round these parts, Ta."

"Damn, dude fucked up! I thought you was still gon' fuck with him, though."

"I was gon' still talk to dude but he ran out of money, so there's nothing we can do. Ol' boy can't even take the kid to get a dollar sandwich. I ain't gon' be in the company of no broke ass niggas, flat out. He better be more careful next time. Hey, he in jail on some petty shit anyway. They will O.R. his ass out eventually. But he need to stop callin' me, 'cause I ain't got nothin' for his ass. Niggas got the game fucked up," she sighed.

Semaj let the words roll off her tongue freely not caring she sounded cutthroat. Shit, she was cutthroat and definitely cut from a different cloth than the average chick seeking handouts. Semaj could see Tala's reflection through the mirror and noticed through her eyes that she was heavily in thought. "Ta, what the heck you thinking 'bout?"

"Fo'real," she sighed. "I'm thinking about getting back into this game wit' you man. My money is damn near on, E, and you know I ain't used to that shit. But then I think about Zyden and don't be on it."

"Is it that heavy? 'Cause you know I can front you some bread."

"Nah, I ain't dead broke. I just can't spend how I use to spend and my expenses are steady rising while my money decreasing. I feel like I got two options: fuck 'round with y'all or start running dope. Paris dude was asking Mercedes to be a transporter for him for a thousand a brick. I was thinking 'bout tellin' the nigga I'd do it."

"So why didn't you?"

"Shit, it's tempting. But then I thought about it and we all know the risk is way higher these days wit' that shit than how you get down."

"I know, right."

"Hell yeah. I'ma have to figure out something though before I really be needing you to front me some dough."

"Why don't you just use some of the money D-Boy stashed away before he went to prison?"

"Girl, you must be crazy! Dude get out of jail and find a dollar missing he'd be ready to kill me."

"Just put it back once you find your new hustle," Semaj suggested.

12

"Or stage a robbery one day when he calls so you ain't gotta pay shit back."

The duo's conversation was cut short due to Tala's blaring phone. "What up, Paris?"

"Ta, I just pulled up at Mercedes house and that nigga is out here beating brakes off her ass again. You better come get your son. Li'l nigga scared to death man. Shaking and shit."

"I'm on my way. Good looking." Tala slid into her kicks. "Bitch, we gotta go. You can just drop me off at home after I get my son. That dumb ass nigga over there beating Mercedes ass as usual. Disrespectful ass nigga know my muthafuckin' baby there."

"I told you to stop letting her watch him. Should've taken him over Ms. Long's like you always do. I know that's yo' baby daddy sister and all, but fuck that. They fight in front of their own kids. Think they give a fuck 'bout yours?"

"Won't be watching mines no more," Tala made clear as they rushed out of Semaj's brownstone in a Brooklyn suburb.

As Semaj drove up the block the girls saw quite a crowd observing the brawl, and of course the neighbors were out being nosey. It was normal for them to fight like savages in the comfort of their home or outside even, and no one had ever bothered to intervene in their quarrels.

Paris spotted the car coasting up and began walking toward the curb with a diaper bag draping her shoulder. The sleeping baby was inside the car seat interlocked in her inner elbow. "Girl, I got here and Zyden's car seat was on the ground. Li'l man was screaming and hollering." She adjusted the seat belt securely and made sure he was strapped in safely.

"Mercedes like gettin' her ass whooped is what I'm concluding," Semaj said, shaking her head at the way he was stomping a mud hole into her. "Couldn't be me, would've been put that nigga into a permanent sleep. Paris, you ain't gon' help your best friend?"

"That's on her dumb ass. I done told her to leave that sorry ass nigga alone and she ain't learned yet. Every time I done helped her, she goes right back to the nigga. Ain't no sense in it."

"I know that's right. I don't get into her problems either. Shit, in the end she gon' be right back with his lame ass and mad at you," Tala explained, happy that Paris had been there to inform her.

"A'ight though, y'all I'm finna bounce. See y'all later." She headed to the black Audi.

Semaj and Tala watched as Paris made it back to the car where Dean-Bean was waiting for her. Tala could look in her niece's eyes and instantly knew she was scheming on something. "What the fuck you up to now?"

"I m-e-a-n, I was just thinking. Shit, Dean been gettin' that money and you know where the trap at. Daddy can just run up in there and you can get some money from that."

"Maj, hell nah! Dean super cool peoples and you know I ain't down with that shit. Dude low-key and don't fuck wit' nobody. Besides that's D-Boy people."

"What that got to do wit' gettin' to his dough?" Semaj asked as she took one more glance before pulling away from the projects.

"The selfish shit in you is a muthafucka. You don't give a fuck 'bout nobody," Tala chuckled, stating true facts. "But on some real shit, I do need the money. But seriously, we gotta make sure your insane ass dad just rob the nigga with no bodies left behind. That's the only way I'm agreeing, Maj."

"That's not a problem at all. I'ma make sure of that," Semaj said with her mouth. But in actuality, her mind screamed money and she didn't care who was hurt. Hell it's all a part of the game. Her fixation was now on putting her old man on Dean-Bean, and she was determined to collect the green by any means. Between him and Big Pat, Semaj figured they could all make a good come up.

After dropping Tala and the baby off, Semaj headed to the restaurant Big Pat had told her to meet him at. As the sun was transforming into dusk, she new her father was following behind her discreetly, so he could start learning Big Pat's routine.

When Semaj pulled up in front, a valet took her car and she headed inside. When she entered the restaurant, Big Pat was already at the table putting in his order. *Just like a fat fuck*, Semaj thought as she walked towards him. By the way Big Pat's jaw dropped, she knew the food he ordered wasn't the only thing his fat ass was trying to eat tonight. But she understood why he wanted to add her to the menu. Semaj was serving everybody in the restaurant with her Gucci liquid leggings, red snug fitted leather jacket and peep-toe, red bottom ankle boots.

After giving her a lingering stare, Big Pat finally pulled himself together to stand and greet her with a kiss on the cheek. "Damn, ma, you look even prettier than the first time I saw you."

Semaj smiled and replied with a "Thank you" before taking her seat and put in her order for a mouth-watering steak and garlic vegetables.

"I thought you weren't coming since you've been giving me the run-around all week."

She smiled, demurely. "I was just working, and honestly I didn't wanna have our time to end early since I really don't stay out late on work days."

"I'm glad you feeling that way. 'Cause you with me for the night."

Semaj blushed graciously and knew that she was about to add Big Pat to the long list of fools she made a come up off of. It only took one slip-up and once that occurred, her father would step in. After Murder Mitch understood how a nigga operated that's when plans went into motion. But there was one thing Semaj made sure of. She was never willing to encounter anyone her victim knew. It was just too much of a risk. It was best to be in and out to alleviate becoming a suspect.

During dessert, Big Pat received a call. From the way his eyes lit up Semaj assumed it had to be either two things: money or pussy. Since he offered for her to ride with him, she concluded that it was money. She accepted and they headed to some projects in Brownsville. "Baby, I'll be out in three minutes," Big Pat said, as he hopped out and walked towards the trap house.

Damn this shit might be easier than I anticipated, Semaj thought as she watched her father who was parked a few cars behind through the side mirror. This was the perfect opportunity and she knew her father was in the cut, ready for the takings. Just then, Big Pat had emerged with a black duffel bag in hand. Semaj was so caught up in thinking how stupid she thought Big Pat was, she almost missed him pulling his gun from his waist and point it in Murder Mitch direction.

Frantically, Semaj zeroed in on her father to warn him, but it was too late. In a swift moment, Big Pat had filled him with lead before he had seen it coming. Five shots to the chest left Murder Mitch's body jerking as if it was hitting switches on an old school Caddy. Instinctively, Semaj reached for the door handle, but wasn't quick enough. "Bitch, you set me up!" Big Pat roared with the gun pointed in her face threateningly.

Terror traveled up her spine as her heart suddenly plunged to her stomach. Semaj knew that this was her end. She fidgeted in her seat and her nerves were so shot she couldn't respond. *Fuck, fuck, fuck,* her inner thoughts screamed as a solitary tear slipped down her face. His 9mm gun was still meticulously trained on her as he drove off at crazy speeds. The look in her eyes confirmed his suspicions. "Bitch, I'ma kill you. You a scandalous ass bitch," he belted as he hit her with the butt of the gun, dizzying her and causing blood to ooze from her mouth.

Semaj couldn't believe that he had peeped game and popped off his cannons at her father. This was the first time anything like this had transpired and she never imagined that this could be the outcome. *It always was so perfect,* she thought helplessly. Now her father was dead and she was about to meet him at the crossroad.

Big Pat pulled in front of what appeared to be a dilapidated house. He rushed over to the passenger side window and pulled the latch back and forth. When he had exited the vehicle, Semaj quickly hit the locks. "Bitch, open this muthafuckin door!" he screamed as he narrowed his eyes to peer intensely through the pane. She was trapped and there was nowhere to run. He pulled out his gun and tapped the metal against the windowpane, aiming it directly at her head.

She sobbed and knew that either she was going to die voluntarily or involuntarily. Semaj surely wasn't about to make it easier for him. Unlocking the doors and following him inside the abandoned home definitely wouldn't be how she met her maker. If he wanted her, he had to do it there inside his car.

Through his peripheral vision, Big Pat noticed a silhouette and not thinking he aimed his burner in that direction. That made for his first and last mistake, because the figure was on the opposite side and fired rounds into Big Pat's body. The dark figure emptied the entire clip, and in a rapid motion replaced the empty clip with a fully reloaded magazine. Although he was already dead, for extra measures, bullets continued to riddle his body, leaving Big Pat on the side of the curb dead as he looked up to the sky with his eyes still open.

Pulling the black hoodie from his head, Semaj looked shocked at her father's breathing body. She just witnessed Big Pat let off cannons into him, and not even fifteen minutes later the same thing was recurring with the opposite opponent being the gunman. Semaj thought she was hallucinating until her father banged on the window frantically, demanding her to open the door so they could flee. Confiscating the duffle bag that lay beside the fresh corpse, they hopped into the car and Semaj skirted off dangerously as her father removed the bulletproof vest.

"Daddy, I thought you were dead!" she cried, softly. "I thought I was going to die!"

Murder Mitch knew the dangers that came with his treacherous profession so for protection he always tried to wear a bulletproof vest and luckily for him that decision turned out to be a lifesaver. "You my baby girl and I'll always protect you, Maj. Nigga slipped up and thought he murked me. That fucked you up, huh?"

"Yeah. Just knew it was lights out for us, Daddy," Semaj sighed in relief as she swiftly wiped her tears away. "We got that money, though!" she laughed it off, knowing sometimes while maneuvering in the streets things went wrong, but there was no turning back. They were already addicted to the stick-up game.

Chapter 3

Fourteen Years Earlier

For the longest Semaj's life was one that most every little girl would dream of. Her upbringing wasn't the typical black girls from the inner city. Semaj's story was different, but also similar to some. Her mother Kasey had been born into a family of drug lords and murderers. She was the daughter of one of the most powerful drug lords that had ever done it. Due to her family's notoriety she had been sheltered. But Kasey was a rebellious child and wanted to be involved in all of her father's dirty work. She used to sneak in the private meetings that were held in the small conference rooms. She even rode around with her father in the limo and listened intensively as he discussed drug business.

Her father didn't want this life for his baby girl but he knew it came natural to his daughter. It was in her blood and there was nothing he could do about it. Her stint in the family business began when she turned sixteen and started delivering packages all over New York. Then shortly after, it escalated to trafficking drugs on the highway interstates and then flying overseas to the Dominican Republic to pick up bricks from the main suppliers. By the age of eighteen, she was trained to empty her bowels once she touched baseline. Kasey was elated with her lifestyle and the dope game gave her a rush. Her father was her first love and she did any and everything for the family business, bringing them in millions upon millions.

Kasey's life forever changed the day she met Mitchell "Murder Mitch" Richardson. Murder Mitch was a well-paid hit man for her family. From the moment Kasey met Murder Mitch he had the "Warning, Do Not Enter" sign written all over him. But Kasey was one to always disobey the warning signs, and the two fell in love almost immediately. Although her father had broken the no interracial dating tradition when he had his son with an African American woman, he loathed that his only daughter had fallen head over heels for Murder Mitch, the daring black murder machine.

He was the head henchman for the family on the streets, the most notorious and prosperous in body count that New York had ever seen. He eliminated everything from the highest prominent individuals to the low-level block boys and even their children. Politicians and pulpit preachers even got touched, and he was known as the killer unseen. Because though his name rang bells like an international superstar, his face was unknown. His slick murder-for-hire tactics got the job done as if he worked for the secret service, erasing any trace linking back to him.

Kasey's refusal to suppress her feelings towards Murder Mitch and their unwavering commitment to each other gave her father the strength to give them his blessings. He knew no other man besides Murder Mitch could protect his daughter, and he hoped that he wouldn't regret his decision.

Nine months into the relationship Kasey and Murder Mitch got married and six months later, Semaj Richardson was born. The first thing everyone noticed was the head full of curly locks and beautiful big bright eyes. The birth of their newborn gave the couple the motivation to grind even harder so their daughter would never have to want for anything. That prompted Kasey to dabble into many illegal activities. She stepped into the world of counterfeit money which earned her a lifestyle that transcended the paper she was making from her father's drug empire. With her making moves in both the dope game and fake currency, Kasey needed additional support so she allowed her best friend Sabrina to enter as her right hand in both profitable business ventures.

Business was booming for the newlyweds. Murder Mitch was knocking off niggas left and right while Kasey went from hustling for thousands of dollars each month to hundreds of thousands in a short span of time. With success came the envy, even within the tight crew she had established. That envy soon turned to jealousy which eventually turned deadly. Semaj would never forget that dreadful night when her mother was brutally murdered. They had just moved from the Brooklyn suburbs to an upscale gated community in Jersey City. The move was supposed to represent their lives getting better but instead it was taking a turn for the worse.

"Father, I know you say it's rough out here and you want me to stop and play housewife but you know that's something I can't do," Kasey said as she was braiding her eight-year old daughter's hair into two ponytails. Semaj was placed in between her legs watching her favorite actress Jada Pinkett Smith in the movie "Set It Off."

"I understand that, K. But I worry about you every day. Being that you are all the way across the states, it makes it difficult for me to protect you. I haven't seen my granddaughter since she was a baby," he spoke in his strong Dominican accent.

"But, Father, it was your choice to move out West. It's not my fault you haven't been back to visit your grandchild."

"But I beg you to come out here, K. The old man misses his family."

"If I come to visit, you'll try to make me stay out West. And besides, Paulie moved down South and you're not badgering him to move out there with you. I'm not here alone. I still have my husband and your overprotective nephew. Never forget about his pestering mother that checks up on me more than necessary," she stressed, knowing it was her father who issued the many calls daily from his sister. "So I'm fine Poppa, I promise. And we'll see each other soon."

"Yes we will. But know that I love you and if you ever change your mind I have a beautiful home waiting here for you."

"This is my home. But thank you and I love you too. I have to go now. Someone is beeping in." Kasey clicked over. "Hey, Sabrina what's going on?"

"This mutherfucka done hit me again but this time I'm leaving him fo'real K, I'm over it. I'm finished," Sabrina, her best friend cried hysterically over the phone. "Please come and get me."

"You always saying that Sabrina," Kasey sighed heavily. "I'm fo'real this time and I will never go back!" Kasey mocked her for the many times she claimed and cried the same tune, but never did anything to change the station.

"This time is different, K. Please just come and get me!" she screamed in a frantic tone.

"Okay relax, Brina. Where are you exactly?"

"Behind that grocery market on Grandly Road in Brooklyn off Bushwick."

"I'm on my way, but I promise, Sabrina, this is my last time coming to rescue you from that no good, pimp ass nigga of yours. I don't even understand why you deal with a dude like that but I'm done trying to figure it out."

"I know. Just hurry please. And whatever you do don't tell Mitch. I don't want anyone to know that I called for your help again 'cause this shit is embarrassing," she sniffed before hanging up.

"C'mon on princess, put on your shoes and jacket so we can go get your Auntie Brina."

"Ooh and Ma can we get some ice cream while we're out?"

"Yes, you can have whatever you want."

After Kasey got her and Semaj dressed, she grabbed her car keys and headed out the door. On the drive, Kasey thought about Sabrina. She couldn't believe that her best friend was continuing to allow this nigga to abuse her mentally and physically. It irked her that after all this time, this bullshit was still going on and Kasey prayed for her best friend's sake that she was telling the truth when she said that she was done, because she promised herself that this would be the last time getting involved with their dysfunctional relationship.

"Semaj, if you don't remember anything else I ever tell you, remember this. You don't need a man that's going to beat on you and use you up. That's not love. Any real man would never lay a finger on his woman," she said as they crossed the Brooklyn Bridge.

"So do Daddy beat you, Ma?"

"Never! Your father loves and respects me. I wouldn't have it any other way."

"Mommy, when I get bigger I wanna be as smart as you. And, very pretty like you too. And have the nice things you have."

Kasey knew there would come a day when she deemed it necessary to school her daughter about the essentials of surviving in a cruel and unforgiving world. But she'd never envisioned that it would be this early in her life. Semaj was smart for her age and with the lifestyle Kasey lived she felt it was imperative to forewarn her daughter about the dangers that came with love and relationships. If anything was to ever happen to her before she left this earth, Kasey wanted her daughter to understand that if she didn't expect the best from a man he would never give it to her.

Kasey lost her mother to cancer when she was a little girl but her stepmother filled the role and instilled the importance of family and unity. If a little girl ignored everything else in the world, she would pay close attention to what her mother had to say. Kasey looked over at her daughter. "My beautiful, Semaj, if you listen to me, you will grow up to be smarter and accomplish even more than I have."

"Really? But you have so much, Mommy. I can have even more?" her cute little voice asked as if amazed.

"Of course. I teach you, so you can learn from me and eventually be better than me. That's what I want for you. One day Mommy and Daddy may not be here to take care of you, so it's my duty to make sure you can take care of yourself. You gotta know how to get dough and be a dough girl like your Mommy," Kasey preached not quite understanding her reasons.

"How do you get dough, Ma? And why?"

"You gotta work to get money, Maj, and always have a hustle. In life nobody owes you anything so you have to be able to make dough so you can get what you desire yourself. This is a new era and most men aren't taking care of their ladies how it was intended. So never look for stability in a man, you look for it in yourself. Even when you find someone you love, you still must have your own. And never settle for anything but the best."

"So the money that's in my piggy bank is the start of me growing up to be a dough girl?"

"Yup! And know, money comes and go so you better enjoy it 'cause no one can predict the future. Got it?"

Semaj nodded, but neither of them had any idea that this would be the last time that they would share a mother-to-daughter talk, and becoming a dough girl would be the conversation left on this little innocent child's heart.

Kasey slowed down when she reached Grandly Road and turned into the alley. She made her way to the back of the grocery market. *This nigga got this bitch hiding in eerie ass places now. This shit has to stop now*, she thought as she noticed a figure standing by the garbage can in dark colored clothing. Kasey beeped her horn to get her attention while pulling alongside of the dumpster.

"Girl, you hiding all the way back here, this shit ridiculous. I promise this my last time…" Kasey fussed as Sabrina hopped in the backseat with a hoodie pulled down over her face. Sabrina didn't utter a word as she raised her semiautomatic handgun and silenced Kasey forever—with no remorse. Her jealous heart now felt whole. She got out of the car and heard the piercing wails coming from her godchild's mouth…but never looked back knowing she'd robbed the child of her mother.

After that tragic night things took a turn for the worst, crumbling the young child's world. After Kasey's death, the streets were talking and Murder Mitch found out that not only did Kasey's father want him dead but he had his people looking for Semaj because he planned on bringing her out West to live with him. After losing his wife, Murder Mitch refused to lose his daughter too. So he put Semaj in hiding at his mother's house in Atlantic City. Murder Mitch knew he couldn't attend the funeral of his late wife because he would be walking into a death trap. He had to lay low so nobody could find him or Semaj. He hoped that Kasey's father would realize that although he vowed to protect her, her murder was out of his control. But he was an unforgiving man so Murder Mitch had accepted that he might have to stay on the run with Semaj for the rest of their lives.

Semaj and Tala, who was eight years her senior stood peering out the windowpane as they watched Murder Mitch back out of the driveway and disappear down the long road. Tears streamed down Semaj's face as she stared, struggling to still see the view of the car that was seemingly long gone.

"Maj, what are you crying for? You don't have to cry. It'll be okay," Tala said, stroking her niece's hair.

"I'm just so sad, Tala. I don't want my Daddy to leave me like my Mother did. And I miss her."

Tala wiped her niece's teary eyes. "I know you miss your mother, Maj. You have a right to miss her. But your father always told me that the Lord above takes some of the best people first because He's ready for them to come home with Him. Your mother was too good for this world," she said. Tala was trying to say all of the right things. "When my father died I was sad too. So that's normal and expected, Maj. And your daddy will never leave you. He loves you. You are his princess."

Mrs. Richardson came in the room and startled the girls. She looked at them with the warmest smile and though she felt her sickened body was weakening, she knew that they needed her. She walked toward them. "Is everything ok?"

"Yes, Mother, everything is fine." Tala said, not wanting her mother to worry.

"I'm glad to know that. I know you both must be hungry so come in here and eat some of this good food."

As the hours passed and the girls sat down at the dining room table laughing and joking, for the first time, Semaj was able to feel some sort of happiness that had been eluding her since her mother's death. But then that moment of happiness soon passed. Although the small box-sized TV was diminutive, the six pair of eyes could see the live media coverage of Murder Mitch's arrest.

"My Daddy! My Daddy! Oh not my Daddy!" Semaj ran to the television and hoped her eyes were playing tricks on her. He was handcuffed and being placed in the back of the police car. An unbearable pain traveled through Semaj as her stomach was performing somersaults. While the girls were entranced with Murder Mitch's arrest, unbeknownst to them, Mrs. Richardson was clenching her neck hoping to find air. She was choking to death, and her face-flushed cherry red as the incident was the last her fragile heart could take. She had been defeated.

Tala was the first to turn and see something was wrong with her mother. Tears formed as her mother died right in front of her eyes. Tala rushed to her mother's aid but there was no saving her. It was too late. Her mother had suffered an unpreventable heart attack.

After getting the details of what happened to his wife the day she was murdered from Semaj, Murder Mitch did what any husband with a penchant for blood would do. He made sure that Sabrina would never take another breath again. But because there was no evidence linking Murder Mitch directly to the crime, they instead hit him with the next best thing, accessory to murder for being near the crime scene. Not wanting the police to dig deeper into his background since it was a fact he murdered Sabrina, and because he made a career out of putting people six feet under, he opted to take a plea of seven years served in the state prison. When Murder Mitch got locked up he still didn't want his daughter raised by Kasey's family because he knew they thought of him as the enemy. So instead Semaj and Tala were left to fend for themselves.

Within a blink of an eye, the girls went from being overindulged to not being sure if they would have food to eat the next day. Tala felt that she had to do something. She couldn't allow the system to separate them. She would have given her left arm before she allowed her niece to be dragged through the system. She wasn't willing to allow her to be a ward of the State. When the authorities arrived, Tala made sure they were long gone.

From pillar to post, not having a house to piss in or a window to throw it out of, Tala made a way for her and Semaj to survive. When she turned eighteen, she knew they could not touch her and that's when she went to public housing for help. Within a week, they had a permanent place to lay their heads. Yes, it was in the projects but at least they had someplace to call home.

Immediately, she applied for jobs everywhere, from fast-food joints, grocery markets and bodegas. She soon found a job at a detail shop and though the pay rate was six dollars an hour, she left with plenty more due to tips from the local drug dealers that frequented the spot. With the pay she was making and proving that she could provide for her niece, the judge granted Tala custody of Semaj under strict supervision.

Being that she had to care after Semaj, she dropped out of school but she did get her GED. That was one of the stipulations she had along with maintaining employment. The state issued her a small monthly check for Semaj and food assistance, but that still wasn't enough. It seemed as if every time Tala got some extra money there was an unforeseen bill to be paid or they needed something around the house.

Tala felt it was a blessing when she met an older lady in the building named Ms. Long. When necessary which was often, she would look after Semaj while Tala worked. She even fed them plenty of nights. But Tala never wanted to seem like they were leeches so often she faked as if she had everything together.

Although young, Semaj's eyes were wide open and seeing her aunt constantly on her grind trying to maintain made her mature at a rapid rate. Semaj appreciated everything her auntie was doing to hold them down but instead of enjoying her youth she wanted to step up and be able to contribute. They were in this together and at the age of thirteen Semaj knew she had to take heed to her mother's last words, which was to have a hustle so you could make your own money. Many nights they went without, but somehow Semaj and Tala managed to survive.

To some seven years isn't long, but to a muthafucka on lockdown it seemed like forever times forever. Murder Mitch, like any other individual that had something waiting on him on the outside, felt despair and guilt. Many would see it as selfish but to Murder Mitch it was fear that allowed him to let his baby sister and daughter be out on the outside alone. But he couldn't allow Kasey's family to take his only child away from him. She was all that he had left in this world and he knew that she and Tala were soldiers and would survive. He never regretted his actions.

The day Murder Mitch said goodbye to those prison walls, he promised himself to never return and before he did, he'd go out with a bang. Guilt weighing down on his soul for being locked up for all those years unable to care for his sister and daughter had turned Murder Mitch's heart even colder. He had changed, but best believe it was in a sick way—he felt the world owed him and he wanted payment in full.

Tala and Semaj was waiting on Murder Mitch as he waltzed out of the wrought iron gates. The girls ran to him as if in a relay race. "Daddy!" Semaj yelled as she jumped into her father's open arms.

"Big bra!" Tala cooed as the three of them embraced one another.

"I'm so sorry. I love you girls so much and a day didn't pass where I didn't think about the both of you. I read every letter y'all wrote and it hurt me so badly that I couldn't even find the strength to write back," Murder Mitch asserted honestly. "And just give me some time and you all will never go through another day of hardship again."

In Semaj's fifteen-year-old mind she just knew that their poverty-stricken life was over and her daddy was going to save the day. Every day she remembered the big houses, nice cars and expensive clothes. She never could forget it, because she longed for the day when she would have it all back.

When they pulled up to Marcy Projects in Brooklyn, Murder Mitch's heart sank. He had left his two favorite girls to live and be raised by the vile streets. He promised himself at that moment he would do whatever necessary to get them out of such despair.

Weeks had passed and the duo had grown close to Murder Mitch. They had quickly become the Three Musketeers and they lived by the creed: *All for one, one for all.* But to everyone's dismay, it wasn't as easy as the trio thought it would be for Murder Mitch to get that dollar.

No doubt, Murder Mitch knew drug peddlers and criminals, but it seemed like there was a shortage of the OGs that he used to work for seven years ago. Either niggas wasn't willing to give up the information on current locations, or cat's drug empires had went into shambles. He knew he couldn't go around asking any and everybody who needed somebody killed for a fee. Now, he was on the verge of hitting niggas' blocks up, but then again, how much money was actually in the petty robbery business on some low-level block boys? Hitting niggas for their pockets was dumb and thirsty, and Murder Mitch knew he had to go for the stash and safe houses.

"I swear I'm not up for this shit. All I got was one hundred measly dollars," Semaj sighed as she flopped down on the couch. "I'm finna start sellin' pussy!" She knew she would never but it was how she felt. "'Cause this going in niggas pockets when they sleep ain't working. The shit is dumb. I'm really tired of this stuff."

Murder Mitch looked at his daughter in concern. "Maj, I'll get out here and take niggas' shit before I let you degrade yourself like that. Don't talk like that," he retrieved his pre-rolled vanilla Dutch. "I'm serious."

"Maj, only reason why you trippin' is because you thought once Mitch came home the money would miraculously begin falling from the sky without any work. But that ain't how shit goes, Semaj. Life ain't that easy."

"You right. It's unfair. And that's why I don't care about nothing," she shrugged. "Daddy, I've been thinking. Mommy always told me that I gotta get money on my own and have a hustle. I think if we put this plan into action, it would be on and poppin' for us."

"And what do you have in mind?" he asked.

"I'm thinking about setting Vega's big brother Boo connect up. I know where that nigga stash house at. I been with Vega when dropping money off for Boo, and they be having close to 30, 40 thou in the trap on an average day."

"Hell nah, Maj. You trippin'! That's too close to home. Vega is yo' man. That shit alone is risky. And you talkin' about having yo' pops run up into the spot. Fuck no!"

"Let me handle the Vega situation. He'll have no idea I'm involved with the robbery. It's not like it's him, it's his brother's connect. Plus, this the only way I can see us getting somewhere. What else we gon' do to get real money? What, you wanna live in the fucking ghetto forever?"

"If I have to, I will. I'm cool on that I just can't get involved," Tala conveyed.

"And I respect how you feel, Tala. But I just cannot continue to live like this. I just can't. I don't see any other option as of now."

"You are only fifteen, girl. You have your whole life ahead of you. You said one day you wanna be an actress. If you work at it, it can happen."

"You know that life ain't for girls like me from the ghetto. I have to figure out how to survive in the world I'm in right now. Enough of this suffering. I can't wait no longer. Something gotta shake. Like yesterday." She paused and continued. "So Daddy, what up?" Semaj stared in her father's eyes.

Murder Mitch looked at his daughter shocked. He felt as if he was having a conversation with his deceased wife Kasey. Semaj had inherited the same love for money. The room fell silent as they searched for the same answer, a better resolution because none of them wanted to continue being broke. But they came up empty.

Murder Mitch's mind was spinning like a merry-go-round. His pockets were filled with lint and he was in desperate need to fill the space with dead presidents. He wanted to see his daughter enjoy life again. "Okay, this is what we can do," he pulled from the blunt, holding the smoke in his lungs as he passed it to Tala. "'Cause I don't want you involved in the least."

Though some may consider Murder Mitch a terrible father for cosigning on a scheme that could easily set up his daughter for an early date with death, in his mind he rationalized it differently. He simply wanted what any father hoped for their daughter—a better life.

"Please tell me that you're not encouraging her?" Tala asked wondering how Semaj's crazy idea was about to come to fruition.

"I'm telling you Ta, this is the only way. We need to get some real money. We ain't gotta do nothing and it's only for a short time until we get our stacks up," Semaj reasoned.

The three of them stared at each other intensely. Though Semaj said it would be for a short time period, they all knew once they got started there was no turning back. Semaj gave her father the details and from there he could manage the rest.

When Semaj came up with the plan to set up her boyfriend's, brother Boo's connect, she never imagined in a million years it would lead to her first love's demise. Semaj was only thirteen when she met Nathan Giles aka Vega. He was seventeen and a brown paper bag boy for his older brother, Boo. Immediately they had fallen hard for each other. They had been each other's first love. Besides Boo, Semaj was the only thing he ever loved. He was the product of a street whore and an absentee father. Since a youngin' he and his brother had been left with their elderly grandmother that secretly had her own drug addictions and paid the boys no mind. When Boo jumped off the porch, things started looking up for the brothers.

Semaj and Vega had met at a Rutgers basketball game in Harlem. She noticed him checking for her as she was doing the same with him. She had heard his name from being in the mix at the city events, and knew mad chicks were checking for him. The fact that Boo was his older brother also made him a target to the girls who thought fucking with him would bring them 'hood fame.

Vega had watched Semaj as she tied her shirt into a knot trying to get a little breeze from the sweltering heat. Between the sweat dripping down her taut belly and the way she licked her Firecracker Popsicle, she was driving the young boy's lust into overdrive. Though she was almost fourteen, Semaj had the body of a twenty-one year old vixen.

Vega had always admired her from afar but was reluctant about approaching her. But this day was different. He was unable to resist. Maybe it was the way her short shorts made her voluptuous ass look even bigger. Her thick hair was pulled into a ponytail to display her beautiful innocent face and though sweaty, her baby hair laid down to perfection. As Semaj walked past to purchase another popsicle, Vega reached out and pulled her to him. "What's up, cutie?"

"Nothing," she answered shyly.

"I want to see if I can take you out."

Oh my God, he wanna take me out! He picks me out of all the girls. Okay, dummy, say something. "Well, I'll have to see what my auntie says. Just tell me your number and I'll call and let you know." He recited his number in hopes of her remembering it. The two clicked immediately and it was as if they were meant to be. From that day on, they were almost inseparable. He would pick her up on weekends and she'd stay uptown with him and his brother, and sometimes Tala allowed him to stay at their spot, prohibiting him staying on school nights. It was truly puppy love, the kind you always remember. That's why it hurt her so much that his death was on her, which made loving another man forbidden. Everyone was a potential victim.

The night when her daddy came home with a bagful of money and the sight of all the white men printed on green paper was what turned the blind eye to the ski mask and bloodstains on his shoes. Murder Mitch went in straight blasting no inquires, hitting anything moving and took all the money that was spread across the table, leaving no witnesses behind.

A few days after the robbery, Semaj was uptown chilling with Vega and his brother Boo. She actually felt bad about what had happened. It seemed as if Boo knew something because the robbery was the main topic of conversation. Call it fate or luck but Semaj had gotten tired of hearing the shit so she excused herself for a brief moment and went to the bathroom.

Not even three minutes later, she heard commotion downstairs. She panicked when a raspy voice, spewed, "Thought I wouldn't find you nigga! Taking my shit." Just like that, Boo's connect had erased him from the map. Never leaving witnesses behind, Vega had been shot too.

Oh my God, please no. Not Vega, please God! Semaj thought as she sat in the bathroom scared to budge, not knowing if the goons were still in the house. As she knelt down paralyzed in fear, she prayed that she would make it out alive.

Chapter 4

The Present

Semaj layed her head on the desk in her class, struggling to stay awake. She was so deep in a mind-numbing sleep the chiming of the bell went unheard. Mrs. Weaver had made the announcement to dismiss the class and after glancing up, she noticed her student, once again, left behind long after the class was gone. Removing herself from her roller chair, the instructor made her way to the sleeping student. "Semaj!" Mrs. Weaver said in a demanding firm tone.

Lifting her head from the small table, Semaj opened her eyes, allowing them to adjust to the light as she wiped the sleep from her eyes. She surveyed the classroom only to notice that the class had been in dismissal. *Fuck, now I gotta hear this lady rant about the same ol' shit,* she thought salty, as she swiftly gathered her belongings from underneath the desk. *Somebody could've woke me up.* But she knew most of her classmates would rather see her in trouble than merely nudge her arm to inform her that the bell had rung.

For the last several months Semaj had been attending college as a theater major. Balancing classes and her side hustle was becoming difficult. But acting was therapeutic for Semaj and there was no doubt she was one of the best at the school, so she was determined to make it work. It seemed though that some of the students were jealous of Semaj's undeniable talent. Her other classmates weren't ready when Semaj stepped on the scene. The combination of what she learned from attending LaGuardia Performing Arts High School, and the fire that burned inside of her from living a hard knock life, made her a natural star when she performed.

"Semaj, we have had this talk numerous of times and the sleeping must stop. We just began our second semester, and you are already starting off wrong."

Mrs. Weaver readjusted her glasses. "Now, I wanted to speak with you after class ended anyway."

"And for what reasons would that be?" Semaj asked in annoyance.

"Semaj, you're extremely talented. You are one of the few students that own the stage when you perform. That gives you an advantage, Ms. Richardson." Mrs. Weaver stared firmly into her eyes. "But when it comes down to the essays for some reason you're not putting your all into the work."

"I'm sorry you believe that Mrs. Weaver, because I do," Semaj countered, speaking truthfully.

"Well, your first paper is due at the end of the month. And turning it in late, as you're aware is an automatic dropped letter grade. This paper also has a vast impact on your final grade."

"I'll have it turned in on time. Trust me, Mrs. Weaver."

"Great and I'm looking forward to reading it." With that said Semaj rose up and stepped around her instructor, anxious to leave. "Ms. Richardson," Mrs. Weaver called out to her before she left.

"Yes?" Semaj turned around.

"Good luck on your performance tonight. I know you'll do wonderful," she smiled.

Part of Semaj didn't trust Ms. Weaver and thought she was a phony, but another part believed that maybe she really was in her corner and wanted her to shine. But to be on the safe side, Semaj felt it was best to keep her guard up. "Thank you. I'm going to do my best," she faked a smile and headed to rehearsal before her performance later on that night.

Semaj, her classmates and her theatre instructor were backstage. Semaj peeked around the black curtain and observed the audience and it was filled to capacity. As the lights in the auditorium dimmed, Ms. Porter sent them out onstage. When the curtains retracted the participants got into position ready to put on the show of their life. The theatrical production was a modern day Romeo and Juliet, and Semaj was a natural playing the leading role. She had a gift of taking a role and making it her own as if she was that character. She captured the crowd's attention and never let it go until the very end.

The crowd erupted in a loud applause as the curtains closed briefly, and then reopened as the bright lights reappeared. Ms. Porter came onstage introducing the cast. Right before Semaj was introduced, she noticed an entourage of thugs emerging from the audience. Semaj wondered who they were here to see and hoped they would be still be outside when she left because they could be a potential target.

When they stopped at the front entrance as she was introduced, Semaj focused her attention toward them as a bashful smile crossed her face. It was one guy in particular that stood out like a superstar rapper in a crowd full of nobodies. Though she couldn't distinguish his facial features, Semaj could tell from his swagger, attire and the way his encourage followed him that he held authority. There was something about this dude. But as quickly as she was drawn to him he just as quickly vanished. *Damn, dude probably would've been a good hit! shit!* she thought as she made her way backstage.

Tala rushed over to her niece. "Girl, and you talkin' 'bout this shit ain't for you," she sucked her teeth. "You killed it. You know you need to pursue this so you can get us into Hollywood. You were the coldest one up there, seriously. You did good, Semaj. You really got talent. There's a lot of money in this profession, too."

The conversation was cut short by her favorite instructor walking up "You did wonderful, Semaj," Ms. Porter cooed, congratulating her.

"Thank you. It felt good to be out there."

"Now, you know there is a huge charity benefit this Sunday and a lot of movie stars, filmmakers, film production company owners, both independent and major are going to be in attendance. I've been getting good feedback on you. I think you should really consider coming just to see how it turns out," Ms. Porter suggested.

"I know it will be fun, but I'm not going to be available Sunday."

Tala nudged her arm and interjected. "Ms. Porter, I will make sure that she is there. I'll be glad to accompany her."

"Thank you, I think that's a wise decision for your niece. I'll see you both Sunday." Ms. Porter winked and walked off to congratulate her other students on a great performance.

The charity benefit was filled with the movie industry elite and A-list celebrities were everywhere to show their support for a common cause. This was a world that Semaj had dreamed of being a part of. Since the sandbox, she practiced her acceptance speech, daydreamed of walking down the red carpet, and watched her favorite actors and actresses on television. Though, this life seemed to be out of reach a year ago, Semaj was glad she made the decision to go to school in hopes of honing her acting skills further.

Semaj and Tala stood in one spot, content with observing the crowd. For once Semaj wasn't on the prowl for her next victim. The primary reason for that was because Semaj felt the men there were out of her league. Although many of the men were eyeing her all night she felt none of them were interested in discussing business. They had other intentions that weren't on Semaj's agenda. *Ain't no need to try to talk with nann one of these niggas. It's hard to get to their money. And far as fuckin' with 'em? Please! They all just want a plaything. I'm cool.* Most young ladies would have loved the opportunity of being in the company of the famous men, but not Semaj. She refused to be like girls that had to keep their legs on automatic open in order to be a part of the industry especially since most of the time they asses still never blew up.

There was one guy, though, who caught her eye. His rich creamy brown complexion, beautiful white teeth, and facial hair that were neatly trimmed made him appealing to Semaj. His five 'o clock shadow blended well with his flawless features and his persona screamed power. Handsome was an understatement and his swagger was just an extra added bonus. His six-foot confident stature and athletic build had Semaj wondering if the most important feature she couldn't see was all she imagined it to be. As attracted as Semaj was to the mystery man, his grown man vibe was intimidating which made her nervous.

Semaj caught him whispering to his man and subtly checking her out. This made her turn her sexy up, and she flung her hair as she leaned into Tala and giving a flirtatious smile. What she didn't know was that he recognized game and knew precisely what she was doing.

He finally stepped away from his man who he had been discussing business with and approached Semaj. "I see you been watching me all night," he said in a voice full of humor while looking Semaj up and down. "Can I speak to you for a minute?"

"If that's what you decide," she responded.

"Aren't we simple?"

"Not really. I'm just waiting for you to get to the point," Semaj said with an attitude as a frown crossed her face. Soon after, her frown turned into a cute smirk. "I guess you're not the only one with a sense of humor."

The guy laughed. "I like you already. Name's Quasim. You are?"

34

"Semaj."

"That's a beautiful name and it's fitting. What brings you out here this evening?"

"My people and I wanted to support the cause. You know?"

"I feel you on that."

One of the guys that Quasim had been conversing with earlier walked over to him while he was speaking with Semaj. "Yo, it's time to handle that one thing," his friend Mike-Mike told him.

"Cool, I'm right behind you. Let me finish up with this pretty lady." Quasim focused back on Semaj. "So can we exchange contact information?"

Never wanting to seem desperate, she said. "How about you take mine."

He pulled out his iPhone and stored her name and digits. "I'ma call you." Quasim was whisked away immediately, and departed with an entourage of five men.

Soon after that, her teacher Ms. Porter came over followed by a guy. "Al-B, this is the young lady that you were inquiring about, Semaj."

"It's a pleasure to meet you." He extended his hand for a handshake.

With a confused expression, Semaj shook his hand and nonchalantly replied, "Hello."

"I saw you the other night and I couldn't help but be intrigued by your performance. You are a very great actress."

"Well, thank you."

"I recently acquired a production deal with a reputable film company. I want to offer you a chance at possibly securing a role in a film I'm producing."

"Really? Is that right?" Semaj remarked sarcastically, thinking this was a weak attempt to try to holler at her.

"Seriously, this could be your big break as well as my own."

"Thanks, but no thanks. I'm not interested at all," Semaj shot.

"If you change your mind you can give me a call me," Al-B said, handing her his business card. "I'll be looking out for you. Trust, I know you'd be huge. I can sense talent and you have it."

She turned to Ms. Porter, "Thanks for the help, but I can tell you he's definitely not it. This was nice, but I have to go. See you in class tomorrow. Tala, let's go," Semaj said. She was upset that the guy wanted to play about something so serious. *Luckily, I'm not stupid enough to fall for the fake hype,* she thought. *Knew this shit was gon' be some bullshit and not for me. Waste of my got dang'gon time!*

Chapter 5

Every Saturday morning, Semaj, her father and Tala would meet at one of their homes for breakfast. It was a tradition that they shared since Murder Mitch had gotten out of prison, and each of them cherished it. On this Saturday, they were going over their plan for hitting Dean-Bean. It had been in the making for a minute and it was time to make their move. "So it's on for tonight then? I'ma meet with y'all at Semaj's in the morning," Murder Mitch said.

"That's what's up. You leaving, Daddy?"

"Yeah. I'm outta here, baby girl. The food was delicious sis." Murder Mitch wiped his mouth with his napkin and rose from his seat. He kissed the cheeks of his favorite girls and departed.

"So have you figured out what you gon' do about D-Boy's money?" Semaj inquired.

"Shit, that's what I was just thinking about. Bills seem to keep coming in this bitch and taking some of the money would be dumb. I'd rather stage some robbery type shit. Act like niggas bust through and demanded cash like you had said."

"You already know I thought that was the better idea anyway. I just didn't know if you'd wanna rock wit' it like that."

"That would be defeating my cause to take some and put it back," Tala admitted as she grew excited. "Hell, I might as well just wait to some of this robbery money come through if that's the case."

"Right. Then if you do that you can keep all that shit," Semaj said as she removed herself from the table and deposited her remains into the trashcan. "That'd be the start of your come back."

"I know right? And I need money, bad. Like yesterday."

"Well, do what you gotta do but my advice is to start getting your acting skills up to par because when he calls from prison your monologue needs to be tight."

The conversation came to a halt by the ringing of Semaj's cell phone. "Hello?"

"Speak to Semaj?"

"Who is this?"

"Quasim. Is she available?"

"Oh, what's up? I thought you lost my number," Semaj said with a hint of sarcasm in her voice. "You called like a whole week later."

"Never that. I just been real crazy busy with this new business endeavor I'm putting together and as if my life ain't crazy enough, I misplaced my phone. I just found it today."

Semaj chuckled. "Umm-huh."

"True story. But I was calling, because I'ma be free this evening."

"Are you inviting me to join you during your free time?" she asked sarcastically.

"Kind of why I called, you know."

"That can work. Where are we going?"

"Everything been about business lately. I ain't had fun in a while. You trying to hit up the Arcade?" Normally, Quasim didn't indulge in these activities, but he wanted to switch it up with this lady instead of the typical movie-and-dinner date.

"Would love to. Where do you wanna meet me at?"

"I can pick you up if you don't mind."

"How you figure I want you to know where I stay?" she asked, cautiously.

"I'm feeling that safety tactic. Meet me at The Tropical Arcade at six."

"See you then."

Semaj was usually not one to wear her feelings on her sleeve, but when she closed her phone shut, a smile crossed her face.

Tala had been eavesdropping and noticed the instant change in her niece's mood. "What's all the smiling about?"

"Huh? What you talking 'bout? Ain't nobody smiling. That was just that dude Quasim and he wanna meet up with me later."

"So what you gon' find out what he working with?"

"Nah, don't even think he that type of dude."

"What? You ain't on the prowl. Shocking! I see you finally try'na start dating on the fo' real side of things."

"Not never. I'm done with trying to get seriously involved with another nigga, ever. True story."

Semaj wasn't normally the shy type, but for some reason when she pulled up to the game room and spotted Quasim waiting for her at the entrance with his hands in his front pockets, butterflies filled her stomach. As she parked her car, he came over and opened the car door for her. "Hey, you look really nice. How you feeling?"

For a moment Semaj lost her train of thought as she caught a whiff of his cologne. He smelled fresh like he just got out the shower and it instantly turned her on. "Good. How are you?" she finally replied hoping he didn't catch the delay.

"I'm straight. Can't complain."

They walked inside as Semaj followed his lead. After grabbing a table and ordering their food, Quasim purchased some coins… rather a galore of coins. They were standing side-by-side shooting hoops when the questions started. "So what is it that you do?" he asked.

"I'ma businesswoman," Semaj replied.

He laughed, finding her answer amusing. "Business huh? That's what's up. I like that, because I'ma businessman. Maybe we can do business together," he joked. He figured she was from a well-off family.

"Hey, you never know what the future may hold," Semaj said as she gripped the basketball and shot it smoothly inside the rim. She wanted to know more about him, and decided to pose questions bluntly to see what he was really about. "So do you have any children?"

"Not yet. No kids, but I do take care of my li'l brother. Our father passed and his mother's a crack whore."

"Sorry to hear that," Semaj said sympathetically. She went on to the next question. "How old are you? And are you a fake that just plays a good role?" When Quasim began laughing, she playfully hit him on the arm with the basketball. "Seriously, a lot of niggas out here be faking."

"I'm twenty-six. But let me be clear about everything now, so we don't have to return to this topic. Everything that you see and that I say is real. I don't know what type of dudes you've encountered in the past, but I'm the truth all day long. I keep everything one hundred percent. I'm not a liar and I hate liars. Not a fake it to you make it type nigga. I'm not for bullshit and I just handle my business. I'm straight up and loyal to everyone that's in my circle. And if you're in my circle that means I believe you're just as loyal as me."

Liking the way his words flowed freely, Semaj nodded her head in approval. "Okay I'm digging that. But lastly, do you have a woman? Because I'm definitely not with the drama."

"If I had a woman I wouldn't be kicking it with you right now. I have friends, and I make it nothing more. If you are around long enough you'll learn this the real me."

"If I am around long enough?" Semaj asked flirtatiously.

"Yeah, if you are around long enough," Quasim repeated seriously as he stared into her eyes. "Being that the interrogation is over," he laughed lightly while turning around and looking towards their table, "And the waitress is placing our food on the table, we can head over and finish this up in a relaxed manner."

Semaj and Quasim sat and conversed for three hours after eating. For some reason Semaj felt comfortable with him and told him everything about herself, except for how she made her money. That was the one secret she kept because she knew it would change his perception of her.

He shared a lot about his past with her too, and for that reason this made them bond instantly. He even shared his feelings about his late father and their close-knit relationship up until he died. His father's death had never been talked about...to no one. He told her how it made him want to change and start moving towards positive things in life.

Semaj was impressed by Quasim. He was a cool dude and she found herself actually enjoying his company.

They practically played every game in the arcade more than twice, chatted like old friends, but both of them hiding secrets that they couldn't tell even if they wanted to. Before they realized it, it was going on midnight. The crowd had already dispersed and the arcade was closing for the night.

"Thanks for the awesome date. I really had a good time with you," Semaj admitted as he walked her to her car.

"You ain't gotta thank me. It was my pleasure and I enjoyed myself too. Maybe we can do this again soon."

"I'd like that," she replied in a seductive tone. He opened her door and Semaj appreciated that he was such a gentleman. She tried to read him, but couldn't. She had never met a man like Quasim before. One thing that was obvious, though, was that he was the closest thing to her mark. Many niggas she simply tolerated to get close to their stash, but with Quasim, she felt a difference already. Plotting had not once popped up in her head, which was rare. He seemed way out of her league, but what she found most interesting about him was how he made her feel comfortable in his presence. The way he handled her was gentle, caring, and genuine. He treated her with respect, and his kindness almost had her open. She admired him, and the serious look in his eyes made her feel as if he was one of the few men in the world who could change her.

The way the two of them carried on a conversation nobody would have known that it was their very first date. They clicked in a major way as if they had been friends for years, but Semaj had to keep it real with herself. Love wasn't in the cards for her at this moment in her life, and although he had her attention, her life was way too complicated. Her main objection was to make sure she got her money up and having a man-distraction was out of the question.

"You are going to make some woman very happy," Semaj admitted as she slid in her car.

Quasim shut her door and stuck his head halfway in the window. "That woman might just be you," he said as he touched her chin and the two of them made eye contact. "Only time will tell." He kissed her on the forehead and walked to his car.

Semaj was reluctant to pull off because she was having such a good time with him. She watched as he hopped in his SUV and blew the horn, flashing him a cute smile as they both waved before pulling out of the parking lot going their separate way.

Murder Mitch crept through the side door and surprisingly it was easier than he had anticipated to pick the lock. For a brief moment, he watched as Paris took tokes from the cigarette as she sat on the living room sofa with a pistol on the end table. Depression and eagerness was washed upon her face but that wasn't going to stop Murder Mitch from moving forward on what he came to get done. He walked into the room with his gun drawn. "Don't move and put your hands up."

Shocked, Paris looked at Murder Mitch as if he was speaking a foreign language. "Damn, Mitch, you done lost your hand in the game? Fuck is this about, nigga?" she raised her hands in the air.

"Didn't come for socializing. Where the money at?" he asked and immediately removed the gun from the end table.

"You gotta be a bold ass nigga coming up in Dean's shit," Paris looked at him fearlessly. "Nigga, you must really got a death wish." She rolled her eyes and sucked her teeth as she shook her head from side to side.

"I don't give a fuck about none of that shit you talkin'. Where the money at?" he asked, waving the .357 in her face.

"Let me tell you something. If you were waiting on Dean so he could tell you where the money at then it's a waste of time, my dude. He'd never give you the combination to that safe. Know you feel stupid, playboy," she chuckled. "Isn't a good feeling to be fucked is it?"

"If I put the gun to your head that nigga wouldn't have a choice but to concede," he said confidently.

"Think that if you want to. Nigga don't care about a human life. For his cake that nigga gon' lay down and die for his. Believe that," Paris expressed. "I see it like this: You help me and I help you."

Murder Mitch stared at her contemplating her request, but then got heated and shoved the pistol in her face. "You Dean's bitch. Fuck I look like trusting you? You might be trying to set me up," he said suspiciously. Murder Mitch was sure that he had put fear in the girl's heart. What he didn't know was that her heart didn't pump fear and to his surprise she didn't flinch.

"Nigga, you ain't gotta be pointing guns in my fuckin' face." Paris forced the weapon out of her face. "Now I see it only working out one or two ways. You kill me and leave with absolutely nothing. Or I tell you the combo to the safe and we split that shit," Paris said truthfully. Fortunately for her, she had watched him put in his code when she faked to be sleeping. "But first we murk Dean."

"What?" Murder Mitch asked in confusion.

"Think I was waiting here just to be accessible to my man?" Paris placed her forefinger on her chin. "Umm… no!" she answered for him. "I was waiting on this nigga to get home so I could murk his bitch ass," Paris said with sincerity in her voice. She was sick and tired of Dean Bean, but

41

the little cash and gifts he threw her way kept her stable. No longer able to take the penny pinching and disrespect though, on this very night, she was planning to kill him and run off with his stash.

"If you gon' murk your man what the fuck I look like trusting you? You probably plotting against me too," Murder Mitch said, letting his suspicions be known.

"It's simple. Nigga petty as fuck and been running around here with all these ratchet hoes, and he ain't generous with his paper. I'm tired of gettin' small duckets and fucking his brains out damn near every night for peanuts. I'm in love with money and I'll do anything to get it. Now you can roll with my plan or just kill us both. But I'm telling you Dean ain't giving up that combination."

At that moment the decision had to be made by a nod of the head, because the sound of keys interrupted the debate. Dean-Bean walked through the door. He had a woman with him. He turned on the light switch to find a gun pointed in his direction. "Damn!" was all he could say.

"Yeah, nigga you been caught slippin'. Both y'all lift them hands in the air."

"So you set me up Paris? Out of all people…you!" Dean-Bean kept shaking his head. Knowing death was imminent regardless, he went for Murder Mitch's gun. But he wasn't quick enough and Murder Mitch pulled his hammer back and placed two slugs into his dome.

When his body dropped, Mercedes screamed out fearfully. Two pair of eyes zeroed in on her and she couldn't do anything but beg for her life. "P, I promise it's not what it looks like! I was just finna help him cook some shit up!" she said, pleading her innocence. She was indeed there to put in work, but there was no way she was declining his offer of a thousand dollars to fuck him. "I got kid's you can't do this!"

"And I was 'pose to be their godmother, but you crossed me Cedes. Bitch, do you think I'm stupid?"

"I swear it's not what you think. It's two coke bricks inside the stovetop and that's all I was here for. Word to my mutha."

"Well, bitch, you 'bout to meet her. Muthafuck you!" In a swift motion, Paris snatched her gun from Murder Mitch's waistband and emptied the clip on her, and left her white shirt crimson. *I was telling this bitch everything about us and she pulls some sneaky shit like this,* Paris thought.

Murder Mitch's intention was to murk Paris too, but after a stunt like that, there was no way he could murder the gangster bitch. She was a thoroughbred and killed as if her heart was black. For that reason alone, he felt she deserved to live. The two of them got the bread from the safe, and found the bricks inside the stove and disappeared into the night.

Semaj was on cloud nine as she walked into her apartment. She couldn't take her mind off Quasim. He seemed to be perfect and she had it bad for him, but she already knew their timing was off. *Maybe in the near future I'll make room for him in my life*, Semaj thought as she stripped out of her clothes and replaced them with pajamas.

She crawled into bed and drifted off to a pleasant dream. Just as the dream had gotten good she heard her BlackBerry ringing. Her last thoughts were Quasim, so instinctively she had assumed that it was him calling. She jumped up to answer but it wasn't. It was a text message from her father. *Hell yeah, that's what I'm talkin' about*, she thought as she read the message:

Maj, it's done. Shit was easier than expected. I'll be over there in the morning with a surprise.

Semaj sat at her dinette table going through her stack of bills, sipping on a glass of Tropicana orange juice as she tried ignoring her buzzing phone.

Tala was reading a section of the *New York Post* about a major drug bust that had her complete attention, so she tried blocking the phone out too, but couldn't. "Damn, can you answer that shit! I'm trying to read 'bout this trap house that got raided. That phone is irking my muthafuckin' nerves."

"Girl, it ain't nobody but Gabe talking useless shit. Nigga ain't got the picture by now. Shit, he gon' make me get my number changed."

The phone started to ring again. "Let me answer it," Tala insisted, retrieving the phone. "What's the problem, Gabe?"

"Put Semaj on the phone."

"Damn, nigga, don't you get the muthafuckin' picture? She don't wanna mess with you no more. What part of it you don't understand, my nigga?"

"Bitch, put that hoe on the phone before you get on my shit list too."

"Empty threats, huh? Why you talkin' shit? You need to be concerned about getting out of jail. Broke ass nigga!" Tala spit in disgust.

"Bitch, that's cute, ha ha. Bet you won't be laughing for too long, sheisty hoes!" The line went dead.

"Well damn, that nigga mad as hell." Tala handed her the phone back.

"So fuck him. Better ask one of his homeboys for the money," Semaj quickly changed the subject wanting to move on to more important things. "Girl, I think it's about time for me to switch it up. I done had the XF for 'bout six months."

"You a fool. Stay changing up your whip game."

"You know how shit grow old to me quick. I want something new. If I'm paying a car note I just oughta be comfortable with how I'm riding. I have to give thanks to Ms. Long for co-signing with her A-1 credit and making it possible," Semaj said as her father walked in with Paris following behind him.

"What the fuck!" Tala whispered as she turned to look at them, then back at Semaj.

"What's up ladies?" Paris chirped being extra bubbly. "Y'all cool?"

"Daddy, what's going on here?" Semaj demanded an explanation.

"Relax, baby girl. Paris down fo'sho and surprisingly I ain't the only one trigger-happy. We gotta murder mama right here in the flesh. Deaded her man."

"Oh…my…Goodness!" Tala covered her mouth. "I thought I told you not to kill him!"

"Dude got out of hand," he said dismissively. He left the part out about Mercedes too.

The room fell in silence. Both girls were confused like a motherfucker. Murder Mitch gave a brief summary of what transpired the night before but Tala and Semaj were still perplexed.

"I always wondered how you were eating so good, Maj. Honestly, I thought your daddy was the brickman and you were a spoiled li'l brat. But after last night," Paris looked at her seriously. "Shit, I learned that you were on your hustle just like the next bitch. I'm tryin' to get put on."

Semaj took a gulp from her glass before responding. "I'ma tell you like this, Paris. You my nigga, but this is a whole nother ball game than you play. That sleeping with hustlers for money ain't gon' get it. Gold diggin' games is on life support. You gotta do too much to get what the nigga want you to have these days. I see it like this: Why waste time when you can hit a nigga real hard?"

"I can dig it."

"This shit real and deadly, Paris. Even if a nigga suspect you to be on some sheisty shit it could be the end. We don't go for just any nigga. Nigga pockets gotta be deep as an ocean, man. That's why you gotta carefully separate the real from the fake. We don't hit no ol' hustling backwards ass niggas," Semaj stated.

"Bitch, I said I want in. Feel me? I'm not green to the game. I just never had a team. I just need y'all behind me and the rest is history," Paris said. She knew Semaj knew damn near every baller in each borough, but she knew niggas outside of New York and it would prove useful.

"A'ight. You gotta make these niggas let you know where the stash at where the cash at. Gotta approach them on some classy, sophisticated shit, like you wifey material. Dope boys don't won't no bird bitch. It's all about the presentation when you approach a hustler," Semaj coached. It was obvious that she was a vet and had hustled plenty niggas out of their money. "You really ready for this shit?"

"Hell yeah," she replied.

"Well, I'ma let you work this nigga from the Bronx I been plotting on. His name is Dank and he something serious in that area. Gettin' plenty paper but like most of these dudes in the streets his weakness is pussy. So he gon' be at you hard. I'ma see if you can prove yourself by going alone. If you pass this test, you're officially the fourth member," Semaj made clear.

Semaj and Tala sat in the back of the sports bar eating spicy chicken wings, as the duo anxiously waited on Paris to approach their table. She was wearing a white jogging suit and designer sneakers. She was toting a medium size knapsack at her side.

"Dang, my dad says you ain't called him or nothing. What happened? You start feeling the nigga somethin'?" Semaj asked.

"Fuck outta here, Semaj!" Paris waved her off and sat down in a seat inside the booth. "What you think I'm just carrying this bag for nothing?"

"Shit, I hope not. And I hope you ain't got no chump change in there neither. That split is four ways."

"Fuck I look like? It's almost ninety Gs. Look!" Paris said pointing to the flat screen television by the bar.

"This is Mildred Baldwin reporting live for News 12. I'm here on the scene where police were called due to neighbors complaining about hearing multiple gunshots. Douglas "Dank"

Rodgers was gunned down in his residence a little after midnight last night, along with two men whose names haven't yet been released. Once officials arrived on the scene witnesses say that they saw an unidentified woman departing in an all black SUV. At this time there are no suspects in police custody. If you have any information regarding this matter, you can call the local crime stoppers."

Tala and Semaj watched the newscast in utter disbelief. It was mind boggling how Paris was able to get away and Murder Mitch didn't have to put in any work. "How in the fuck you pull off that shit?"

"It was simple. I was in the bathroom when some niggas bust through. They didn't even know I was there. They sho' in the hell wasn't finna get off with what we were after. The Dank nigga keep guns all over his crib and lucky I found the gun that was underneath the sink. Once they nearly beat him to death Dank gave in and popped the safe open. When they thought they was leaving I came out blasting. Two to the head for both niggas." Paris shrugged casually.

"You murdered them?" Tala meant for the words to come out in a whisper, but her voice raised a few octaves.

"Hell yeah! After I let off on them niggas, I popped Dank just to be cautious. Snatched up my shit after a quick wipe down on what I touched and dipped out that bitch. Did I do good?" Paris asked. "Am I in?"

"Most def. You're in," Semaj replied with a confident smile. The average chick probably wouldn't have made it through the situation to speak on it. Paris not only lived to tell about it, but most importantly she had the paper. She was grimier than they were. Now she was a part of their squad.

"Cool, 'cause I got some niggas in B-more we can hit right now!"

Chapter 6

Three Months Later

For the last few months Semaj had been on her grind so she decided to treat herself to a day of shoe shopping. Ever since she put Paris down, Semaj had come into more money than she could have ever imagined. She discovered that having Paris put in work with them was the best decision she'd made thus far. She was the perfect asset for the team. They were living a secret society lifestyle and drug dealers were no longer their only targets. Anybody that had deep pockets could get it.

It seemed like the more they hit a lick the wiser and slicker they became. Their hearts were cold and none of them thought twice about leaving the victim dead once it was done. Semaj had turned off her emotions a long time ago and detached herself from feeling sympathy. The only agenda was money, and the payoff was all they were focused on. Some may consider it cold-blooded, but Semaj was just on a paper chase. This was her grind and how she ate. It paid the bills and she treated her hustle seriously. Just like a person who worked a nine to five, this was her full time gig.

One thing Semaj wasn't built for was the murder game though. Her heart was hardened, but she knew she couldn't indulge in an actual killing. She could watch a nigga get murked right before her eyes, but it was a different story if it meant her pulling the trigger herself.

That's what set her apart from Paris—because Paris killed as if she was placed on earth to murder. She was the product of a mother/father homicide-suicide. Her father had killed her mother in front of her and then turned the gun on himself. Paris was never the same after that fatal day.

Semaj had also found out that Paris was a snort head, but she wasn't a messy one. The thing that had Semaj livid though was that Paris turned her auntie on, and Tala was getting sloppy with it. Instead of being an occasional social user, Tala was snorting the shit almost daily.

Semaj tried to urge her to stop but when Tala was set on something nobody could tell her otherwise. When Semaj tried to confront her auntie about her frequent drug use, she snapped on her and Semaj was done with it.

"Semaj. I'ma grown ass woman and I raised you. You don't tell me what I should and shouldn't do. You act like I'm addicted to this or some shit. It's just something to do for fun. Leave me the fuck alone. Do you and let me do me. Damn!"

"Fuck it then! That's on your dumb ass," Semaj said and vowed to never say anything else about it.

As she stood in her large walk-in closet, Semaj chose to wear a comfortable white strapless knee-length sundress, an oversized pair of designer shades and jeweled sandals. She pulled her hair off of her face in a neatly loose high ponytail. After locking up and grabbing her handbag, she headed out. She was ready to get her shoe shopping on at her favorite store, Gucci.

Semaj walked into the flagship store and felt like she was in shoe heaven. The sales associates immediately flocked to her as she was a regular. As she breezed through the store, She decided to buy two pair of stilettos, a pair of flat sandals and some sneakers. A pair of loafers caught her eyes so she got them too. She debated on the two thousand dollar handbag, but elected against it. She had one almost similar, and the price was way too high for the simplicity of the bag.

"I see somebody shoe shoppin' today," a voice behind her stated.

Receiving her change from the salesman, Semaj spun on her heels and smiled when she recognized the familiar face. "Yes. Everyone knows that a girl's shoe game must be on point," she beamed.

"How you been?" Quasim asked. "You are the hardest woman to catch up with. You stop answering my calls and everything. You making me feel like I'm an ugly nigga or some shit."

She blushed, surprised that he was still checking for her. It had been months since their date and even though he hadn't spoken to her in forever she thought of him all the time. But her life had been hectic, and she was committed to the hustle and a man was the last of her concerns. "Now you know you need to quit that. You're really making me feel bad. I've just been

48

crazy busy that's all," she replied. "What up, though?"

"Shopping for my li'l brother some school clothes," he said. "Can you help me out? This li'l dude need's a woman's touch to get him straight."

"Of course," she agreed. Semaj thought she was shopping as if she was a rich bitch, but when she saw how Quasim was doing it, it made her look like a lightweight in the game. From store to store, she picked out things for his brother and he purchased items without being distracted from his cell phone. While he handled business, Semaj tore down the high-end designer stores. She grabbed everything from clothing to shoes and games sparing no expense. Every time he whipped out the Black Card to foot the bill, she wondered how he made his money. Semaj was impressed at how he handled things and also surprised as she listened to him discussing business ventures sounding like a Wall Street stock broker. Semaj knew that Quasim was her dream man.

"Dang, you were definitely caught up in your phone conversations leaving it all up to me," Semaj said as he finally ended his call.

"Sorry about that. Business just gets kinda crazy," he said stepping close to her. "Tell you what. I wanna make it up to you. I'm having a party at my cabin next weekend to celebrate this new project that's underway. It'll be fun and it will give you a chance to meet my crew. I can see if you fit in. And if I really like being around you," he smirked.

"Well damn! Aren't we blunt? How you know I wasn't thinking the same thing?" she asked, slightly offended.

"Seriously though, I want us to get to know each other. Is that fair?" he asked with a charming smile.

"Yeah that's fair. So I guess I'll be there," Semaj said as she reached up to hug him. She walked away, letting the natural sway of her ass hypnotize him. *I think he wants me,* She thought smugly, knowing that she didn't want a relationship at this time in her life but it surely felt good to have someone she was interested in paying her some attention.

Quasim sat discussing the issues they were facing with his latest business venture. The screenplay was well written by Jah-Jah the screenwriter, but the dilemma was coming from finding a leading lady for the starring role. The filming date was set to start in just under a month, and they were no closer to finding their star. Quasim was irritated because they had auditioned over fifty females and none fit the part. "Can't we just call and get Megan Goode? This shit just ain't working. She the last actress I can think of that fits in the age range we need. We done went through damn near everybody and even the highly trained actresses ain't delivering what we want."

"I spoke to her manager but she's in the middle of filming right now," Al-B, Quasim's childhood best friend and business partner said. Quasim was the financial backer and Al-B was the brains, which made for the perfect combination. Al-B was the film producer for the movie, and the one who had the major connection with Christopher Cunningham, who had acquired the motion picture deal. Christopher was a well sought after director in the film industry, and had worked with many big names.

Quasim and Al-B had a few independent films out under their production company, *Street Life Entertainment* and the two-year old company was surprisingly beginning to get off the ground. Quasim believed in his man and didn't hesitate when he came to him with his vision that could make them both rich... as for Quasim, richer. He had invested from the door. They felt this was the big one though, and wanted no mistakes.

"Yes, we really need to find somebody immediately. Time is of the essence. I'm not trying to have this project delayed," Christopher told them.

"I see it like this: It's simple. We re going to have to do an open casting call this weekend for some raw, unknown talent. It's a lot of stars out there just waiting to be discovered and we have to find the one for this role," Quasim said as he rose from his chair and walked over to the large window. Crossing his arms, he looked down at the busy New York streets as he stood in deep thought.

"No doubt. We need a young lady that has that same fire that Mary J. Blige had when she first hit the scene with that 'Real Love'. The music world had never seen a female singer like that. She was hip hop, soul and street all in one. But we need an actress that's giving that same passion but on the big screen," Al-B stated.

"I know exactly what you mean. This might not work but at this point it's worth a try. There might be a young lady that can bring this character to life. She definitely got the attitude but I'm not sure if she has the acting skills," Quasim admitted wanting to be cautious.

"Who is she?" Jah-Jah asked as everyone waited on his response.

"Bad li'l broad I was talkin' to at the charity event. You 'member her,

Mike-Mike?"

"Oh yeah, shorty was bad and had that urban swag we need."

"Get her on the phone. She can audition right now. We need the lead role filled as soon as possible and you better hope she's what we're looking for. If not, shooting would be pushed back to a later date indefinitely," Chris told both Quasim and Al-B.

Semaj was counting big faces and wrapping them in rubber banded bundles as she heard her phone ringing. Her father had just dropped the money off to Paris' apartment. It was from their latest hit, which was on one of the guy's Paris used to date out of Baltimore, Maryland.

While Semaj and Paris were counting money, Tala was on a date with their next potential victim. To Semaj's surprise, Tala was going hard and hipping them on some low key but big time hustlers. She also knew where their stash was at too.

"Hey there," Semaj said answering the phone cheerfully. "I'm surprised to hear from you since the trip isn't until next week. Oh, wait... let me guess... you're calling to cancel?"

"Never that," Quasim chuckled. "You're silly...that's cute. But ummm...I was calling 'cause I need a huge favor from you. It's serious."

"A serious favor?" Semaj asked. "I don't even know you like that to be doing favors."

"It could be beneficial for me and you," he replied.

"Oh, really?"

"On some fo'real shit, I have a role I might need you to play."

Semaj immediately assumed he wanted her to set up a nigga for him. "Oh, that's cool. What do I get out of the deal?"

"You don't even know what role I'm talkin' about." Quasim said.

"If it's paying then I'm with it."

"Okay, I see you about your money," Quasim laughed lightly. "But first you gotta come down here and audition to see if you're the right fit for the part."

"Audition?" she asked in confusion.

"Yeah. Me and my peoples are finna start shooting this movie and we got every role filled except for the leading lady. What you thought I was talkin' 'bout?"

"Fuck outta here!" she shouted in excitement. Semaj didn't know if it was a low budget film or what, but truthfully, she didn't give a damn. "First, do that shit pay?" In truth, She didn't care she needed the exposure and experience.

"I wouldn't ask you to do nothing free for me. You should never do a thing if it doesn't benefit you."

"Where do I come? I'm on my way!" she said barely able to contain her excitement.

When they pulled up, luxury rides were lined up in front of the building. It resembled a car show instead of a place of business. Quasim had met them downstairs and they headed up to the 32nd floor, and entered a vast lounge-styled room. The way Semaj's designer jeans hugged her wide hips had the dudes drooling. She was dressed simple, but captured attention unintentionally. She rocked a white V-neck, a pair of Mauri kicks and large superstar sunglasses perched on her head. She had a distinctive look about her and a style of her own.

Semaj smiled as she waved at all the men and the one woman that was in the room. Her mind was so far in the distance that she didn't notice the man sitting at the desk staring at her intently.

"Where I know you from?" The man's question had everyone in the room's attention, and they all turned their direction towards Semaj.

"I have no clue," she replied as her heartbeat became erratic. She searched her memory bank on where the man could've possibly recognized her from.

"Hell nah! I know exactly where I know you from! I was tryin' to give you this part, months ago. And you thought I was bullshitting. You're the young lady from that acting school where Ms. Porter teaches. Qua, that's the one we saw performing that play Romeo and Juliet. That's her. She the truth. True story, y'all."

"That's you?" Quasim asked surprised. "You was tight in that role."

"You thought I was selling you dreams, huh?" Al-B asked and laughed.

"I mean, yeah. Know how many dudes will sell a chick a dream just to holler at her?" The room fell into an abundance of laughter.

"You been in reach all this time and I ain't have a clue. Let's get down to business."

"Great. She's here now and all we have to see is if she can deliver," Chris said, handing her the script.

After grabbing the paper, Semaj walked into the hallway to look it over. Reading the role first, she learned that her character was a girl from the ghetto who lost her parents due to an assassination by the government. This lead her to becoming an orphan and once she turned eighteen she was determined to murder everyone responsible for her parents' death. She was willing to do any and everything to seek revenge and had with a very shocking ending. The setting was placed in Washington, DC and the film was titled *Murderess in DC*. Semaj read over the ten required lines and memorized them in under twenty minutes.

Taking a deep breath, she sighed, anxious and excited all at the same time as she made her way back into the room. She was no longer Semaj Richardson. She transformed into her character, Nina Simone Brown. The way she brought the character to life flowed as if she was actually born Ms. Brown. Her own suffering and heartache during her childhood made it all too real for her. It gave her the creditability to land the role and potentially becoming a star. The decision of if she had gotten the part was unquestionable by the looks on each of their faces.

"I knew you would be the perfect girl," Al-B said breaking the silence.

"Yeah, you the truth. You kept that shit gangster and I can't see nobody playing the part but you," Jah-Jah said as Semaj prepared to leave. "I'm glad the casting is over," she smiled with excitement.

"Me too," Quasim added. "You out of here, Jah?"

"Yeah, I'm already late for this appointment in midtown."

"A'ight, I'll speak to you later on." Quasim turned to face Semaj. "Damn! I never knew you were the one I saw when I was up at that school. This shit crazy. It's amazing how things always come full circle."

Semaj now remembered him the day he was leaving out of the auditorium. She blushed, knowing that this was destiny bringing her dreams to life. *Maybe this could finally be it,* she thought gratefully. "This is too crazy."

"But umm, is you gon' even have enough time for shooting and things like that, Maj?" Paris questioned, interrupting Quasim's and Semaj's conversation.

"Why wouldn't she?" Al-B inquired. "If she don't I'm sure she'd make time. She has a lot of potential and I knew that from the first time I saw her performing. This is a once in a lifetime opportunity, I doubt Semaj is going to blow it."

"Damn straight I'm not! I'll make this work, I promise you." There was no way Semaj would turn this down, though it all seemed so unreal. She could hear her mother's voice in her head: *You said you were going to Hollywood to be an actress one day. And this is where you'll get that legit dough, baby girl. This is the hustle that I never had a chance to get, but you gettin' it so you better take it for all it's worth.*

"Well, filming starts May 1st. My assistant will call you tomorrow morning to go over the paperwork," Al-B smiled and walked out.

"This is big, Paris! I can't believe I'm finna be in a motion picture. If this is a dream, I hope I never wake up from it," Semaj gushed with happy butterflies in her stomach. She grabbed her phone from her bag and called everybody she knew to inform them that she would be starring in a major motion picture not no straight to DVD shit, although she would've taken that too.

Semaj still wasn't one hundred percent comfortable with Quasim coming to her residence, so she opted to have him pick her up from her father's brownstone. She sat on the stoop with her father as they shared a blunt filled with cush. It was during these times her father would keep it a hundred with Semaj, schooling her on her advantage over men and how to survive in the treacherous streets. They respected each other and his baby girl was his best friend and vice versa.

"You gon' have to let me meet this li'l friend of yours," Murder Mitch said as he took a deep drag of the blunt, letting it rest in his lungs before he released it out.

"You know I don't be on no meeting the parents type shit, Daddy. Plus it's too soon for all that. I might come off desperate," Semaj replied as she heard the sounds of a bass-filled car coasting up. "This probably him right here," she smiled graciously as she stood up and sat back down after realizing it wasn't Quasim.

"What! If it ain't my nigga, Block! What's poppin' li'l nigga?" Murder Mitch said as he stepped out his vehicle. "Block, what the fuck been good nigga? I ain't seen ya li'l ass in so muthafuckin' long time," Murder Mitch said, pulling him close for a brotherly embrace.

"Million-Dollar!" he said, referring to the old name the streets had given him years ago. It was because some folks knew that he got paid millions of dollars to lay niggas down for a notorious Dominican Mafia family. "It's been a long time, big homie."

"Now what do I owe this unexpected visit?" Murder Mitch asked as he puffed on the blunt once more.

"I got some business that I think I'ma have to have you handle for me. Niggas been on some ol' other shit. Every heard of the nigga, Santana?"

"Heard a lot about him but who hasn't. Few have seen him in the flesh though."

"Yeah, but I know a little more information about the cat than the average nigga."

"I'm sure. You got a ton of goons on your squad over there in Brick City," he said referring to Jersey.

"You know I do, big homie," Block nodded. "But I got a lot of live wires. I need some shit done right and on the low. I know you an OG with this shit. I 'member how you used to rock niggas to bed and they'd never find the bodies." Murder Mitch laughed reminiscing on how he used to put in work for Block's Uncle Bennie. He was a major kingpin in Newark and Murder Mitch was his number one hit-man. '

On one occasion, Bennie had hired Murder Mitch to wipe out an entire block for his nephew. It was then he gave his nephew the nickname "Block". And being that he was running major blocks by the time he was fourteen made it stick. That was over a decade ago and Bennie had been ambushed leaving his home. This tragedy left Block next in line to take the head of the family heroin business.

"I'm feeling that. So when you need these niggas mind lost?" He was referring to him placing one in the dome. "And what's the pay nigga? You know I don't murder for chump change."

Block chuckled. "I know how you rock, big homie. I'ma pay you good. But check, the reason I'm here is to invite you to my son's party. It's gon' be huge and that is where we can continue to talk business."

Murder Mitch laughed at the fact that he taught Bennie who had obviously taught Block to never just discuss business anywhere and the safest place is the place you lay your head. At times that wasn't even safe, because it was easy for the Feds to bug anyone's home. "I'm feeling you on that li'l nigga. I'ma be there to show my love and we can finish discussing our business there."

"It's on. But for old time sake we need to catch up, so let's do lunch at one of my favorite joints, Uncle Mitch."

"I don't never turn down a good meal." Mitch turned to his daughter "Semaj I'ma holla at you. I gotta handle something with my little man."

"Okay, Daddy," she yelled before he hopped into the coupe.

Hours later Quasim and Semaj was being chauffeured up to the massive cabin as the driver of the Escalade truck navigated his way up the spiraled hilltop. The wrought iron gate opened, admitting them in as the driver drove to the back entrance where the celebration was taking place.

Quasim's driver opened the truck's door for them, and quickly escorted Semaj to the backyard where he made his rounds with her on his arm. Everyone seemed to show her mad love except for the girl that wore the mean mug.

His uncle, Quentin was impressed by his lady of choice for the night and he had never seen Quasim bring any woman as his official date to one of their many functions. "You must be special, because my nephew never brings dates to our affairs. But I'll admit you are truly breathtaking." Quentin admired her beauty and stared longer than necessary. He had a feeling that he had seen her before. She looked too familiar but he dismissed it, assuming she resembled a woman he had known in the past.

There was a massive white rectangular shape table that seated ten people in the high-back, black-and-white chairs, which was positioned atop an onyx-glossed platform. Quasim took his place at the head, positioning Semaj directly beside him. The sun was setting graciously and the backyard's automatic lights shone, emanating a pale yellow-hue to brighten up the yard. Waiters in black-and-white military uniforms came to serve them the gourmet cuisine.

"Do you always do things this big?" she asked as she leaned into Quasim, curious as to what his response would be.

"Why you ask that?"

"Because you coming all the way out to the mountains to celebrate and how you having your people catered to like this is normal or some shit."

"This the only way to do it. I can't take no armored trucks to the funeral homes. May as well live it up. This a day in the life. I told you this what you can get if you act right," he laughed.

"Oh, is that right?" Semaj asked and hit him right back. "But you better hope you act right. Let's not leave that out playa."

Al-B stood with his champagne bottle in hand. "I'm toasting this one out to my man, Quasim. Mutherfuckas don't wanna see us out here living and though they took out our people, he shining down on us and telling us to keep doing what we doing so we can make him proud. Here's to you big bra, to us, to our fam, and to getting money, my nigga. They can't stop the movement, and all the li'l hatin' these hoe ass niggas doing is small thangs to a giant. We in here and taking it to the top."

"No doubt, baby," Mike-Mike added, slapping hands with his li'l brother, Slim. "Congratulations to you niggas on this project."

"You already know, nigga," Quasim said. Though he didn't drink, he raised one of the many bottles in the air graciously. He figured he had to stay focus and always had to be on his toes. Matter of fact, he wasn't drinking, smoking or nothing. He was strictly about his paper.

Everyone there was in his inner circle and as expected, he didn't allow outsiders in and everyone not present was considered an outsider. Semaj could feel the honor, respect and loyalty amongst the crew. They were family and it seemed like everyone had the same level of respect for each other and she admired that about his crew. They were doing major shit and a part of her wondered what they all did to live such a life of luxury. He would've had to be in the film business a while to be moving how he moved, so she assumed Quasim dabbled into illegal things also.

As the evening proceeded, Semaj couldn't stop smiling. She played her position as queen of the dynasty while enjoying the celebration. She felt special that Quasim was catering to her every need and showed her all of his attention. By midnight, the invitees were dispersing.

"Yo, Qua, this nigga keep calling my phone talkin' bout you duckin' his calls and shit," Slim said.

"Who?"

"The Jerz, nigga. Talkin' 'bout he gotta rap some major business wit' you."

"I'ma grown ass man. What I look like dodging calls? Fuck, that nigga buggin', B," he said. "Yo, bay, I really need to take this call." Quasim excused himself from the table.

She watched as Quasim rapped with the caller and after a few minutes he terminated the call seemingly angry. Walking to speak to his man's briefly, he returned back to Semaj. He quickly dismissed the madness and welcomed her inside his opulent vacation home.

The place was the most amazing thing she'd laid eyes on. This wasn't the average cabin. It was something ripped out of the magazines for the rich and famous. "This cabin is too beautiful," Semaj said, admiring the tri-level brick entrance. The modern interior design was breathtaking. Saying it was plush would be an understatement.

"You like it?"

"What, boy I love it!" she exclaimed still in amazement of the whole idea of her being in this man's company.

"I'm glad you do. I bought it last year."

"What planet you come from? Mars? Because they don't make niggas like you where I come from." Semaj said as she walked by his side.

Quasim looked at her like she was crazy. "Mars? What is that supposed to mean?"

"It's like you got everything in your life in order. You a young nigga and a black dude at that doing good for yourself. You don't find dudes like this often and definitely not around my parts."

"Maybe you need to find new parts then, because everybody I know living life like this."

Semaj giggled. She was waiting for Quasim to deliver the punch line but he didn't. Dude was serious with his response. She knew undoubtedly that she was dealing with a major nigga. "So what are we going to get into tomorrow?" she asked, changing the subject.

"We're going hiking and if you wanna go fishing we can do that too. I ain't enjoyed no different shit in a minute."

She smiled graciously. Dudes that she had dealt with in the past always thought the ordinary shit was the crème de la crème, but he was proving that he was extraordinary.

She followed him up to the master bedroom where they got comfortable. Semaj expected for Quasim to push up on her, but to her surprise, he didn't even make a move. For that reason alone, she respected him even more and they sat up and pillow talked for hours—having a deep conversation about goals... dreams... the future. Semaj had felt that her life was changing right before her eyes. She had even forgotten briefly that she was a cold individual. She had never experienced anything like this before and she wondered could this have been what she'd been missing all along. That night she fell asleep in Quasim's warm arms as he stroked her hair, and for once in her life she felt loved by a man.

The next morning the ringing of Semaj's phone interrupted their sleep. They tried ignoring it, but it wouldn't stop. It was irking the shit out of Quasim. "Yo, you need to answer that shit or turn it off."

Leaning over to retrieve her cell from the nightstand, Semaj tried adjusting her vision to the light. Her intentions were to turn the phone off until she saw Tala's picture pop up on her screen. "Is this you really blowing me up like this," Semaj asked groggily.

"Oh shit, I still see you got that smart ass mouth. Shit ain't changed after two years, huh?"

"Who is this?" Semaj frowned as she sat upright to try and recognize the voice.

"D-Boy. I hope you got my fifty Gs since you helped this bitch spend my hard earned money."

"Wh… what you talkin' about? Some niggas ran in Tala's spot and took your money D-Boy," Semaj said, standing up as fear entered her heart. "Where is my Auntie?"

"Dumb bitch lying out on this couch high as a fuckin' kite. I'm about to beat this bitch up until she tell me where my money at. What, you bitches done snorted up all my money?" he asked.

"What are you talking about, D-Boy?" she asked, hopelessly.

"I know y'all bitches try'na swindle me out of my mu'fuckin' bread. Real cute and brilliant notion. Bet you betta come up wit' that cheese 'cause a nigga a do whatever to you bitches for my fuckin' cheddar, hoe." With those words he hung up in her ear.

Shock and disbelief formed in her eyes and Quasim didn't know what was going on. "What's wrong? What happened? Are you okay?"

"No. That was my Aunt's baby's father. I need to go."

"Now?" he asked.

"No… right now!"

Chapter 7

Semaj hated that she had to end their trip, but hearing from D-Boy had her on edge. All she could do was replay his threat in her mind. *Bet you betta come up wit' that cheese 'cause a nigga a do whatever to you bitches for my fuckin' cheddar, hoe.* Semaj shook her head in disappointment. *He think she took his money to get high,* she thought regretfully. *I should have never encouraged her to take that man's bread.* No matter how hard she tried to ignore her nagging gut, the bad feeling in her stomach let her know something was wrong. She stared blankly out of the window in order to avoid Quasim seeing the fear in her face.

The whole ride Quasim didn't say a word, respecting that she obviously didn't want to speak on the situation. Out of care, he did often caress the back of her neck in comfort to let her know that she could talk to him about anything.

The ride seemed to take an eternity and Semaj wanted to roar at the driver. It seemed as if he was outside of the car pushing it himself. He was driving extremely too slow and she desperately needed to get to her auntie. Her mind was so gone she hadn't once thought to phone her father. All she wanted at this moment more than anything in the world was to get back to the city. *Father Lord, please don't let D-Boy have harm my auntie. Oh God, let her make it through this and I will get her help,* she promised silently. *How did she get to this point? Please keep her safe, Father.*

Semaj had never experienced anything close to God, but she desperately needed the higher power to watch over her auntie's welfare. Semaj knew that the reason it was hurting her so badly was because she hadn't reached out to help her. She assumed that she would eventually shake her drug habit. In the beginning, Semaj battled with Tala over the drugs she was abusing, but soon gave up on her. Her heart was filled with a twinge of guilt for giving up on her auntie so easily. *But I never knew it was that bad. She knocked out on the couch and don't even know he's there,* Semaj thought in disbelief. *All this is my fault. Why did I tell her to go into that nigga's stash? Why didn't I tell her that the lifestyle we all are leading isn't the way it's supposed to be? All I had to do was help her.*

When they pulled on her father's block, Semaj quickly gathered her belongings and waited for the truck to come to a halt.

"Baby, whatever there is that I can do for you, I'm only a phone call away," Quasim said sincerely.

She nodded her head and tried to give him a comforting smile but to no prevail. "Thank you, but at this time there's nothing you can do. But I'll call you at a later time." Semaj opened the door and stepped down from the truck. Noticing her father's car was gone, she called his phone and left him an urgent voicemail while sliding in her car and driving away.

When she arrived at Tala's apartment, she threw her car in park. She hopped out of the vehicle and rushed into the high-rise building. Her heart pumped out of her chest. She immediately knew something was wrong. The door was ajar. As soon as she stepped inside a horrible smell filled her nose and through the corner of her eyes Semaj saw her auntie laid out on the sofa. Blood was soaking through the throw pillow and dripping onto the tan carpet, leaving maroon specks. She had blood leaking from her head. Semaj ran over and knelt down beside her as she broke down crying.

"Auntie! Tala, wake up man! Wake up! Stop playing!" Semaj screamed as she cradled her face with her hands. She grabbed the thin sheet and tried pressing against the bullet hole in her head, but the sheet was nothing compared to the blood flowing profusely. "Tala you can't die on me! We don't die! We bad bitches!"

Tala started to cough and gag up blood as more blood poured from her mouth. "Don't let me die like this," Semaj heard her faint whisper and realized that she was alive.

"I'm here, Ta. Don't think about that right now. You gonna make it through," she said in a panic as she frantically pulled out her phone, her shaky hand barely able to dial 911. "Please, I need help. My auntie has been shot in the head," she muttered urgently. She gave the operator their location and dropped the phone as she concentrated on her auntie, and attempted to hold her.

"My baby boy, Maj. Please make sure Ms. Long takes him because she's all I trust."

"Stop talkin'…Tala save your breath ma. I'ma make sure, but don't talk. The ambulance is on the way."

"I'm sorry for not listening to you. You always been my favorite person in the world. I love you. If I could do it all over again, I would've raised you better. I would've done better for the both of us."

"I love you too. But you raised me to the best of your ability. I'll always be grateful. Just hold on a few minutes longer. You have to be strong for us Tala. We been through it all. You can hold on I know it, Ta." She could hear the paramedics from a distance as she rubbed her hair softly. "Just hold on Ta," she cried. Semaj had tears streaming down her face, partially obstructing her vision.

"Please… don't be mad, Maj," her words were barely audible. "But the pain…" Tala whispered before her eyes shut against her will.

Mobb Deep was pumping out of the speakers as Murder Mitch cruised the interstate pushing 85 mph in the CLK rental, blowing purple haze. In all his years, he never owned a car. It wasn't because he couldn't afford one. But in his profession he believed that it was mandatory to switch up whips like he switched firearms so that nobody would recognize him when he rode down. He liked being incognito. He took an extensive toke from the blunt and briefly held the smoke in his lungs.

Since he had been home from prison he hadn't been in the murder-for-hire business. Actually, he assumed he'd been forgotten about regarding that line of work. He'd been robbing niggas for so long that his most skilled trade being a hired gun had been placed on the back burner. With the proposition Block had offered him had been a long time coming. He was ready to put his murder game back on.

"This li'l nigga try'na keep the legacy going," Murder Mitch laughed. He pulled off the expressway and entered a small city in the suburban section of New Jersey. After a few turns onto a couple back streets he arrived at

Block's residence. Murder Mitch looked down at the paper the address was on and smiled. *I see the nigga doing well for himself, making his peeps proud of continuing what they built.* He observed the elegant mansion and the tall, black wrought iron-gate that kept the onlookers at bay leading to the entryway. He gave his name to the security guard occupying the booth before entry.

After a brief moment of silence, then the sound of the metal clanking, Murder Mitch was admitted inside the private property.He maneuvered his automobile through the gate and followed the signs that led to the back of the French-style mansion. The scenery was amazing and Murder Mitch promised he hadn't seen a place so beautiful since working for Kasey's father. The lawn appeared to be freshly mowed and the flowers that lined the front complemented its entry. The driveway was filled with exotic vehicles and Block's henchman took their positions around the borders.

Murder Mitch slid out of the car where an obvious pool party was taking place. It was obvious that it was a children's shindig and the parents watched their activities attentively. Block was laid out in a beach chair by the bar, accompanied by his wife, Kandi. The soldiers kept their eyes glued on Murder Mitch as he approached their boss.

"My man Million Dollar! What's good?"

"You know what I'm ready for. This business, son."

"Always been a businessman." Block chuckled and stood to slip into his linen shirt. "Let's go inside the pool house," he suggested, signaling for his wife to prepare him a drink.

"That's a beautiful wife you have there, little homie," Murder Mitch commented as he admired her shapely body and flawless dark skin as her hips swayed from side to side.

"Thanks man."

Block's wife led the way as Murder Mitch closely followed behind them. He walked inside where it looked like a large apartment in itself. "Can I offer you something to drink?" he asked as he entered into his office.

"I'm good."

"So I guess we can get straight down to business?"

Kandi came over to pour her husband a glass of grapefruit juice and placed it on the coaster that sat atop the shiny oak table.

"Most def," Murder Mitch replied.

"Hand me that briefcase." Kandi retrieved the briefcase from the desk and sat it in front of him. She finally popped it open. "This fifty thousand and you know how we do. When it's done, I'll have that other half for you."

"Fo'sho. But check, how you want this done?"

"Like I said before, I know you can get the shit off, but I want you to take it slow! 'Cause I don't want this to be a fuck up. Nigga very wary and stay on his toes. Take your time so this shit won't be messy," Block said as his phone rang. It was his cousin. He hadn't talked to him since he'd been released from prison so he had to take the call. "I need to take this. Hold on a minute." Block answered, "What took you so long to call me, nigga?" He leaned back in his chair relaxingly as he focused in on the call.

"Man, unfinished business, B."

"Well did you get that li'l shit taken care of?" he asked.

"Tried to, but let me put you on game, nigga." D-Boy filled his cousin in on how his baby mother had played him on his money and how he assumed it went down. "Guess they thought I wasn't gettin' out, family," he sighed in frustration.

"Yeah I tried to tell you about them all-about-money NY bitches. Can't trust 'im, family."

"I know. But before I say anything else, B, I really 'preciate everything you did since a nigga been away. Thanks for covering all funeral expenses for Mercedes too. A nigga respect shit like that."

"Y'all my family. You ain't gotta thank me. 'Cause I know if it was me, you would have done the same thang for me," Block said surely.

"No doubt."

"So did you ever find out what happened with that whole situation? Who I gotta *holla* at, cuz?"

"Streets ain't talking. But when I find out I'ma handle that one personally. But I am definitely gonna need you to handle this li'l bitch for me. My source told me she be around ya man's, Santana." D-Boy was a street nigga to the core. There was nothing or nobody that he hadn't heard about on the East Coast. He kept his ears to the streets, in and out of the prison walls. He hated Santana. How funny it may seem. It wasn't personal, because actually D-Boy had never seen the dude let alone knew him personally. It was from a business perspective. He was bred to never like the competition and he envied Santana. "Never liked that nigga anyway. This shit gives me more of the reason to dead both of the muthafuckas."

"What's crazy is I'm currently paying my OG to eliminate the competition right now," Block laughed, "I'ma just add extra for the bitch."

"Damn! I thought that was ya mans" D-Boy said.

"Some bullshit went down, fam, giving me the reason to annihilate that man…and now his bitch," Block said. Just the thought of Santana cutting him off left a bitter taste in his mouth. No longer receiving his supply had Block's drug business suffering significantly. A hustler's worst nightmare was a decline in business and Block wasn't having it.

"It's on. I'ma be to see you in a couple days."

"You already know and welcome home." Block hung up the phone and refocused his attention on Murder Mitch. "Plans have been stretched, OG. I need you to get at his girl too for my peoples."

"Never a problem," he said nonchalantly as if murder was nothing. To him, murder was nothing.

Block smirked, pleased. "You know Ox, my Jamaican connect?"

"Yeah," he replied. "I used to put in major work for that nigga too. Matter fact, he the one introduced me to your peoples."

"Yeah. Well his freighter was seized by U.S Coast Guards. Ox had a shipment of about a half million bricks of that shit on its way over here to the States when it got hit, making it one of the biggest heroin busts of my run in this business. Quality heroin is so scarce it's ridiculous. Niggas so muthafuckin' thirsty they stretching that shit so much that the *boy* has lost nearly all of its purity. This shit out here is straight garbage. It's hard to move. Santana is the only nigga eating on the East Coast, besides his plug and clients. It was cool for a minute, because he was selling me them thangs at a reasonable price. But now nigga talkin' some scary shit and wanna cut me as being my supplier. Some bullshit about 'cause the bitch ass feds, lurking. Tried to tell the nigga I got that situation under control. This my muthafuckin world," Block paused to spark up a blunt and continued on. "That's one disrespectful li'l nigga. I gotta show 'im this shit deeper than just getting money out of the game. That's why I personally want you to tell that nigga I send my regards."

Murder Mitch agreed with a nod of the head.

"My fam just said something about this bitch he just start seeing. The nigga never have bitches with him so you're gonna be able to get at her like nothing, 'cause she gon' be the only broad around him."

"You know that ain't never been a problem for me." Block nodded pleasingly. He went inside his desk for an additional twenty grand. "That's for the girl." He gave him all the known information on Santana before walking him out to his car. "I'll get with you in a week or so to let you know how it's coming along."

"That's what it do." Murder Mitch popped inside his car. As he pulled off, he honked the horn as his phone rang.

"Daddy, Tala been shot! Hurry up and get to the hospital!" Semaj screamed into the phone, causing him to drive at dangerous speeds as he attempted to gain all information necessary. Somebody was about to die.

Entering the waiting area, Murder Mitch spotted his daughter sitting on the floor. Her hands and clothes were still covered in Tala's blood.

"Tell me what happened, Maj," he said and rushed over to her. He hugged his daughter tightly. He could see that his baby girl was distraught, causing his heart to break into pieces. An emotionless man, nothing had ever made protective feelings come out of him except for when his family was in pain. He needed answers. Semaj didn't respond and he understood why, quickly dismissing it as her being in shock. He sat beside his daughter on the floor to hold her as a sense of solace and security overcame her.

"Daddy, I thought she was dead," she finally uttered. "He called me and said he was going to beat her. I didn't know he was going to shoot her. Daddy, I hope she make it through this," she cried in her father's arms.

"Who, sweetheart? What are you talkin' about?" he asked, rocking her back and forth.

"Her baby father, D-Boy. He knew about Tala lying about his money. He said he was only going to beat her up. I really never knew he was going to shoot her." Snot and tears mixed on her face. "If I'd known I would've called for her some help."

"Don't worry about that, baby girl. But, I thought that nigga was still in jail."

"I assume he got an early release for good behavior," she sniffled.

"Well I'ma be lookin' for that fuckin' nigga and as quiet as kept you know the rest. Stop crying, Maj," Murder Mitch wiped the tears from his daughter's face. "Believe that. You know I'm going to handle this shit. Don't you?"

"It wasn't supposed to turn out like this, Daddy. Between me and you,

I just told her to take the money for all the wrong he'd done to her. I felt this was her get back for all the things he took her through with the bitches and fuckery. For him having a main bitch and her not finding out until he went to jail…all that."

"Don't worry about it. I'ma handle it" Murder Mitch gently stroked her hair for comfort. As the hours passed the two were growing impatient. It seemed as if they had been there for days instead of hours, anticipating the outcome of the emergency surgery Tala was undergoing.

As daylight approached, the nurse came out to update them. "Ms. Richardson is a tough one. She's been through intense surgery and has made it through the operation. She is still in ICU. The room number is 3728. Now, she is under heavy sedation and will probably sleep into the next day."

"Can we see her please?" Semaj asked, whispering.

"Sure. It will be good to sense loved ones around her."

Murder Mitch stood up and assisted Semaj onto her feet. Grabbing her hand, they walked to the elevator and rode up to the third floor. Exiting, the pair walked down the long hallway and into the dimly lit room. The sight of Tala lying there battered and bandaged up with a gunshot wound to the head sent him over the top. He loathed seeing his sister like this. He hated himself more for not being there to protect her. A defeated feeling overcame him, and he could no longer stand it. To mask his watery eyes, he left the room without informing his daughter on his departure.

When he left, Semaj knew he was on a rampage and actually hoped that he murdered D-Boy before the next morning broke. She hated him with every fiber in her. Easing her way to Tala's bedside, she focused on the needle marks on her arm. Teardrops instantly hit the bedding and guilt consumed her. *Damn, I ain't know she was shooting up. Was it this bad really?* Semaj asked herself, shaking her head as she gently grabbed her auntie's hand. "I'm sorry auntie. I should've never let it get this far. I know you can easily be influenced and let things get the best of you. I hate that we've been so distant lately. I'm sorry. I will never leave you again. You could've…" the tears were flowing like a heavy rainstorm. "I mean, I don't know what I would've done. I love you Tee-Tee," she said, calling her the nickname she hadn't used since she was a little girl.

Suddenly Tala squeezed her hand weakly, causing Semaj to jump. Her heart warmed knowing that her auntie gave her a sign that she had heard her speaking to her. Never releasing her hand, Semaj pulled a chair close to her bedside and took a seat. Resting her head on the diminutive space on the bed, Semaj prayed slightly and thanked God for sparing her family. Conversing with her auntie on the good times, unintentionally Semaj drifted off to sleep all the while never releasing the hold of her auntie's hand.

That morning Murder Mitch robbed three innocent individuals of their lives: D-Boy's girlfriend of eight years and the two daughters they shared. D-Boy had violated and had disrespected him. Now it was payback and he deleted his most cherished loved ones. He had to pay the cost for shooting his sister in an obvious attempt to murder her.

His cold heart had no remorse for taking the lives of the blameless woman and her children, because it had to be done and it was all a part of the game. Call it tit for a tat; an eye for an eye or a life for a life, but this was the result of retaliation and Murder Mitch showed retribution at its highest intensity.

When D-Boy found them that afternoon his entire reason for living died right along with them. He was determined to find out who he had beef with that was sick enough to brutally murder a woman and her children. But deep down inside of him, D-Boy knew this was a message sent to him personally. He promised himself that he would get revenge on the people responsible, even if it cost him his very own life.

Chapter 8

"Okay, it's a wrap. Great work," Christopher shouted to the movie crew. This was the final day for shooting and Semaj couldn't have been more elated. She was even more euphoric that the production company had cut her first check to the eighty thousand dollar movie deal. Her part had been delivered and it was a blessing for the thirty-five days of straight filming to be over. She woke up early, but four in the morning was pushing it, especially because of the fact that she only went to sleep two hours before that. Semaj was getting no sleeping literally.

"Hey, know you're glad that this shit finally over," Quasim said walking into her trailer.

"Yeah. But my heart is in this. I love it! So I can see myself doing it all over again," Semaj said.

"I feel you. It's definitely a grind though," he said as he gently massaged her shoulders. "I have tickets for this Broadway play tonight. What you have planned?"

"Nothing really," she replied.

"Well, you should come. I think it's Phantom of the Opera. Al-B said I need to expand my mind and try some different shit," he chuckled with a handsome grin on his face. "Usually I don't get into shit like that, but that nigga insists I experience it. And besides, they say it's calming and I need some peace in my life. You game?"

"I've always wanted to attend a Broadway play. I'd love to go," Semaj said as she stood up and stood face to face with Quasim.

"Okay, I'll arrange to have a car pick you up."

"Great."

"How does six sound?" he asked, gazing in her eyes.

"Perfect."

It was as if Quasim loved everything about this girl and still so far their relationship hadn't been sexual. That was cool with him though, because he wasn't going to pressure her into anything. He was still completely turned on by Semaj. He ran his fingers through her hair and softly kissed the top of her head. "I'ma call you in an hour or so, when the car is on the way." He kissed her once more, and disappeared out of her trailer as she smiled graciously at the man she had secretly fallen hard for.

Semaj drove down the BQE heading towards her house. Her mind drifted back to Quasim. It had been so long since she'd been actually attracted to a guy. It was freaking her out. Since Vega, a man hadn't impressed her up until now. Semaj felt that there weren't any real niggas left and figured Vega was the last of a dying breed—that was until she met Quasim. There was something unique about him. He wasn't her man, but then again he wasn't just her "friend" either. They shared a bond that was on a level of its own, and on the outside looking in a person would assume she was his woman. Honestly, it hadn't bothered Semaj, because she could see herself being his lady. She just hoped that he looked at her the same way.

Semaj felt a vibration on her lap and it jarred her from daydreaming about what her life with Quasim would be like. She looked at the screen and noticed it was her father calling. She answered it. "What's up, Daddy?"

"Hey, baby girl. I see you done with filming."

"Yeah I'm finished. But I'm anxious to see what people are gonna think of me and the movie as a whole."

"I know you are. I'm very proud of you on some true G shit. This shit big. You just seem so humble about it all."

"I mean, it still seem like I'm dreaming, Daddy. Maybe I'll feel it is reality once it's released and talked about in the press. Feel me?"

"Yeah. But you always been like that. Wait to things explode before getting excited, just like your mother. You remind me so much of her."

"I miss her, Daddy. I wish she was here to share this moment with me. She'd be so happy and proud."

"She would," Murder Mitch said. "But believe it baby, Kasey smiling down on you. Trust and believe she's your guardian angel."

Semaj changed the subject quickly, knowing it was always hard for her to discuss her mother. "So have you got any info on D-Boy?"

"Still nothing. It's like dude fell off the face of the earth. But he'll come out trust me. And when he do I'm going to send him back to hell where he belong."

"Well, you know Tala is being moved out of ICU in two days. I'ma go see her when I get out of school."

"It's about time. They had my baby sis in intensive care for close to two months."

"They had to do that so she could recover," Semaj said. "She still gon' be temporarily paralyzed for a minute. Her whole right side fucked up and the doctor said there is a chance she'll be like that permanently."

"But if she sticks to her physical therapy she might be able to come home sooner than we expect."

"Yeah, that's why we gonna have to stay on her ass," Semaj suggested, getting off at her exit.

"You already know. But I'll be in touch in a couple days, baby girl. I'ma be out handling business and my phone gon' be turned off so I don't have no distractions. Gotta be completely focused on this job I'm handling."

An eerie twinge shot through Semaj's spine and she wanted to speak with her father about how they had been living a life of self-destruction, but she knew that Murder Mitch was a murderer first and there was nothing that she could say that would change the way he lived. So she simply said, "I love you and be careful, Daddy."

"Love you more," he said and hung up the phone.

Semaj pulled up to her crib and popped the trunk to grab the manila envelope with some important documents inside. She headed straight inside and walked into her room to prepare herself for her night out on the town. Semaj didn't exactly know what to wear to a Broadway play so she went the casual route to be safe. She decided on a pair of black True Religion skinny jeans and a black, gray and purple plaid flannel shirt. The limited edition black suede Jimmy Choo ankle boots set the outfit off. They were a gift from Quasim before filming started. Pulling her hair up in a genie ponytail, complimented the pair of diamond studs and the Chanel lip gloss made her succulent lips glossy.

Quasim had Semaj picked up by a limo. Never having been in a limousine before, she felt special. When the driver pulled through the Theatre

District, she noticed men in suits and slacks and the women in dresses and pencil skirts. She immediately knew she put on the wrong thing. She felt underdressed as the chauffeur coasted up to the theatre's front entrance. She dropped her face in her hands in embarrassment, and no longer wanted to step out. "Only if I would have went the LBD way," she seethed, scolding herself. "You can never go wrong in that!"

As the limo came to a stop, Semaj spotted Quasim standing at the entrance waiting for her, dapper from head to toe. He wore cream slacks and a plain snug-fitting brown Ralph Lauren sweater, and a pair of brown designer loafers. He didn't wear any jewels and still looked like a million dollar nigga. His fresh Caesar haircut was trimmed to perfection and his facial hair seemed to be cut by an expert. Semaj couldn't stunt, the man looked sophisticated like a motherfucker.

The driver stepped out the limo and walked around to let Semaj out. Reluctantly, she walked over greeting Quasim with a sad expression across her face.

Instantly, he felt her vibe was off and asked. "What's wrong? You cool, ain't you?"

"Not really," she whined, displeasingly. "I feel out of place and I wish I could go back home and change clothes. Or run down to grab me a dress out of a store on Madison." She lowered her head in her chest.

Quasim grinned and found her to be amusing. "What you buggin' for? You look beautiful, ma. You straight."

"But don't nobody got on jeans here," she complained.

"Quit trippin'. Ain't nobody looking at it like that. You act like you got on some gym shoes or some shit. Stop buggin'. You cool. C'mon, the play is about to start" Quasim grabbed Semaj's hand, dismissing her insecurities. He warmed her heart instantly and she followed his steps. He guided her into the building and down the long corridor that led to their premium seats.

They arrived right on time because when they sat down the lights dimmed. Semaj was completely intrigued by the play and even more elated that she was enjoying it with Quasim. She knew he really didn't care for plays but the fact that she was his invited guest made it all the more special. After intermission when they sat back down Quasim reached over to hold her hand and Semaj willingly obliged. By the time it was over she wished it would start all over again. That's how much Semaj enjoyed the show.

"Man, that was a really good play. I can see myself doing Broadway some day" Semaj glanced at her wristwatch as they were walking out. "It's only going on nine. It's still early."

"I know. Why don't you come to my house and chill out for the rest of the night with me? We always go to my condo in Midtown because it was more convenient while we were filming, but you ain't even seen my home yet." He pulled her into his chest. "I wanna welcome you into all of my life, Semaj. If you just let me in."

"I want that too, Qua," she admitted, as the mood changed into a more serious one.

"Then let me. That's all you gotta do is let me. A lot of people talk for the sake of talking because they have ulterior motives. But with me, like I told you from jump, I'm the truth and what you see is what you get. I just wanna make you better…make your life better."

"That's all I ever wanted was to be better," Semaj mumbled underneath her breath, getting sensitive. It brought back so many memories. It was the first time that she actually had that feeling of guilt to overcome her from how she was living her life. Being around a man like Quasim brought the emotions out of her, and she had to forcefully choke back her tears. She'd almost lost her auntie over some bullshit, and with an opportunity like this she'd be a fool not to change the lifestyle she led. She was grabbing it, and running as far as she could.

"It will be okay," he said as he rested his head on top of hers. Wiping her tears away, Quasim helped her inside the vehicle and they headed out to his place.

Semaj sat in the backseat of the limo as it navigated through the hilly, wealthy gated-community in Bergen County. She tried keeping her composure as she was being transported to their destination. She observed the multi-million-dollar homes as they bypassed and was secretly in awe. She knew Quasim was getting it in, but she wasn't green to the game either. This was major dopeman living, and a newly independent production owner couldn't afford a place with such extravagance. Quasim residing in a ritzy suburban neighborhood had Semaj's assumptions in overdrive, figuring he had to be the Brickman. He didn't have to admit to it now but the proof was slapping her in the face. He was moving major weight. *But, damn, I never*

heard this nigga name once, and I know everybody that's getting money in New York, she thought to herself. Semaj surely wasn't sleeping on his status in the streets, but something still seemed to be missing. For nothing in the world could she place her finger on it.

Finally, they pulled through a chrome iron gate after it split apart and traveled along the extended driveway. "Omigoodness!" Semaj gushed unintentionally. From the way the front was bedecked with exotic flowers to the opulent miniature, fountain-pond embedded in the front yard to the luxurious vehicles screamed P-r-i-c-e-l-e-s-s, and she couldn't help her excitement.

"Here we are," Quasim said as he opened the French doors to admit them inside of his home.

As soon as she stepped foot inside she couldn't believe her eyes. She had entered a world of pure luxury. The floors were cocaine white with crystal flakes. The stairs that led to the top were chrome with an indestructible glass partition. Exclusive albino mini-sharks were within and platinum railing was atop. It was the most amazing thing her eyes had ever seen.

Quasim's place was pristine and stately. It made her feel like she didn't belong. She was totally out of her element. She was just a girl from the 'hood, raised in the roughness of the ghetto in Brooklyn's Bed-Stuy Projects to be precise. The fact that he had gotten her a lead role in a movie was already beyond her, but to introduce and expose her to something so superb had her on some new shit. The crazy thing was this was Quasim's reality and a life that Semaj only dreamed about. Semaj lived a life above average, but this here life was the made life that rappers showcased this in their music videos but here it was all in arm's reach. "This gotta be a dream man," She kept repeating.

"It's the real deal. You ain't dreaming."

"You live here alone?" she wondered.

"For a long time I did, but my li'l brother moved in after our father passed. He's over at our Uncle Quentin's for the weekend right now though."

"Damn, I know he love living here," Semaj stated unable to grasp that people really lived like this and she knew one of them personally.

"The house he lived in before my father got killed was just as nice but yeah, I'm sure he's happy to be living here now."

"Well, I know you gon' take me on a tour," she said ready to see each room.

"Follow me," Quasim said as he began to walk towards the kitchen.

The gourmet kitchen was equipped with state-of-the-art stainless steel appliances with a skylight above the island. Semaj had never seen so much granite and marble in a place you cooked your food. It had the most beautiful countertops she'd ever seen. From there they went through the many living rooms and then he led her upstairs where there were seven spacious bedrooms. From room to room and floor to floor, Semaj got more excited.

Quasim showed her every inch of the home, including the indoor swimming pool and game room. The place even had a glass elevator in case you weren't in the mood to take the stairs. It took them an hour to view the entire house and when he was finally finished, Semaj shook her head, speechless. "Walking around this big ass house has made me thirsty as shit," She laughed.

"You hungry too?" he asked concerned.

"Don't tell me you got a chef too."

"Well, I do but they're off right now."

"So what, you wanna go get something to eat?" Semaj asked.

"Nah. I'll whip us up something."

"Shut the front door!" she blurted, laughing at the idea of Quasim cooking. "Boy, please! I'm trying to live."

"What?" he looked at her, pausing briefly. "Oh, so you think I can't cook, huh?"

"So you telling me you can?" Semaj stood face to face with him.

"Well, I'll let you be the judge of that." He nodded his head for her to follow him, and she accepted his invitation. He pulled out a chair for her and she sat down. She smiled, loving his charm. Quasim then walked over to the refrigerator and opened it up. "What you prefer baked or fried meat?"

"We gon' go with the baked," she puckered her lips and laughed. "'Cause you know it's easier to fry than bake."

"If you say so. You eat pork?"

"Nigga, I'm black, from the heart of the ghetto. Duh, I eat pork."

"Just making sure. I don't want you having any excuse to hate on my cooking." They both burst into laughter as he grabbed out the meat package, raw potatoes, rolls, gravy, sliced green-and-red peppers and everything to fix steamed vegetables.

For the next hour, Semaj watched Quasim and couldn't stop smiling. He looked so sexy as he prepared them their meal. He made her feel like a queen the way he was catering to her. When he was finished he placed a plate in front of her. It was a full-course meal too. Handing her a fork, he playfully said. "Now eat up and give the kid his props."

She cut a piece of the pork chop and took the forkful into her mouth. Chewing, she turned up her face in disgust. "Ewww... this shit nasty!" she played, clutching her neck as if she was choking.

"Fuck outta here!" He joined her at the dinner table. "I see you one that likes to hate."

"I'm just playing, baby. This shit banging fo'real. How did you learn how to cook like this?"

"My grandmother taught me when I was a youngin'. You thought I was bullshitting, huh?"

"Hell yeah, I did. I guess I'ma have to show my skills one day," she joked.

"Yeah you is. 'Cause I bet you ain't fuckin' with me," Quasim said confidently.

"Psss!" she rolled her neck. "Nigga, please! Just call me Rachel Ray," she replied with the same confidence as him.

"Well, we will see how you do tomorrow night," Quasim challenged.

"Tomorrow night! How you know I'ma be here tomorrow night?"

He dug inside his slacks and pulled out a set of keys. "'Cause I'm giving you a key to my home. You my girl now. So I hope you gon' be here tomorrow night."

"Really?" she asked in disbelief.

"Yeah you mine...unless you know you not—"

"No, no. I'm just surprised."

"I feel you on that," he said. "It's to the point that I believe we're both ready to take our relationship to the next level. It's obvious that we really feeling each other and I think you might as well have a key to my spot. I can see a future with you and us building something great together."

"Hmm!" Semaj sat there puzzled. She never knew that his feelings ran this deep, and out of all the women in the world, he was choosing her. The shit made her feel better than great. "Qua, I'm feeling you too, baby, and I wouldn't want it to be no other way." She reached over and hugged him tightly.

They laughed and chatted like they had known each other forever. After they ate, Semaj removed their plates and put them in the sink so she could wash the dirty dishes.

Watching as she washed the dishes, Quasim admired that she was so girly-girl, but yet loved that she was street all in the same. Instead of utilizing the dishwasher, she kept it 'hood, washing and rinsing the dishware one by one. He eased up behind her as she placed the last skillet underneath the sink and kissed the nape of her neck all the while wrapping his strong arms around her tiny waist.

She could feel his manhood poking her in the small of her back. Her pussy instantly got wet as her clitoris blossomed like a flower. "I want you to make love to me," she whispered erotically.

That's all that had to be said. Scooping Semaj up from the floor, Quasim carried her to his room. Items of clothing flew all around the room as they scrambled to undress one another. Their lips seemed to be glued together having been they had not parted.

Finally, the moment they had both been waiting on. Semaj wanted him bad sexually, but she didn't wanna seem too forward and eager. Quasim was just waiting for her to be ready; he didn't want to make her feel obligated to have sexual encounters with him. Now they both were ready to take it there.

Quasim led her over to the bed and gently laid her down. Her head fell back in delight as he took both of her breasts and pressed the pair together, licking her nipples into erection. He sucked on them and gently bit them as she moaned softly in his ear. The way his mouth explored her could have made Semaj cum alone. His hands moved down her leg and he parted her thighs as he slipped his finger inside her pussy. She was so wet.

She saw the excitement in his eyes as he gazed at her pleasingly. Passion filled her as she grabbed his length and then stroked him slowly, and separated her legs further apart so that he could enter her gushy entrance.

She desperately wanted him inside of her, but he wasn't ready for his man to meet her girl yet. However, he introduced his lips to her pink pussy as he feasted on her pearl. The smell of her was so sweet, he treated it like it was a piece of candy and sucked it into his warm mouth while toying with her hot opening. Quasim wasn't shy with her. He was a grown man and knew there was no half stepping with her. He was going all out and he stuck his thick tongue inside her ass. Her butt cheeks in his hand, her lower body lifted off the bed, Quasim alternated with sucking on her hole and nibbling on her clit.

"Ahh!" Semaj screamed in pleasure as she began to shake uncontrollably.

Quasim definitely knew what he was doing and his head game was firm. He had her feeling a way that no man had ever made her feel. "This shit feels too good!" she shrieked as she crawled the sheets. She couldn't take it.

"Stopping running," Quasim groaned and in a swift motion he tugged her back down.

"I can't…it feels that good!" she whined as her hands found his head, deciding to take it like a champ.

He made her cum twice and she attempted to rise up, but he shoved her down. He was determined to take control of their first sexual escapade. It was something about a man being in control of sex that drove Semaj over the top, and she stayed in her spot like an obedient naughty girl.

Semaj was aroused and didn't hesitate pulling him inside of her warmth. His ten inches filled her insides as she arched her back, and her walls allowed him in acceptingly. The anticipation that had built up to this moment made the sex that much more explosive. Her slit seemed to fit around his thick girth perfectly, and with each thrust he explored depths of her that she never even knew existed.

"Maj, your pussy so tight," he grunted as his slow grind turned into full swings. With her legs in the air pinned upward, it was hard for Semaj to throw the pussy back at him with intensity. Implying for him to release them, she began to roll her wide hips around and around, up and down, back and forth, which sent Quasim to cum prematurely.

Gaining control again, Quasim rolled her onto her stomach and started hitting it from behind. The snug of her pussy had him grunting from pure passion. It sort of felt like he was fucking a virgin.

"Qua, daddy, I'm finna…damn!" she whined.

Her voice was even sexy and the hotness that spilled out onto his dick felt good as he continued to thrust in and out of her with long and hard strokes. "What are you doing to me," she moaned, sexily.

"You ain't seen shit yet." He pulled her by the waist to the edge of the bed until she was standing; never had he pulled out. Slapping her big brown voluptuous ass sent chills up her spine as he picked up his pace.

More comfortable with the size of his penis, she got into the sex even more. Wanting to please her man, she pulled out every man's favorite trick and tightened up her pussy muscles. She contracted herself around his shaft, sending him out of this world. "Yes…Quasim!" she called out softly as he pounded her love button. "Yes…Quasim!" she repeated as he sped up a notch and pumped her hard, clutching to her hips. Letting her know that he was the controller, he laid her upper body flat onto the bed and continued to pump all of him inside of her vagina. Licking the back of her neck and having her in places she never knew caused her to nut everywhere, and cream streamed out of her slit like a much-needed rainstorm in a forest. "I'm… awl…shit!" she squealed, reaching her peak as her body tightened up.

"Ahh…yes!" he moaned. His entire body shut down on him as the semen built up at the tip of his penis. "Shiiittt… fuck…girl!" his pump grew with more intensity from the orgasm he was experiencing until he erupted. Breathing heavily, Semaj panted as he collapsed on her back, releasing a long hard nut inside of her.

Afterwards they cuddled, kissed and stared into each other's gaze. Finally, Quasim broke the silence. "That was the best pussy I ever had."

"So that means that I was worth the wait?" she asked as they laid there with the sheets wrapped around them.

"Fuck yeah! It was beautiful, ma," he admitted as they got out of bed and stepped onto the balcony and stared up at the night sky. Springtime in New York has some of the most beautiful nights of the year. The slight breeze kissed their faces, refreshing them as they gazed out at the darkness. With Semaj's back leaned against his chest, she and Quasim looked out at the glittering full moon and the shooting star as all stress seemed to melt away from their tense bodies.

Chapter 9

The knocking on the master bedroom suite door had awakened Semaj the next morning. "Come in," Semaj said, wondering why Quasim would be knocking on his own door. To her surprise, it was an older heavy-set Spanish lady with berry red hair. She carried a platter of breakfast food.

"Hello Ms. Richardson. I'm Mesh, Quasim's maid. I fixed you breakfast and was ordered to give you this letter," she said in a thick Spanish accent.

"Thank you." Semaj said after retrieving the cream & red envelope and the platter that consisted of pancakes, turkey sausage links, white eggs and a bowl of cheese grits.

"You're welcome. If you need anything just let me know."

Semaj smiled as she thought, *damn is this how its gon' be? I can get used to this treatment.* As soon as the door closed behind Mesh, Semaj opened the letter anxious to see what this was about.

> *You on your way to the top anyway, ma. May as well get you used to the good life. Plus, you deserve it from the performance you gave last night. Smiles! Nah, but for real it's a limo outside waiting for you. It's gon' take you to the mall. Get whatever you like. The black card is inside the limo, but just be a li'l easy on me now. LOL! But I had to step out and I'ma be out 'til later on tonight. I, had something important to tend to. Enjoy yourself though and call me whenever. Don't forget about that dinner you owe me! See you tonight!*
>
> *Quasim*

By the end of the letter, Semaj was all smiles and couldn't believe it. *Black cards and shit. This nigga on some 'ol bossing me up shit.* She couldn't stop the cheesing as she ate her food and dressed for a day of shopping.

From the moment the driver pulled through the opulent open-air shopping mall, Semaj went into shopaholic mode. From one designer store to the next, she purchased items whether it was something as simple as a key chain from Juicy to an alligator Prada bag, Semaj made sure to visit each store. Not trying to overdo it, sometimes she didn't purchase a single item. She just loved the fact that she was privileged enough to have whatever she liked.

Her phone began vibrating as she was departing one of the stores, but she had so many shopping bags that she had to wait to call the person back. When She got to the limo, the driver took all her bags so she was able to retrieve her phone and returned Paris' call.

"Damn, bitch, what the fucks good?" Paris exclaimed.

"Hey, girlie. Yeah, I been crazy busy. Just finished wrapping up the film. But what's up, I miss you!"

"Yeah right. Quasim done took my friend away from me."

"Girl, bye. I was barely seeing him during my shooting. Hell, I barely got any sleep," Semaj admitted.

"Yeah…yeah…anyways. What's up with you today? You hanging with your girl?"

"Yeah, we can hang, but shopping is so out of the plans. I just tore down this mall. I mean, I have never shopped so good in all of my life," she said excitedly.

"Okay, are we bragging a bit?" Paris asked sounding irritated with her boasting.

"Nah, it ain't never like that. I'm just excited because I thought I used to do damage up and down Madison."

"Girl, stop it already. This movie shit ain't even out and it has gone to your head already," she joked but was serious.

"I think I sense alotta hate. What's really good?"

"No! What's really 'hood with you? Humph! I hope you don't let this Hollywood shit get to your head and you forget where you come from."

"Not never! I'ma do Maj, regardless. Rich or poor, famous or infamous in the 'hood. You know me, baby. I ain't never changed and it won't start 'cause my bank account changing. Feel me?"

"Just hope your word is bond," she laughed it off.

"Shut up, P. But what's up, though? You trying to relax with your girl so we can play catch up? I'm in desperate need for a spa treatment," she sighed in exhaustion. "Say relaxation."

"You? Me too. Which one you wanna hit up?"

"Lavish Perfection. It's on me."

"It oughta be. You a rich bitch now."

It was around noon when Quasim entered his semi-empty club. He glanced up at his office at the fourth level and noticed his man's standing at the glass front. He made his way up the back wraparound chrome stairs and walked into his office. He slapped hands with Mike-Mike and Slim, and took his place in the white, oversized, executive, leather chair. These was the two underbosses in his profitable street operation. The brothers were the enforcers, his muscle. They were the reason Quasim stayed so low and didn't have to get his hands dirty in no form. Ruthless was an understatement for them.

Slim grabbed the seven Hefty trash bags from the corner of the room and the trio began counting the week's take. Most hustlers allowed women to count their money, but Quasim didn't trust women and completed the task with his right hand men only. What appeared to be profits from his nightclub was in actuality drug money. He was smart, though, and opened up several front businesses with his dirty money. Quasim dabbled in as many legitimate businesses as possible; the nightclub was one of many.

"Yo, so what you gon' do about, this Jerz nigga, fam? Nigga talkin' real, greasy. Word in the 'hood he got a contract on your head, son. Pride is getting to that nigga head," Mike-Mike stated, placing the stack of bills inside the money machine.

"Pussy-nigga mad you ain't cutting him in on this potency dope no more," Slim added.

Quasim glanced up but didn't reply immediately because he hadn't felt the need to be offended by the threat of the next man. "Niggas like that is my sons, B. I teach 'em how to do this shit nigga. Y'all know I always stay ahead of niggas. So I know he pissed and he might be coming, but when have you known me to be worried about the next nigga? I ain't let the best nigga strong-arm me, and it won't start now because a lot of these clowns try'na play mob." He paused to wrap the money into bundles. He finally continued. "Beef is always a distraction and brings too much heat. I ain't gon' let a nigga get in the way of me and my paper."

"I already know, fam. But I can get it poppin'. I got one of my Jerz soldier's that's cool with a loudmouth nigga in dude's circle. All you gotta do is say the word and its lights out. It can be done within the next couple days," Slim said matter-of-factly.

"What you want me to do, Qua?" Mike-Mike asked. He stayed ready for street war, and that's why he was Quasim's shooter.

"Fall back. We'll handle it when it presents itself." His goons obliged because they knew once Quasim gave the green light on that gunplay, there was no red stop signs available.

As Semaj stood in the mirror, she applied a nude blusher to her cheeks and replaced that bristle brush with an eye cosmetic tool. Applying the bronze shadow onto her eyelids, she dolled herself up. The smoke alarm interrupted her primping and she realized she'd forgotten all about the turkey wings that she had simmering in the oven. She hadn't even smelled the food burning until she ran downstairs to the kitchen.

Mesh had emerged from the sliding door simultaneously. Swiftly moving toward the oven, Semaj opened it up as masses of smolder surged out of the range. "Fuck!" she yelled out in frustration. She was pissed at the fact that this was her chance to prove herself, and she ruined it. She already wasn't an expert at cooking, and deciding to prepare something simple, she figured it'd work in her favor. Having no clue when Quasim would be walking through that front door, she looked at Mesh with worry in her eyes. "What should I do?" Semaj had wanted this night to be so perfect, something like the previous night with more of a romantic mood, but from the look of things it wasn't happening tonight.

"Would you like for me to whip up something tasteful and quick?" she asked in an attempt to be of assistance. "It could be our little secret."

Shaking her head, Semaj replied. "We both know he knows your cooking, and I don't wanna chance it," Semaj said dismissively.

"Order something out and I can pick it up for you quickly." Mesh wanted to help her. She'd been Quasim's head maid for so long, and had never heard him speak so fondly of a woman like he did of Semaj.

"What's a place that he never orders from, but he'd enjoy?" Semaj asked.

Mesh smiled widely as she opened the cabinet drawer for the yellow pages. "I have the perfect place."

"Thank you so much, Mesh," Semaj said, relieved. However, she did feel like she was cheating and thought, *I'll do anything for this man and if that mean tell white lies to keep him happy and smitten, sho' nuff will,* she smiled at the thought of the good man she'd stumbled across. Semaj watched as Mesh thumbed through the phonebook. After a list of restaurants, she put in her order and Mesh was out the door to pick up the food.

After clearing the kitchen out, Semaj headed back up the stairs to prepare for their intimate night after the dinner. Pulling off her robe, she dressed in a chocolate brown La Perla negligee with gold detail. The expensive fabric looked good against her sun kissed brown skin.

Darting down the stairs, she retrieved the prepared bucket of fruit and wine that she'd grabbed from the storage wine cellar. She figured they'd have dessert in the bedroom. Strategically placing apricot-scented candles around the bedroom, Semaj set the fruit basket in the center of the bed. She left a trail of rose petals from the room door to the bed and sipped from the bottle of wine. *If he don't drink, he gon' drink with his shorty tonight,* Semaj thought as a naughty grin crossed her face and she checked herself one last time in the mirror. Her reflection gazed back at her as she admiringly stared at her glowing face, and fixed her hair into soft curls.

"I'm back!" she heard Mesh call out from downstairs. Looking down from the hallway balcony, she noticed Mesh with a brown paper bag in hand. "Would you like me to set this up for you Ms. Richardson?" she asked as she looked up at her.

"You've done enough, Mesh. I don't know how I'll ever be able to repay you for this," Semaj said appreciatively. She took the bag from Mesh and went into the kitchen as the doorbell rang. "Can you answer that, Mesh," she called out as she prepared to remove the food from the plastic container and onto two serving dishes. *I hope that ain't Qua.* She hurried and disposed the evidence.

"BOOM!"

At that moment, Semaj dropped the dish onto the floor as the first thing that popped in her mind was the word "intruders". As if her legs had given up on her, she stood paralyzed in fear. Her brain begged the muscles in her legs to move but her frozen terror prevailed. This was the end and she knew it. Once the masked gunman entered the kitchen, tears gushed from her eyes. She was unable to hum a sound. With the gun pointing at her, Semaj's survival instincts finally kicked in and she took a leap for the back stairs that led to the panic room.

In mid-stride, she heard a voice call out her name. "Semaj!" She recognized the voice. Totally shocked, she spun around on her heels and felt that she had to be bugging the fuck out. But she knew she wasn't. Just by the way her name had been called, she knew exactly who stood behind the black hoodie. Her mind was racing a million miles per second. Not green to the streets, she could pretty much place the puzzle pieces together before her father said a word.

"Fuck are you doing here?" he yelled angrily and loosened the hoodie from around his head. His gun shifted from side to side just in case he would have to hit a moving object.

"Put down the gun. It's only me here," she told him. "Question is what are you doing here?"

The wheels in Murder Mitch's mind were turning and immediately he knew he'd been paid to take out his own daughter and her boyfriend. "Maj, you telling me that I was paid to kill you!" he said in shock.

"What?" she yelled out harshly. "Fuck you mean you was paid to kill me? Fuck would pay you to kill me? Daddy, tell me what's going on here." Her words came out in a panic and she could barely get them out clearly.

"You remember that day you was going to the cabin and that dude stopped by my crib? Well, that was one of my old client's people. He ordered a hit on your dude. You know I don't ask too many questions, I just do my job. His people called when I was at the house and said he wanted me to get at his girl too." He looked at his daughter attentively. "I had no idea that it was you and your man." He began to pace back and forth in confusion. "This shit crazy as it fuckin' gets."

"Daddy, he has to be warned there's a hit out on him!"

This could go either two ways: he could wait for his victim to come home and possibly lose his daughter forever, or not go through with the hit and possibly go to war with Block. Then there was the thing about having his daughter hit that had him make his choice immediately. "Definitely do that. But I gotta see why and who called for your head, Maj."

"I know," Semaj said wondering as she tried calming her erratic heartbeat. "I have to tell Qua to come home so I can explain everything to him."

"Call that nigga," Murder Mitch insisted and sat on the barstool. He massaged his temple with the tip of the gun.

Semaj knew he was in deep thought because it was a habit of his to always rub his head when contemplating. "I'll be right back, I'm finna change and call him," She whispered and slowly walked off. What she stumbled into next bothered her heart. Mesh was sprawled out on the marble tile floor with one single gunshot wound to the head. It was a sad sight and it instantly brought tears to her eyes. *She was the most innocent one and wound up getting killed on the job,* she thought remorsefully as she stepped around the fresh corpse.

Semaj slowly made it to the bedroom and picked up the phone to dial Quasim.

"What's up baby? I'm on my way. You got that ready?" he asked smoothly.

"Qua. Something very real just went down and I need you here. How far away are you?"

"Like ten minutes. Why, what's up?"

"I don't want to discuss it over the phone. I'll talk to you about it when you get here. But I'm cool and my Dad is here with me."

"Are you sure you're cool?" he asked concerned.

"Yeah, I'm good. I just want you to hurry up," she said, completely shaken up but trying to maintain her composure while talking to Quasim.

"Be there shortly," he said and hung up.

On her way back downstairs Semaj was passing by Quasim's brother's room and unlike yesterday the door was open. As if wanting to escape to a place of peace that only an innocent child's room would have, she went inside and turned on the light switch. She flopped down on the bed and buried her face in her hands.

Semaj was afraid and confused. Her mind was so cluttered she could not even think straight. *What was Quasim gonna think of her once she had to confess to him her father's profession? Would he still look at her the same? What would he do once he knew that a hit was out on him? Why was someone out for his head anyway? Hell, what would be the reason for a contract to be put out on her? What if it just so happened to not had been her father hired?* Her mind was in a jumble of confusion and it would not stop thinking dire thoughts.

Shaking her head at the unbelievable event, Semaj knew nothing worse could happen until she rose and met the portrait staring at her on the wall evilly. It was as if the air in her lungs had been knocked out, but instinctively she screamed piercingly. "Agh!" her heartbeat stopped and Semaj felt her knees cripple from the sight of Big Pat's face. Her pulse was thumping so hard it felt like the beat was in the back of her throat. Her breathing shallow…her vision blurry…the spinning room made her dizzy and the white walls seemed as if they were closing in on her. She became hot and drenched in sweat.

She had no idea that she crossed the man that she'd fallen completely in love with. Quasim, the man that was heaven-sent was Big Pat's son. He was the man she had witnessed her own father kill on her behalf. If not guilty for pulling the trigger, Semaj was an accessory to his father's murder and guilty for capturing the heart of a good man. She was the reason for the empty space he held in his heart.

Murder Mitch heard the fright in her voice and instantly began running full speed, barely hitting the three steps he was taking at a time. "What is wrong with you, Maj?" he bellowed, waving his .357 magnum frantically around the room.

Semaj was slightly bent over as if something was bothering her stomach, but her eyes never averted from the photo on the wall. When Murder Mitch directed his attention to what she'd been staring at, he shook his head slowly as he studied the portrait. The picture was Quasim and Big Pat. Big Pat had his arm thrown around his son's neck and the gesture was mutual. At the top in white fine cursive print it read: *Death b4 Dishonor*.

Many people didn't know about the magnitude of Quasim's power in the streets and there was good reason. He had New York's heroin trade on lock, but under the name Santana. Only a few people were aware of him being one in the same person. Quasim wasn't the average kingpin; in fact, he was the opposite and moved through the streets more like an untouchable drug lord. He was a faceless name. It was virtually impossible to touch him. As many people had been in his presence, they were oblivious of being next to one of New York's biggest dope kings.

"Fuck outta here!" Murder Mitch mumbled not believing his eyes. He was aware that he'd killed Santana's father because word spreads throughout the 'hood grapevine quick. But never in a thousand lifetimes would he have known that his baby girl was dating the infamous Santana…the unseen king of New York. The two men were one in the same. "This shit is unreal." His eyes grew wide in disbelief.

An overwhelming sick feeling overcame her and still in shock, Semaj was unable to make it to the toilet. In the middle of the room floor, she violently expelled the contents from her stomach.

"We will talk about this later, Maj. Snap out of it okay?" he said encouragingly. "It'll be alright."

"But we killed his father. 'Cause of me, his dad is dead. The one he always talks about and would do anything to have back. Because of me, Daddy!" she cried hopelessly.

At that exact moment, Quasim had entered the house and yelled, "Semaj!"

"C'mon, Maj, you gon' have to get straight baby girl. We'll talk about this later." He picked up his daughter's shuddering body and descended the stairs.

"Fuck happened to Mesh?" Quasim shouted in both confusion and fury. "Fuck wrong, Maj?"

"Man! Some crazy shit went down and I'm sort of glad it went like this despite the death of your maid," Murder Mitch said apologetically.

"No disrespect, Mitch man. Fuck is going on, son!"

"Semaj shaken up from this, so just follow me in the other room so I can explain."

Quasim followed him into the sunken living room, and watched as Murder Mitch carefully placed Semaj onto the couch. Quasim looked at her with a weak heart as her body trembled violently. He rushed to sit by her side. "You cool, baby?"

Tears started gushing out even harder. Immobile to move her mouth, Semaj nodded her head as if afraid to speak. Her eyes indicated her horror and terror, and Quasim signaled for her to rise up. She obliged and fell right into his embrace. Her breathing became very deep. "What happened, Semaj?" he asked as he looked down at her. The agony on her face was one of pure heartbreak. "Talk to be, Maj!" he begged as he kissed her on the forehead. To see her fucked up inflicted an immeasurable amount of pain within his heart. "Mitch, what the fuck is good, big homie?"

"You know my daughter is my heart."

"Mines too," Quasim admitted and sat down, holding Semaj in his arms.

"Well, you know I only met you a few times, so I never knew too much about you, son." Quasim nodded, waiting on him to continue. "I was paid by Block to have you murdered and my daughter also."

"What?" his eyes bugged wide in alertness as he stood back up.

"He paid me a nice amount to have you rocked, my man." He went on to explain to him in more details on the contract that was out on them, but left out the part about Semaj being requested because of her own personal wrongdoings.

Quasim was shocked and was at a loss for words.

"All this because I ain't wanna put this bitch ass nigga on 'cause he hot ass fish grease and feds is closing in on him. What part of the game is this? Nigga wanna go to war over some shit as simple as this. It'd feel better if I was battling a turf war… drug war—somethin' worth a beef!" Quasim said fuming.

They both could tell he was vexed from the bulging veins in his forehead, and the sweat forming on the bridge of his nose.

"Nigga really tried to get you to get at me 'cause I ain't selling him none of my dope. Nigga mad foolish yo," he seethed angrily and all he could do was shake his head pissed the fuck off.

He gazed into Semaj's eyes intensely feeling guilty for involving her. He knew that he didn't have a choice now but to inform her on his hidden lifestyle. "I'm so sorry for putting you in this situation," he said trying to console her as he rubbed her hair soothingly.

Quasim had no clue that her tears weren't from what had transpired, but from the demons that she had erased from her memory bank throughout the years but were now coming back to haunt her. The tears were from the betrayal she veiled as his woman. Her breakdown was for all these reasons, and her emotions were spilling right out of her.

"Whatever he paid, I'll pay double that. I want you to leave as many casualties as possible on his end. I'ma have you meet up with my mans and them tomorrow." Quasim paced the room back and forth in frustration. "Shit just got real and after the stunt they pulled today, there's no turning back!"

"I feel you" Murder Mitch turned his attention on his daughter. "Do you wanna come home with your old man tonight?"

Knowing she had to pull herself together, Semaj inhaled heavily and slowly shook her head. "No Daddy…I'll be fine with Qua."

"I understand." He gave her a look that meant she had to pull it together. "What you gon' do about this body?" he asked turning to Quasim.

"Already called my cleanup crew. They on the way." With that Murder Mitch made an exit and Quasim led Semaj upstairs by the small of her back.

The tepid water sprayed out of the massager showerhead as it cascaded down Semaj's body. Lathering herself with soap, she softly washed herself with a sponge as hot tears slipped from her eyes. She wanted so badly to tell him the story about her life up until now, but feared the repercussions. She wasn't willing to risk his trust by telling him the details of her past. Quasim was the type of nigga that hated sheisty bitches, and had said it during plenty of their discussions. Semaj hadn't outright lied to Quasim about who she was, but instead lied by omission and there was no turning back now.

There was no way Semaj could admit to the bad. Even leaving the part about his father out still wouldn't be a good idea. Believing that she'd weathered the troubled storm of growing up without a mother, and her father being absent from her life for so long made him feel like she was a soldier. He worshipped the ground her feet graced. He praised her for her nobility and overcoming. Not willing to risk his admiration, Semaj would have to carry the burden around that she was responsible for his father's demise.

Stepping out of the shower, Semaj grabbed the red towel as she heard the front door close. Quasim had made it to the bedroom once Mike-Mike and the clean-up man left. *I can't believe I'm deceiving someone as good as him,* she thought looking over at Quasim. He was on the bed with his hands clasped behind his head staring up at the ceiling as if in deep thought. After slipping into a nightie, Semaj lay down and cuddled up in a fetal position on the opposite side of the bed.

Leaning over, Quasim wrapped his strong arms around her and his soft lips kissed the back of her neck. It felt so good to have her secured in his arms. She made everything in his world feel right. "I'm really sorry about this mess I involved you in," Quasim said in a low tone.

And I'm really sorry about what my father did to your father, Semaj thought, not saying a word as the tears began to flow down her face once again.

Quasim fought with himself about putting her in such an ominous predicament. He tried so hard to avoid beef, because it always brought unwanted attention and fucked up niggas getting money. But when provoked he didn't have a choice but to send his gunners to the battlefield. He hated this part of the game, but it was the most important, because it would determine who would end up on top.

Quasim scooted her close to his chest so that she could feel his presence. Semaj felt his heartbeat in her back as some of her pain eased. "You know I never meant for this to come on you," he began as Semaj listened to him tell his story about getting into the game at a young age. "I always wanted to stay low key and keep a low profile, because the least known you are the longer your run will be in this game. My father on the other hand had been a street nigga since the eighties. He's the one who taught me the game. But I was different from him. He loved the attention street fame comes with. He was a ladies' man and an attention seeker. I was a little nigga when I first got my dope plug.

"Being so, I jumped in headfirst and put my people on. But I was smart about it, and never looked back. I let my old man still hold the front while I played the back. But, I was actually the one supplying the streets. While all the niggas around me wanted to be seen, I used my last name, went unseen, and left that up to them. I was the source, and as long as I stayed relevant in name and irrelevant in flesh, I already knew I'd last a long time in this business. That's why too many people don't know that Quasim and Santana is the same nigga on either ends. And if so, you have to be deeply rooted into my life, or a well-connected, muthafucka."

Semaj listened to him for about five more minutes and then the room fell quiet.

"I love you for you…and I don't wanna lose you for nothing! Please don't ever leave me, Qua." Semaj felt compelled to say, breaking the silence.

"I love you too, ma. I wouldn't leave you for nothing in the world."

"Nothing? You promise?" she asked.

"I promise," he confirmed.

On her way to the hospital, Semaj couldn't stop what transpired from the previous night from plaguing her mind. She wasn't surprised that Quasim was a major drug dealer, but the fact he was the infamous "Santana" had her head messed up. *I would've never known. How could I?* She'd heard so many stories about the kingpin. He lived a lifestyle that doughboys only dreamed of. The way he articulated himself didn't display notorious in Semaj's mind, but from hearing his name throughout the years, Semaj knew he could have the most powerful man touched. And just to think…this was her man.

Fear entered her heart at the thought of him finding out. She knew of his power in the streets and had heard of the murders that he had ordered to those who crossed him. Her heart skipped a beat as her phone rang. The chiming jarred her from her frightful thoughts and she answered. "Hello?"

"Why you ain't call me? I thought you got out of class at 3:30." Although Semaj had starred in a major film, she still wanted to perfect her craft and decided to finish the semester out.

"I was finna call you once I got to the hospital to see my auntie. I'm cool…I got that thang you gave me this morning riding shotgun." She glanced over at the chrome .25caliber handgun and focused back on the road ahead.

He laughed. What he didn't tell her was that he had one of his goons following her just to be cautious. He didn't want to spook her. "Well, I'm finna meet your old man, so just call me when you on your way home. Love you."

"Okay, love you too." Semaj pulled up to the hospital and rushed inside.

Standing at the entryway, Semaj looked in at Tala's fragile body. She had IVs inserted in her arms and was hooked up to a machine. The machines were monitoring her condition. Walking to her bedside, Semaj stood watching over her. Her eyes were closed, and though time had moved on Semaj still felt responsible. It was a blessing that she survived the gunshot wound to the head. Though her right side was stiff and her mouth had a slight twist, Tala's appearance hadn't changed a bit. The doctors said the bullet was so close to hitting a major nerve that it sent off damage to the nervous system. Her brain had to learn how to send correct signals for her to walk again. It would take time at a recovery center for her to heal fully.

As if she could feel her presence, Tala opened her eyes and looked over at her niece and though she couldn't form a smile, her heart fluttered. In the beginning, Semaj had visited her nearly every day but Tala didn't want this life for her niece. Even during filming, on her break she'd shoot to the hospital to check on her auntie. Semaj would come, sob and continuously apologize for something Tala knew wasn't her fault. She felt her niece needed to rest and didn't have to be at the hospital all the time. After begging her to lessen her visits, Semaj did but she would call every day, a couple times throughout the day. Semaj would sit over the phone with her and reminisce about old times for hours. The love she had for her niece was everlasting and the friendship she held onto over the years was important to her and had withstood the bullshit. When Semaj insisted that she stopped using drugs, she wouldn't listen. So it was her own fault that she was caught slipping when the intruders came in. She never once blamed Semaj and hated that she blamed herself.

"You alright, Maj?" she asked with a voice that sounded like it no longer belonged to her; it was rough and raspy and almost inaudible.

Tears instantly started to fall, and Semaj began crying silently. "Stop that crying, Semaj." Tala was annoyed, and loathed seeing her becoming fragile. "All that crying should be out of you by now," she said and coughed weakly. "Hell, if anybody should be crying it should be me," she teased.

"I know, but something else has happened, Auntie. I'm tainted and not good enough for Quasim." Semaj recounted the events of the prior night, and explained to her who Quasim's father was. Tala was in shock as she attentively listened to her niece's story. "Ta, enough about my drama for a minute. I never asked you about that night you were shot. Did you know D-Boy was going to shoot you?"

"D-Boy didn't shoot me, Maj. We got into a huge fight. He couldn't believe I was fucked up on these drugs. He beat the shit out of me 'cause he was pissed and he cared. I remember, because I went to the bathroom and looked in the mirror and saw my face fucked up." She paused momentarily. It was bothering her to talk but she forced herself to continue on. "If D-Boy wanted me dead, he would've killed me before leaving. The last thing he said to me was, his son better be here next time he came by, and I better have myself together. He was talking shit about the money, but he was more so ranting on that I let you convince me into some shit and had me doing drugs. I was so angry that he went off on me because I knew he was right. But I didn't want to admit it, so what did I do—found my stash and started shooting up again. I was so high I kept going in and out of consciousness. It was like I blanked out. So whoever shot me did it after D-Boy left. But I know for a fact it wasn't him."

Semaj stared at her like she had just spoken Chinese, and though she didn't say it, Semaj knew that Tala was protecting D-Boy. But it was too late for that, and her father was out for his head. "I understand what you saying Ta," Semaj said. She didn't want to upset her and brushed the situation off.

"Can you promise me one thing niece?"

"Of course, Tee Tee," Semaj replied.

"If anything ever happens to me, could you go on with your life and let Ms. Long get the baby?"

"Why would I do that, Ta?" She looked at her in confusion. "You took me in, why wouldn't I take your seed in? That's stupid and selfish."

"Because I didn't want you to get lost in the system. You're so young and you need to live your life and accomplish your dreams. Zyden gon' be more than good with Ms. Long. She has him while I'm here, and is caring for him well. She never could have children, and I don't want you losing yourself with the responsibility of having to care after my load."

"Yeah, I hear you talking, but this dying shit is over. You pulled through," she said soothingly. "You good and gon' stay good. Bad bitches don't die, fam!"

"I'm just saying, Maj. I learned that a person never knows when they might take their last breath. I'm telling you so you will know this is what I wanted. I don't want you to feel obligated to take him because I took you. Just make sure you stay in my baby's life and make sure he remembers me for the good."

"Of course I'ma do that regardless. That's my li'l man too, and I'ma make sure he straight and Ms. Long. Even if I'm not they will always be good. He'll eat before I eat. Believe that."

"You gon' be forever good, Maj. I see something in you that's rare. You are a star. Always has been. Why you think I sent you to that special high school and kept you in different activities? So don't be afraid to grab that shit and never let go."

"Thank you, and I love you."

"I love you too." Emotions were filling the room making this the most profound conversation that they had ever had. It tore Semaj up inside just knowing that her auntie was suffering for some bullshit. Semaj wiped the tears from her face and in sync the pair burst into laughter.

"Now get out of here and enjoy life. You finna be in movies and all that shit," her Brooklyn accent rolled off low but thick. "I need to be getting prepared for my six 'o clock physical therapy, so I can be up and about too. I go to the recovery center in about three weeks. I'ma be back jumpin' in no time," she teased and got back on a serious note. "Keep Quasim by your side. He makes you happy in a way I haven't seen since Vega. You understand?"

Semaj nodded her head and replied. "I understand, Tala."

Chapter 10

In the streets jumping ship once a deal was sealed was considered disloyal, but Murder Mitch felt it was either Block or his daughter. His allegiance was with his child, and it didn't matter that he'd already been paid for the hit. Besides, he didn't have any loyalty, and anything was game when it came to his murderous mentality. Murder Mitch was a natural born killer and becoming head henchmen for Santana after all the years of being out of work had given him a hard-on. Some niggas loved pussy, some money, some the fame, but Murder Mitch loved to kill.

Murder Mitch pulled up in the alley behind *Kandi* hair studios and parked the car. He slipped his fingers inside the black pair of gloves. He knew getting the nigga would be getting to his wife first. He prepared the perfect setup, so that Block would run right into him alone. Block usually traveled with a goon with him, and going to his house would have been suicidal. Bodyguards usually surrounded the premise for protection and this way was his only option.

There was no personal beef he had with Kandi. She was just guilty by association. Murder Mitch had waited on her to come out to the wolves all day. He had gotten elated when her cranberry-hued Lex finally turned out of the gated-community. He tailed behind her with caution.

Kandi was headed to her beauty salon to collect the weekly booth rent and was oblivious that she was being followed into the inner city. It was 8:30 p.m. when she coasted up to the empty parking lot. With Kandi being on her cell for the duration of the ride made her careless and she wasn't alert to her surroundings.

When the flawless dark skinned beauty climbed out the vehicle, Murder Mitch noticed the pistol print in the small of her back. Though she appeared feminine in a cream-colored Armani pantsuit, he knew that she was gangsta. *Ol' Block got 'im a classy and thoroughbred bitch,* Murder Mitch thought as he meticulously watched every move Kandi made. She was setting up a meeting with a potential supplier, and was deep in conversation. She failed to notice the silhouette that had slipped behind the garbage device. Murder Mitch had hid behind the vast dumpster and waited for her to return.

Murder Mitch scanned the area. He tried to figure out how many people were around and possibly inside. His intention was to sneak up on her when she emerged, but instincts pulled him toward the car. Unfortunately for Kandi, she had been so preoccupied on her phone call that she failed to lock her car door, practically welcoming Murder Mitch to hide inside her ride.

After about twenty minutes, Kandi emerged with the apparent shop manager who jumped into the vehicle that awaited her in the front of the hair shop. Walking towards her car, Kandi hopped inside, having no clue that her life was on countdown until she felt the cold steel pressed against her head. "Who sent you?" she asked calmly.

"If you do exactly what I say I'll let you live. Put your hands on the steering wheel." She obliged and he told her, "Call Block."

"Nigga, you think I'm finna call my husband so you can murder him! You gotta be one dumb muthafucka if you did. Nigga gotta have a death—"

"Bitch, I ain't got time for the rah-rah bullshit. Either you call that nigga up or I leave your fucking brains splattered."

Kandi looked through the rearview mirror and noticed it was Murder Mitch with a crazed look etched across his face. She shook her head and though not surprised, she couldn't believe this nigga was bold enough to get at her bare face. She tried informing Block about trusting niggas, especially them grimy New York niggas. They didn't have no loyalty or respect for the game.

Kandi went to reach for her handbag when Murder Mitch said, "Don't try no slick shit, either." He pressed the gun to her temple. "Tell the nigga to meet you here and come alone. You need to speak with him on something concerning the feds."

Kandi knew that she was about to die. But she knew that she'd have one up on Murder Mitch in death as she dialed her husband's number.

"What up, Kan?" Block answered.

"Your man Murder Mitch killed me."

She was so calm, and it shocked the hell out of Mitch. He wasn't expecting her to chance her life over Block's. He figured she'd call him in hopes of him saving her, and thought her bad girl image would die once reality kicked in. But what he didn't know was Kandi wasn't green to the streets. She knew precisely how grimy niggas played, and being married to a hustler could end her precious life at any moment.

And yes, if losing her life in the process knowing that Block wouldn't sleep until he found Murder Mitch, then she was willing to deal with death. She was a true soldier, and the Bonnie to his Clyde. Their love was only fathomable to real streets niggas and real street bitches. She was riding for hers and knew that Block would ride for her.

"Pssst!"

The gunshot through the silencer made it virtually inaudible as the bullet erupted in Kandi's skull. Blood spilled from the side of her head as her body slumped over on the window. Murder Mitch quickly went for the latch as he heard yelling coming from the phone.

Opening the door, he stepped one foot onto the pavement. He was so pissed that he had swiftly glanced back at the fresh corpse and aimed the gun at her head. He emptied the entire clip on her, leaving her head and upper body filled with several holes. He jogged to his car and then pulled away, disappearing into the black night.

The thing about a 'hood killing, most of the time family, friends and nosy motherfuckers arrive on the crime scene before the police. Street gossip spread like wildfire.

Block was on the opposite side of town when he received the surreal phone call. His phone had been chiming relentlessly since he had gotten the unexpected call from his wife. Hoping that this was some kind of prank, he rode shotgun as his driver flew him to the west side of town. He arrived at the hair salon in record-breaking time. The car barely came to a halt and Block hopped down from the truck. He rushed to his wife's Lexus.

"Block, man I don't think you should go over there," one of his young soldiers warned.

"Fuck you mean? Move, nigga!" He forcefully pushed the young thug and headed for the car. Opening the car door, reality kicked it and the horrified sight devastated Block. "God no...no Kan...why her!" Tears filled his eyes as he kneeled down and held Kandi in his shuddering arms. Shortly after, her parents arrived and her mother's hysterics were something straight out of a street movie.

By this time police officers, homicide detectives and an ambulance had showed up. The officers had directed everyone to move outside of the crime scene yellow tape. That sent Kandi's mother over the top. "Nooooo! This is my baby! She can't die!" She ran around the tape and tried to pull her daughter from the car. "Wake up, Kandi! Baby, get up!"

The officer could understand the reaction of the mother. She had seen it many times, but she had to do her job. "I'm sorry ma'am, but I will be forced to have someone remove you from here. This is a crime scene. I just need you to move behind the tape," the female officer ordered as the mother cried uncontrollably in her husband's arms. There was nothing in the world worse than losing a child.

Block paced back and forth on the sidewalk, and replayed Kandi's last words: *You're man Murder Mitch killed me.* He didn't understand it as a pounding migraine plagued his brain. A million thoughts boggled his mind as the detective walked up. "Sorry, Mr. Stevens for your loss. I will do everything in my power to solve this case. I just need your help and the names of anybody that could be a potential suspect."

Block ignored the detective's statement and walked off furiously. He was never willing to speak with the pigs. He hated them with every fiber in his body, and hated everything they stood for. Just like any street nigga, he was bred with the "fuck the police" mentality. He knew they couldn't bring no justice in his situation better than he would—that meant street justice—that meant an ugly death—stream of deaths. This was the beginning of a war.

Semaj sat beside Quasim on the sofa sectional as they watched breaking news. Mike-Mike sat across from them.

"Homicide detectives are on the scene of the latest murder in Newark. Authorities are saying this might be a hit for the husband of the victim that has been under federal investigation for the past nineteen months. We'll have more details coming up on the eleven o'clock news. Now back to your regular programming."

"Well damn! Did the nigga get at Block or what?"

"That's the shit I'm trying to figure the fuck out." Quasim replied and picked up his phone.

Semaj looked at Quasim and felt bad for the woman that had lost her life. She was used to people dying but she felt guilty that her father had to switch teams. Semaj hated that she had broken the deep line of loyalty that her father had with the Stevens'. *Fuck it! It was either him or me and my father chose family. 'Nough said.*

"Hello?"

"Did you get the job done?" Quasim asked.

"I'm about to walk inside the house right now." Murder Mitch hung up the phone and after five minutes, he entered the home. "Man you ain't gon' believe this shit." He immediately told them what had gone down.

"Damn, Block had him an ol' gutta bitch, huh?" Mike-Mike asserted.

"Now it's gon' be hard for me to get at that nigga." Murder Mitch shook his head in disappointment.

"Fuck that nigga! I mean niggas wanna beef. When we get done wit' these muthafuckers, they'll regret they ever got this shit poppin'," Mike-Mike said, letting him know nobody was inaccessible. "Nigga ain't no mu'fuckin' Carlo Gambino! Might act like it, but nigga's camp ain't that untouchable."

"I know that, B," Murder Mitch stated seriously. "Any nigga can be touched. I'm just saying he gon' be extra careful now."

"The murder of his wife is enough to show that nigga that shit's real out here. I'm not playing with niggas no more." Quasim said calmly. He knew that Block had to be terminated and the sooner the better. But as of now he'd have to wait and stay two steps ahead of him, because it would be damn near impossible to touch him anytime soon. Quasim was a man that never cried over spilled milk, so all he could do was wait it out. "Just let shit die down and get at the nigga when he least expects it. But for you Mitch, you gotta lay low for now. I know that nigga got blood in his eyes for you."

"Niggas bleed just like the next man, fam. Nigga run up try'na clap, best believe I'm taking a couple mu'fuckas with me," he said coldly.

"Daddy, stop talkin' like that!" Semaj demanded.

"That's the only way I live. You know that Maj."

"Yeah, I know," she replied not hiding her anger and went upstairs to take a shower.

Chapter **11**

It was one of those days that started out fast and time was the last thing on your side. Several weeks had passed and finally the day for Tala to be released from the recovery center had arrived. Excited that Tala was better, Semaj decided to have a dinner party to celebrate. She had already been running errands all morning trying her best to get things in order.

She'd shopped for Tala some new clothes, but wasn't even halfway through her list of things to do. Her itinerary was full and Semaj still needed to get her hair and makeup done by the Dominicans and her brows Indian threaded. *Least they all in the same vicinity,* she thought, trying to find ways to save time.

When Semaj got home the first thing she did was unload the many bags in her auntie's new room. Quasim had agreed to let her stay with them once Semaj expressed her reasons. She wanted Tala close to her. Semaj felt she could finally return the favor for all her aunt sacrificed to raise her after her mother died and her father went to prison.

"S… Semaj…" Paris summoned from downstairs. "Would you come the hell on with the outfit you want Ta to put on? You gon' make me late picking her up."

"Come up here for a minute, P," Semaj countered as she went into her bedroom to slip on a jogging suit to be more comfortable.

"What's this?" Paris asked, entering the room and walked to look at the things on the bed.

Emerging from her walk-in closet, Semaj finally noticed the gorgeous items that were on the bed along with a shimmering silver and black envelope. She opened it and the card read:

I'm proud of you. Through all the bullshit you always remain strong and for that you exceed the respect level I have for any woman. This is a little something I put together for you to wear to dinner tonight.

The items that lay on her bed consisted of a multi-hued beautiful short silk dress with draping long sleeves. It was pearl with teal, fuchsia, dark purple, royal blue, bright green and golden yellow splotches that flowed effortlessly together. Atop the dress was a turquoise box containing a pair of fuchsia diamond earrings and a watch with a pearl face incrusted with diamonds. The pearl and fuchsia open-toe Giuseppe stilettos Quasim picked out was the perfect finishing touch.

"Now Quasim know you don't dress like that. Please!"

"You don't like it?"

"There's no denying the shit is hot, but you know you ain't never dressed like that before. Nigga try'na turn you into something that you not."

"I mean...I guess you right" Semaj's insecurities exuded and she knew she'd look dumb in the classy, yet sexy dress. But since Quasim went out of his way to think about her, she figured she didn't have a choice. Instantly, she dismissed the self-doubting and knew she would wear the dress. "Anyways, I wanted to speak to you about something before Tala came home."

"What is it?"

"I know Ta is a grown ass woman, and though she told me that she is finished with the drugs, I'm asking you to not do drugs around her."

"I feel what you saying Maj, but umm...Tala is grown and she gon' do what she wanna do regardless."

"You right." Semaj grabbed her bag from off the bed and draped it over her shoulder. "But I'm just saying don't influence her, and don't do nothing in front of her. You know how she can easily fall victim to temptation."

"Why would you think I'd try to manipulate her into doing drugs? You act like I'm just this big blow head. I just do that shit when shit heavy on my mind. And, I ain't never put a gun up to her head to start fuckin' with coke. She wanted it herself. And I sure in the hell didn't get her into shooting up. I don't even fuck with that shit, so you can't blame me, Maj."

"I'm not blaming you, Paris," she huffed as they exited her room and descended down the left set of stairs. "I'm just saying you know Tala's need for drugs can easily be triggered by the littlest thing. We don't need that for her. She don't need it for herself," Semaj said, trying to protect her auntie's well being.

"I feel you. I'ma make sure she don't go back down that road," Paris replied sincerely as she followed Semaj out of the house.

"A'ight fam. Thanks for picking her up for me too. My day is already hectic," she sighed, unlocking her door by the keychain. "I'll see y'all when you get to the salon."

"It's on." Paris climbed inside the rental car and pulled away.

Semaj was sitting underneath the hair dryer flipping through a popular fashion magazine at her favorite Dominican spot Lulu's when Tala and Paris walked in. She smiled widely as she watched her auntie strutting through on her own twos, looking beautiful. Her dark skin looked as if it had been kissed by the sun and she had a healthy glow to her.

"Auntie! You look good!" Semaj gushed excitedly.

"You too, Ms. Thang!" Tala kissed each of her cheeks. "Now what's up? You know I gotta get it back jumpin'. This ponytail shit gots to go. I'm seriously in need for a doobie so I can feel like a true diva."

"Only how we can," Paris added as the stylist immediately called them to the shampoo bowl. Before they knew it, the trio were all underneath the dryer with a head full of large purple rollers, conversing and joking like old times. It felt good for them to all be inside the same room outside of the walls of confinement that Tala had been in.

"Well, I still got a million errands to run, but least I got the big shit out the way," Semaj said, finishing up first.

"We'll catch up with you at the dinner party. Love you Maj."

"Love you too. See you guys later on tonight," Semaj waved and blew her aunt a kiss before leaving.

Climbing down from the Range Rover, Quasim handed the valet Semaj's truck keys and the duo walked inside the venue. Everyone had arrived before the couple had, and were already seated at the table. The place was exquisite and the décor was something snatched off of a sexy South Beach scene. The bright colored lighting and modern furnishings set it off.

Taking her seat, Quasim sat beside Semaj and before they knew it the entire table was being served. They drank champagne and ate good as they laughed and talked. Semaj loved being surrounded by the closest people to her and looked forward to the next chapter of her life. Clanking the glass with her dinner spoon, She stood with her champagne raised in the air, preparing to show her appreciation.

"First, I would like to make a toast to my auntie. If I never told you before, I'm telling you now. I appreciate everything you've done for me, and the many sacrifices you made to ensure I had decent clothes on my back and good meals in my stomach. We been though it all, but now it's like the game allowed us to throw in our bad hand and gave us another chance with a totally different hand, a winning hand. Again Tee Tee," Semaj smiled, excitely. "I love you, ma, and thanks for everything. Know if I'm rich, you're rich too. No questions." She had to hurry up and move from that speech because her eyes were beginning to water.

"And I have to thank my lovely father. You know we been through it all, but managed to get through all the bullshit." She winked. "I'll always be grateful. You the realest nigga I know, and will always be." She blew him a kiss.

"Now, lastly," Semaj turned to Quasim who stood up and took her hand in his. "Baby, you don't know how much joy you bring me. I haven't been complete since before I could remember, but with you, I'm like completely complete, if that makes sense," Semaj laughed optimistically. "Seriously though, with you, I feel like a different woman. I can't thank you enough for the way you shifted my direction in life. I love you, boo."

Oohs and awws erupted followed by everyone applauding and yelling.

The parking attendant emerged and approached their table. "Sir, sorry to interrupt your dinner but a tow truck is outside towing your vehicle away."

"What!" Semaj shouted. She headed for the door as everyone followed with smirks and sly grins. She was pissed as the tow driver loaded her truck onto the back. "Why are you towing my car?" she asked as she raced towards the tow truck.

"I'm just doing my job, ma'am."

"Qua," she turned around to a grinning Quasim. "You need to see why he towing my truck. And what's so funny?" She looked around at everyone who had smirks etched on their faces. He nodded towards the car approaching them. Turning to see what he was looking at, she spun around.

The valet was driving a pearl white Mercedes-Benz E 63 AMG wrapped in a red ribbon. The car stopped right in front of her and the driver climbed out and left the driver side door ajar. "Nice car and the gadgets are out of this world," the valet smiled.

"This you, ma. My girl ain't gotta lease shit. We owners on this end," he whispered in her ear charmingly.

She jumped up and down in excitement like a kid on Christmas, and hopped right inside. Semaj explored the top-of-the-line features in her brand new car. But with all the newness that surrounded her for some reason it made her reflect to the past. Semaj couldn't help to think about the secrets she had concealed that enabled her to get into a car like this. Now times had changed and she was a different person. However, the deceit she kept buried was tearing her apart. But she was different now and after tonight there was no way she was carrying that heavy burden around any longer. She had the man that would bring her joy and happiness. Sometimes the past was best to stay exactly where it was—in the past. *This the way it's supposed to be. Finally I have a life to be proud of,* she thought pleasantly as she jumped out to hug Quasim tightly. The attendant moved her car back to valet parking so they could enjoy the rest of their evening.

"You must like it," he commented with a cute grin.

"Nigga! Like? Like? I love it!" she screamed, hugging Quasim again.

"This is a day in the life when you fuckin' with a boss. 'Member I told you that," he joked, and kissed her on the top of her forehead.

The handful of guests applauded cheerfully as the couple was a picture of happiness.

But some happiness is only for the moment because in a matter of seconds love, joy, and excitement deserted the atmosphere. Death took its place as two black vans crept up and the ringing of different machine guns signified that. Everyone ducked for cover and Quasim's henchman shielded the duo as his goons fired back. They chased the vans down the street with automatic handguns.

"Oh my God!" Semaj muttered after the shooting had ceased.

"You okay?" Quasim asked, freeing his body from shielding hers.

"Yeah. Where is my Daddy, Auntie and Paris?" She frantically looked around as a crowd started to form a couple feet from her. She spotted her father and darted over. Some people tried to block her path, but she broke loose from their hold. The entire scene felt too familiar. She'd already been through this tragedy, now it was like a movie that was on replay. It was like she was reliving Tala's shooting all over again. Tala was lying in a puddle of blood, barely holding onto her life. Semaj broke down and began to cry uncontrollably. She fell to the ground and picked up Tala's head to lay it on her lap. "Auntie, you just got better. You can't leave me now… hold on please, Ta! You strong, Tee Tee. You took a bullet to the head so these chest wounds ain't shit. You a solider. Please don't go."

"Maj," she heard her whisper faintly as her eyes rolled slowly around.

Semaj looked at her in shock as she realized that she was trying to hold onto her life once again. "Shhh, don't talk, Ta. Just hold on like last time. You gon' make it." Covered in blood and looking at Tala's white baby doll dress now crimson, Semaj heaved violently as she rocked back and forth still pleading for her auntie to hold on. "You the baddest bitch I know…you always been the shit. We still gotta shine. You can't leave me like this. Please stay with me!" her words cracked.

"Apply pressure," Quasim said, removing his shirt and Murder Mitch repeated the same gesture.

"I can't, Maj. Just please don't be mad at me. I love you and so proud of you."

"Yes you can!" Semaj demanded as her fear turned to anger. She pressed the shirts against her chest wound, desperately trying to stop the blood flow but there was too much blood. In her heart Semaj knew that her efforts were useless. Tala was slowly slipping away. "Daddy, where the fuck are they? Qua, where are they? Just hold on a little longer, Ta!" Semaj screamed out, hoping the paramedics would arrive quickly as she looked around.

"The pain is bad and I… I can't," Tala muttered. Her eyes closed as she took her last breath.

Murder Mitch banged his fist with his head and departed ready to go to war.

Semaj, not, immediately knowing that Tal was gone was still pleading to God until she glanced down and saw her auntie's lifeless body. She shook the corpse forcefully, but it was too late. Tala had made it to the light. "Wake up, Ta! I know you ain't gon' leave me like this! We got too much shit to do! " Semaj cried out now completely distraught.

At that moment, EMTs came rushing and Semaj jumped up and started screaming on the paramedics, swinging wildly, scurrying towards the police, but Quasim scooped her mid-stride. "What the fuck took you bastards so long? You bitches seem to make it everywhere else on time, but when it's a shooting you racist fucks take your precious time!"

"I'm sorry for your loss ma'am," the officer said.

"Fuck you! She's not dead!" Semaj was becoming delusional as they loaded the body onto the stretcher and covered it with a white sheet. She bolted toward the coroner's van in a swift motion, and lifted the cover from Tala's face and tugged her into an embrace. Semaj begged her to wake up as she cried over her lifeless body in total disbelief. The officer tried talking to her in a negotiation for her to release the body, but the words fell on deaf ears. She wouldn't let go. Well she couldn't let go. To Semaj to release her aunt from her clutches would mean letting her go forever and she wasn't ready for that.

The officer looked at her in frustration, whispered to the family to get her. Seeing her mourning over the body even brought tears to the onlookers and some of the toughest men in New York. Quasim's goons were fighting back tears.

Quasim wrapped his strong arms around Semaj. "You have to let go, baby. She's in a better place now."

"But she just got better. She didn't even have enough time to enjoy her welcome home," she said not understanding it.

"She wouldn't want you acting like this. She stuck around long enough to see one of the most important days of your life."   "But we had so much more to accomplish together. That's my auntie. She was there for me when I had nobody. Nobody!"

"And she still is gonna be in spirit. But you have to let go so these men can do their job."

She nodded her head profusely as she pulled her auntie extremely close to kiss her cheek one last time. "I love you, Tee Tee, forever and ever. Wait for me too," she whispered as her knees crippled her and her body went limp. She collapsed in Quasim's embrace.

For the entire ride home, Semaj cried silently. The stiff body gestures expressed true hurt, and it broke Quasim's heart to see her like that. He did not know what to say to ease her pain, so he remained quiet. When his father had died he hated the thousand apologies from people who would never bear his agony. Telling her it was going to be all right was useless. From past experiences of losing close loved ones, Quasim knew for a fact that the pain never waned. He did, however, reach over and intertwined his fingers with hers to let her know that he was there to help her bear the cross.

He pulled through his gated community and after punching four digits into his newly installed security system, the chrome gate clanked, parting and welcomed them to their home. Semaj's body was still in shock, so he carried her into their house. He headed straight for the master bathroom where he laid her on the white suede sofa. By this time, Quasim's ivory colored threads were covered with blood as well as the sofa, but the material things could easily be replaced. Semaj was what was important to him and he was going to make it his personal mission to cater to her. He turned on the knob and let the warm water surge. He removed her dress and wrapped her hair into a rubber band, hating every second of her grieving.

He helped her up the three Jacuzzi steps and gently sat her on the edge as she continued to sob. Soaping the sponge, Quasim lathered her body, softly washing every part of her skin. He did not leave a trace of blood as he rinsed her with the unhooked sprayer device. Wrapping her into a towel, he laid her onto the bed and dried her off. After massaging her body with oil from head to toe, he dressed her in a nightie, and tucked her in like she was his little princess. "Let me know if you need anything."

Semaj hadn't wanted to respond, but her father was heavy on her mind. "Just call and make sure my Dad is okay."

He nodded and walked back into the master bath. Hearing the door slightly close behind her, Semaj still heard Quasim. She stifled her cries so she'd be able to overhear the conversation that was on speakerphone.

"We got to get rid of that nigga a sap, dawg," Mike-Mike expressed. "Me and Mitch just shot up Block's main spots and laid several niggas down, forever!"

"From the gate, when he sent Maj's own people to get at her I should've bodied that nigga. Fuck all this back and forth shit. It's pointless, yo. He try'na get at anybody close to me."

"I feel you. I knew you ain't forget how this shit was done, fam. That's what you got soldiers for. For crab ass niggas like that bitch muthafucker."

"This nigga gotta go, like yesterday. He disrespectful and feeling like he got something to prove. Nigga gotta be dealt with before things get even worse, son."

"That's the Qua…Nah fam, that's the Santana I know my nigga. You already know we gon' handle this shit."

Chapter 12

As Semaj dressed a dreadful feeling filled the pit of her stomach. It hurt her badly, because she knew this would be the last time she would ever see her auntie's face. It felt as if someone had snatched her heart from her chest. For nearly her entire life, her auntie had been there for her and now she was just a memory. There was a void in Semaj's existence that no one could fill, because nobody would be able to take the place of the woman that gave her own life for hers.

Seeing her like this tore Quasim's world up. She was always so live, energetic and assertive. This was the second time he witnessed her so fragile and vulnerable but this time was different. Semaj stayed locked up in the bedroom up until the funeral. She didn't speak to anyone. She even gave him the silent treatment and pushed him away unintentionally.

Quasim was patient with her though. He understood the grieving stage. He knew that eventually she would have to deal with it and in its fresh stages were the worst. He knew that she was mourning, so he turned a blind eye to her silence. Wanting to give her the space she desired, his heart couldn't allow it though—her pain was like a magnet to his soul—it drew him close. He catered to her, fixing her food, though her appetite was nonexistence and cuddled with her for solace.

With every passing day, Quasim was becoming increasingly annoyed that no one could find Block. Many members from his team had been knocked off or severely injured at Quasim's order. Through Murder Mitch's hatred it pretty much ended Block's reign over his own city. For Quasim, that wasn't enough though. He wouldn't be able to fully relax until Block was dealt with and he was marked a memory. It surpassed the dope game. The situation was deeper than that. It was about respect. As long as he was still alive, Quasim would not be able to regain his complete sense of security, expecting him to strike back at any moment.

Emerging from the bathroom, Quasim looked at his beautiful lady as she sat on the bed in a snug sleeveless, black, designer tailored dress and clasped the straps on the Christian Dior black stiletto pumps. She stood and grabbed her python clutch bag. The black flower bedecked at the front of her pinned tresses, and the black delicate python gloves made her look like a modern day Billie Holiday. Quasim took her arm in his, and the couple walked outside to the awaiting limo.

When they arrived to Omega Baptist Ministry it was filled with Brooklyn's street elite. From hustlers and haters known and unknown to Semaj poured into the church to pay their respects to the young woman that had fallen victim to street violence. The limo had let them out directly in front of the popular black church. As if the universe was in synchronization with their somber mood, the sky formed dark gloomy clouds, transforming the day into a dreary afternoon that matched the occasion. It was like the Heavens felt her pain.

Knowing her auntie wouldn't want her to have breakdown for all to witness, she gathered her bearings and buried the pain.

Murder Mitch walked in first with Ms. Long, followed by Quasim and Paris who was on each of Semaj's side. She held onto both of their hands tightly as they walked down the long aisle. A cream and gold casket sat at the face of the pew.

"Semaj, know I'm right here with you," Quasim whispered to her as he noticed her tense up. "I'ma be right here with you. Don't pay these other people no attention."

Semaj stared straight ahead. The entire casket sat amongst hundreds of gardenias, Tala's favorite flower. The closer they got to the casket the sweatier Semaj's palms became. She stood over Tala's coffin and unable to hold the tears any longer she allowed them to fall. Staring at Tala made her feel at ease. She looked beautiful and more at peace than she ever had.

Semaj bent down and kissed Tala's cheek. "Even in death, your beauty shines through. You still the baddest bitch and I got us Auntie, I promise. Tell my mom and Vega I love and miss them so much when you get there." Semaj kissed her again for the last time and said her final farewell. "I love you so much and will miss you dearly. Look over me while I'm in this ill world."

Semaj took her seat at the front of the pew and prepared herself for the service to begin in memory of Tala Richardson. Murder Mitch sat next to his daughter, and held her hand with nothing on his mind but murder.

What they saw next astounded the attendees as everyone noticed D-Boy approach the coffin. Many had already heard that he was behind the shooting at Tala's home. People felt that he was one bold individual, and even though he felt the daggers burning a hole through him D-Boy did not care. This was his child's mother.

"This nigga got balls!" Murder Mitch muttered displeasingly as he reached for his gun.

But Semaj stopped him. "Daddy, please. Not at Tala's going home service. Please! I can't lose you too. Remember we're in public, Daddy. He's not worth it."

He nodded in agreement, and released his grip on the gun as he watched D-Boy. *The one time I see this nigga, it gotta be here*, he sighed to himself as he watched D-Boy and one of his goons take a seat.

The entire eulogy was a big blur. All Semaj could focus on was the fact that D-Boy showed up to the funeral, and Tala's lifeless body lying in the casket in front of her. It was as if she'd been absent from the service because the sermon from the pastor was inaudible. It was as if she'd temporarily turned deaf.

Once the service was over, Semaj stood to depart because she desperately needed air to breathe. It had felt like she was suffocating as she raced to the door, and waited for the pallbearers to load the body onto the horse-drawn carriage.

Once they arrived to the cemetery, Semaj looked on as her auntie went home in style. She was carried in a clear icy case by white horses and in sync the family allowed one hundred white doves to fly away. Semaj promised herself that she would not cry once they lowered the body into the ground. Tala was never coming back and this was a reality she had to deal with. Seeing it all was heart-wrenching, but Semaj was all cried out.

D-Boy on the other hand broke down. Murder Mitch had to walk back to the limo. It burned him up that he couldn't kill D-Boy right then and there. If it wasn't for Semaj's pleas he would've murdered him the moment he saw him. But for his daughter, Murder Mitch saved his blood for later.

As Semaj prepared to walk off, D-Boy approached her. "I know you probably hate me right now but all I wanna know is if I can see my son."

"You one daring ass nigga. After you shoot my gotdamn auntie, basically taking her away from her son...your son... you wanna see him! D-Boy, please! Word is bond, you'll never see him again. Now get the fuck outta my face!"

"Damn, you gon' give me shade like that, Maj?" he looked at her square in the eyes. "Just know I ain't have nothing to do with that shooting at her house. Word to my mutha, me and Ta was on speaking terms. I don't know if you heard or not, but I've been going through some issues of my own," he tried playing victim, but Semaj knew he was full of shit and if she had the heart she would've blown him away herself. "I loved Ta, on my son, Semaj. I visited her several times while she was in the recovery center. I don't know if she told you that or not."

At that moment, Murder Mitch and Quasim both appeared behind D-Boy. "Is there—"

Murder Mitch cut Quasim off mid-sentence as he pulled out his strap and pointed it at D-Boy's temple. He was unable to hold his composure any longer. "Nigga, you don't ever in your mu'fuckin life try to approach my daughter. I mean don't say shit to mine. That one belongs to me, son."

D-Boy looked over at his mans. As if on cue, he had his ratchet pointed at Murder Mitch in a defensive stance. "We don't move unstrapped, baby," the goon smirked mischievously.

Semaj didn't want this situation to brew any hotter and intervened to try to eliminate the problem. "Daddy, let's just go, please," she said with frustration. All this was too much to deal with and for God-sake her auntie had just been buried.

"Yeah Daddy let's just go please," D-Boy tried making a mockery out of the situation.

"Yo, my man, you need to get back in your car before you make this an ugly outcome, son," Quasim stated without raising his voice but with enough authority to establish his dominance.

D-Boy didn't know it at first until he looked around and noticed several goons with assault rifles pointed in their direction. All were sharp shooters too. Quasim never left the house without his goons for situations like these.

"Quasim, please lets just go." Semaj stepped in to avoid the situation turning deadly.

It wasn't the name that made him smirk, but the person that he'd seen for the first time. *So this is the Quasim Santana nigga,* D-Boy thought excitedly. *Now it all makes sense.* "You know what? A'ight. Y'all be easy," D-Boy said and walked away.

"I'm going to kill him!" Murder Mitch promised as he watched the man pull off.

A couple weeks had passed since the funeral and this day was going to be the first time that Semaj got up and stopped moping around the house. She'd been doing it so long it started to irk her. She had to pull herself together. She knew her auntie wouldn't want her to be in isolation. It wouldn't bring her back. And while still missing her auntie, Semaj decided that her days of depression was over.

Semaj shook her somber emotions out of her system as she impassively climbed out of the comfort of her bed. First thing on her agenda was to cleanse her mind, body and soul with a long hot shower. She needed it badly and scrubbed her skin clean. After the soothing shower, she got dressed. She smiled at herself in the mirror. For the first time in a minute she felt cute and refreshed.

When Semaj got downstairs she heard noises coming from the master living room and hoped to find Quasim but he was nowhere in sight. Instead Slim and his girlfriend were sitting on the couch. Quasim made it clear that Semaj was never left home alone. "What's up, Slim? What up, Chi?" she greeted amiably.

"What's good Maj? You cool?" he asked with sympathy in his voice.

"Hey," Chi replied nonchalantly. It wasn't a mystery that the girls didn't care too much for each other, but neither was rude.

"Yeah, I'm cool. Just decided to, you know, get up and get to moving again. Ain't no need for the moping."

"I feel that. You got a movie finna come out too and all that. That's what's up."

"True that. But Paris finna pull up in a few. When she gets here tell her to come upstairs," she said and exited the room. She made a turkey sandwich, and washed it down with grape Kool-Aid before heading back upstairs.

Semaj wanted to pack up Tala's belongings and clean out her room. There were bags and boxes everywhere. Quasim had asked her if she wanted him to hire someone to move Tala's things to an inner city charity. She agreed on the newly purchased items, but decided to keep all of her auntie's other belongings. As she went through her personal things, Semaj found a photo album. She reminisced and laughed as she flipped through the picture book and surprisingly not one tear dropped.

"What the hell are you doing in here?" Paris asked as she walked inside the room.

"Looking at these photos." Semaj thumbed through the album never taking her eyes off the pictures. Paris kneeled down to sit beside her.

"Oowwee, you mu'fuckas know y'all looked like some true birds."

"Shut up," Semaj laughed. Coming across the next picture really made her reminisce.

"Why you staring at that picture like that?" Paris asked.

"Girl, this was the last photo I took with my first love. It's bringing back so many memories."

"You talking 'bout that one that died?"

"Yeah," Semaj replied.

"Man, I promise that nigga look mad familiar. I think I seen dude out in Baltimore," she said, surely.

"Must be somebody that looks like him because he died a long time ago."

"Damn! That's weird as shit," Paris said as she searched her memory bank, but came up empty. "They say we all have a twin somewhere."

"I know right?" After they finished looking at the photo album's for the next couple hours they went through Tala's clothes putting them up in the closet and drawers. Semaj hung up the last outfit and then turned around to walk out of the room.

"Well, we've finished up here. Now let's get you out the house," Paris stated.

"I know right?" Semaj said as she slipped into a pair of silver gladiator sandals. She grabbed her handbag out of the closet. "Let's go. I got an appointment for a doobie at Lulu's. Then let's head to Midtown so I can get a facial," she said, ready to treat herself to a day of relaxation.

The blue cloudless sky had faded into a pretty orange sunset as they walked out of the spa conversing. Semaj now felt like a brand new woman after the deluxe spa treatment. It seemed as if it had been an eternity since she'd had a whiff of fresh air. "It feels real good to be out and about," she said, inhaling the fresh breeze.

"I know an—" Before Paris could finish her sentence, she screamed, "Semaj get down!" pushing her down to the ground as the items in their hands went skyrocketing in the air. Paris was on point, because a second later a darkly tinted truck sped up and stopped. A ski masked man pulled out a Tommy Gun as he leaned his body half way out of the window and bullets rapidly spit from the gun, piercing their ears. Semaj and Paris both stayed crawled behind a company van as the terrifying sounds of bullets shattered windshields and side windows. Semaj's heart was pounding like a jackhammer, but her body was as stiff as a statue.

Glass was strewn across the walkway's concrete and finally after what seemed like forever, the sound of gunshots blaring came to a cease, leaving them with minor cuts from the car's shattered glass. But to be safe from the danger, the two remained on the ground for a couple more minutes to make sure that the attackers had vanished.

"Man, what the fuck! Is Qua and 'dem in a fuckin' drug war or something? Why the fuck is niggas busting at us!" Paris squealed. They both looked at each other and swallowed hard before standing to their feet. "I ain't never in all my years had some mu'fuckas deliberately target me in a gotdamn shooting. And it's obvious that they were aiming for us."

"I know. This is getting too ridiculous," Semaj sighed. By this time people were coming outside and the sounds of sirens were within distance. She'd phoned her father who was with Quasim. She explained to him everything that had happened and told him to come pick them up immediately.

"And that's the reason you need somebody with you at all times!" Quasim barked upsettingly as soon as they arrived. "If I knew you were leaving the house I would've had somebody following you."

"At all times somebody has to be with you, Maj," Murder Mitch added. "No exceptions. At least for a while."

"I know," Semaj replied, knowing that they were serious and could understand why they felt she needed the protection.

Chapter 13

Several weeks had passed and things were gradually getting back to normal. Nothing had been out of the ordinary since the one-sided gun battle, and as promised Semaj's security had been enforced and she traveled with a bodyguard everywhere she went.

It was four days before Semaj's movie premiere party and her initial introduction to the entertainment industry. The overwhelming process of preparing for a movie release was draining albeit rewarding and a distraction from the tragic events encompassing her life. It was rumored that she purposely structured the shooting as a publicity stunt, but Semaj took it as a warm welcome to the industry. Magazines and radios had called wanting interviews, and it was good for her because it kept her mind on the positive side of things. Semaj was embracing the film business. She was finally stepping into the life she felt she deserved since she was a young girl. She dreamed about becoming an actress, but no dream or vision could actually prepare her for the reality of it all. This was how life was supposed to be.

For the first time, she and Quasim's life was semi-calm and he deliberately made certain that he had shown her how a woman was supposed to be treated. It seemed like their relationship happened so fast, even with the mayhem surrounding them. But to Semaj, he was the best thing that had ever happened to her. Quasim respected her to the fullest and came home every night at a decent time, and although he ran a drug business, he conducted himself like a corporate businessman. When he was home, he left the dope game in the streets, and her father and his trusted friends handled all dirty business within.

Under a course of a month, Quasim had put his property on the market. He didn't want niggas knowing where he laid his head. Because of how Block sent Murder Mitch over to his crib, Quasim knew it had been time to make a move. He felt Semaj would feel more comfortable knowing that nobody knew of their new residence. The gated mansion was nice, too... way nicer than the other crib.

Semaj decided to give him the remaining balance of the forty thousand dollar advance check she received to go towards the purchase of their new home. She felt any real woman had to keep it all the way real with her man, especially if his mentality was vice versa. Being independent was a plus in Quasim's book. But he felt he was her provider and tried to give the check back because she had worked hard for it. But Semaj shunned his persistence vehemently. Out of respect of her wanting to show she could contribute he accepted it, and secretly Quasim found her trying to exercise her independence real cute.

Their relationship was an easy-paced one, because they stayed on point with communication and it seemed as if they clicked well as lovers. They both had been extremely busy the last few weeks, but any free time they had the couple spent together in the comfort of their new home. They were always lovey dovey and cuddling. Semaj had found her king, lived in their kingdom and they both had careers. She had her dream career and it seemed as if life was on its way to happily ever after.

Al-B had informed her months earlier to prepare a list of the guests she wanted to invite to her premiere party. With one-week left she'd finally gotten around to her list. With not many friends, Semaj called a few acquaintances from the Brooklyn projects. And she made sure to invite the important people that impacted her life...especially Ms. Porter. *If it wasn't for that woman, I would've never met the man of my dreams and have my career fall in my lap,* Semaj thought gratefully.

Semaj woke up the morning of the premiere with nervous butterflies in her stomach. She had run around damn near all day with Paris to find something to wear. By nightfall they'd both found outfits but were in a rush to get back to the hotel so their hair and makeup could be done

The makeup artist was applying smoky shadow to her eyelids when Quasim walked in the presidential suite. "Oh, babe, I thought you were gone already," Semaj said, happy to see his handsome face.

"I couldn't leave without giving you this," he said, pulling out the velvet Harry Winston box. "You already a star, but rocking pieces like this makes it official."

"Baby, I'm not a star. I been through too much to be a star," she stated seriously. "I think I'ma survivor."

When Semaj opened up the box she almost lost her sight, the jewelry was so icy. It consisted of a three-piece set containing earrings, a garland necklace and a matching black and white diamond bracelet. "This is the best jewelry I've ever had! The pieces are gorgeous! Thank you so much!"

"It's all love. Diamonds last forever. We forever, baby."

"Omigoodness, I love you so much." Tears formed in her eyes.

"Here you go with that mushy shit, and you try playin' gangsta. G's don't cry, we shine, ma." Quasim smiled and swiftly ran his index finger across her cheek. "You look beautiful. I'll see you in a bit."

After getting professionally dolled up, Semaj dressed for the movie premiere. Looking in the three-way mirror for an once-over, she admired herself. She felt sexy and glamorous. The white sleeveless puffed blouse revealed ample cleavage and fell slightly over the black fitted skirt that had a long slit on the side and showcased every curve on her body. Black Prada peep-toe heels trimmed in white completed her outfit.

They arrived to the theatre in a white Maybach. Exiting the car, hundreds of fans were screaming for Christopher who was an actor-turned-movie director. The flashing cameras gave the girls a rush as they stepped out onto the red carpet and Semaj got swarmed by paparazzi and reporters to get a quick interview from the starlet. She slightly waved and air-kissed the fans who were chanting her name as they made their way inside. Quasim had already arrived through the back door. He wasn't with the popularity in this business either, and deterred himself from being on-scene.

The movie premiere was huge to say the least. Everybody who was anybody in the New York entertainment industry came out to show support. Her teachers showed up and the 'hood came out like they were the stars.

"You look stunning," Quasim said as she took a seat next to him.

"Thank you." Semaj sat in her seat calmly listening to the reactions of the audience and she couldn't believe it. All the attendees were on the edge of their seats, and were so enthralled in the action-packed film. Once the movie was over, people went into an abundance of applause. As she moved through the crowd, people complimented her and congratulated her adoringly.

For the next week, Semaj was traveling to other premiere parties. The next stop was Cali then it was Atlanta and the following night it was Miami. This all seemed like a make believe world and a figment of her imagination. But Quasim always reminded her. "Baby, this is reality and it's our world. The sky is the limit now."

That it was. If anybody would have told her that she'd be living this life a year ago, she'd told them they were a fucking liar. As the days passed by, the film finally hit theaters that Friday. Semaj would have never imagined that starring in her first movie would have gotten her immediate recognition. Movie theaters across the nation were sold out at every showcasing. Her name was ringing, and that Monday morning she was the main topic of every newspaper headline, magazine and television show and they wanted in-person interviews.

People were amazed by her and more so moved by her story. Witnessing her mother being murdered and an absentee father for important years of her life had people rooting for the underdog.

Learning about her background but still able to pursue her dreams made Semaj an inspiration to every black girl from the 'hood. Despite her tragic childhood, she was making something out of her life. Within the first weekend the movie had did numbers way beyond anyone's expectations. The movie debuted number one at the box office, competing against major names. It was bananas, and though Semaj tried to remain humble about it the girl was definitely on a high.

All sorts of agencies were trying to recruit her, but Semaj was going for what she knew. Al-B and Christopher had recently incorporated their very own entertainment agency. She was loyal and decided to stay down for the team. She was willing to build her career at Screenplay Inc., which she was now contracted under. Over the course of a month, Semaj had many inquires and major production companies potentially wanted her for upcoming movie projects.

This day in particular, Semaj was having a meeting concerning the companies that were reaching out for endorsement deals. She was having dinner with Christopher and Paris at an upscale restaurant discussing the business matters ahead. "It's unbelievable how much press you are receiving. Major deals are coming across my desk daily. But we had to get you the best endorsement deals offered," he explained. "Trust me, I been in this business since I was a kid. It can get very dirty."

Semaj knew he had years invested in the film world. So she trusted his judgment. "I understand where you are going with this."

"Now I have something lined up for you with the Adorable cosmetic line that was just launched this year. They're running ads with top magazines in the next few months and they want you featured in all six. It pays two hundred and fifty thousand. What do you say?"

Semaj was floored. "Are you serious?" she asked as her smile widened.

"Anything concerning business I'm always serious. This is just the beginning. I have a few other things lined up, but I'm trying to get the best deals. So once you sign the paperwork we can get this ball rolling."

"Well, I'll call my lawyer up so we can go over the paperwork. If everything is in order, I'll have them signed and personally deliver them back to you within a few days."

"Great."

Semaj's dreams had come true but not in all of her days could she have imagined that such wonderful things would be within her reach. Her schedule was filled by the weeks.

Christopher kept Semaj's schedule tight. He knew that he had to get her as much exposure as possible, because this business was very rocky, here-today-gone-tomorrow-industry. Booking business meetings with major production companies had gotten her more exposure, and it seemed as if everyone wanted her to be a possible candidate in their new movie project. Between the industry business meetings, reading scripts for potential parts and the Adorable campaign had Semaj physically drained. Her mind could barely function. She was worn out.

Finally, after a month she was able to get away from her hectic schedule and chill with her man. Her first available day consisted of mind-blowing sex, and the lovers slept through the evening into the night. Yes, it was that good and they had missed each other that much.

The next morning, Semaj crawled out of bed while the birds were still chirping. After brushing her teeth and washing her face, she walked over to the sliding door. She slid the door back and stepped out onto the marble veranda. She sat down on the ivory vintage chaise and looked out at her beautiful home, and watched the rising of the sun. Their place was one that only people imagined and Semaj loved the fact that Quasim had chosen her to share his life with. With the cool wind breezing at an easy pace, Semaj stared off into space, and for once allowed her mind to be thoughtless as she meditated for the next couple hours.

Emerging into the bedroom, Semaj slipped out of the negligee that she wore for her man the previous night and threw on some sweats to run around their track. She was adamant about buying this house because not only was it gorgeous but it had a track. Not the one for a treadmill, she loved running laps. Knowing the Hollywood business was primarily based on appearance Semaj felt she was really obligated now to stay in shape. She pushed herself three times out of the week to run ten laps.

Perspiration caused her clothes to stick to her body and sweat dripped from her face. Semaj slowed up as she caught her breath during her last lap, and walked back through the patio door. She made her way into the kitchen where she fixed her and her Quasim a big breakfast.

"You finally getting the cooking down a li'l huh, bay?" he joked. "Oh, I forgot you only know how to cook breakfast food."

"Shut up, punk," Semaj giggled, playfully slapping him across the arm.

"Go get dressed. We spending the day together."

"Yes. It seemed like I haven't spent time with you in a minute."

Semaj raced upstairs on cloud nine heading straight to her spacious closet and rummaged through the many clothes and shoes she'd owned. Her closet was so loaded it resembled a medium-sized designer boutique. Her garments were color coordinated and tidy too. She liked for her clothes to be extremely neat and organized.

After deciding what to wear Semaj placed her clothes on the bed. She took a quick shower as she was excited to be spending the day with Quasim. It was very rare for them to enjoy each other's company outside of their home because Quasim was a homebody, and although she loved to watch movies in the theater room while eating popcorn or bowling against him in their bowling alley, Semaj was the total opposite and very much outgoing. In that particular way they were different but Semaj didn't mind. It felt good to just be in his presence no matter where they were.

After getting dressed and doing her hair she went downstairs to meet Quasim who was out front. "Where are we going?" she asked kissing his lips when she got inside the car.

"Just sit back and relax." Quasim smiled at her eagerness. This was one of the reasons he loved her so deeply. Though she was his woman, she acted like a spoiled baby always faking with her child-like voice.

Semaj knew that was the hook, line and sinker move right there, and it usually got her what she wanted. Acting spoiled once in awhile allowed Semaj to be obedient and respectful without being too passive. She listened to Quasim and did most of everything he asked of her, but still stood her ground like a lady when necessary.

Semaj sat back, enjoying the ride through the suburban streets. When they pulled up to a park she was all smiles. The park was so beautiful and the grass was green as fresh steamed broccoli. The leaves on the trees were starting to turn colors for the fall season. "Oh…my…Gosh, this is so romantic!" Semaj gushed, tugging him out of the car after she noticed the setup.

"I know you like the outdoors and like to be out period. This is your treat, ma," he said charmingly, and pointed as they walked arm-in-arm up to the blanket that sat atop the grass. It had a picnic basket filled with snacks, fruits and a bottle of her favorite wine.

Beaming from ear to ear, Semaj searched the park noticing they'd had it all to themselves. She loved the surprise and felt special, knowing she was getting her man out of character. She sat on the quilted blanket and laughed at the fact that Quasim couldn't quite figure out how he wanted to kneel down into position. "You got it baby?" Semaj asked as she helped him. The young couple mouth-fed each other fruits while enjoying the sweetness as they made small talk about the beautiful cloudless sky and the birds that were flying above them.

Deciding to walk around to tour the massive park the couple sauntered through the many walkways when paradise all came to an abrupt end due to the disturbing phone call. It was Slim. "I need you to meet me somewhere. Some shit happened to Mitch. You know homie go out of town to see some stripper bitch he fuck with ev'ery now and then."

"Yeah, I know. But why you think something happened with that situation?" He tried being discreet as possible so Semaj wouldn't catch on. He didn't want to cause her to fret for what could be nothing.

"I haven't talked to dude since he left two nights ago for Atlantic City. You know he call at least once a day to let us know how the streets operating."

"I'll be there after I drop Maj off. Meet me at the club."

Quasim hung up and by his facial expression Semaj knew they had to go quick.

"Is everything cool?"

"Should be. Just gotta go holla at this nigga and see what he talking 'bout."

"I was just getting comfortable, too. Dang! I don't wanna go home."

"I tell you what. Since I'm headed towards Midtown call Paris and see if she home. I can pick you back up from there once I get finish handling this shit."

"Okay." Semaj replied softly and he noticed that she was saddened that their date was ending early but he had no choice. Quasim hoped like hell that Semaj wouldn't have another reason to be hurting all over again, but his gut told him that something dreadful had happened. For her sake, he prayed that he was bugging and paranoid.

Paris leaned forward towards the compact disc to scoop the cocaine with her French-manicured pinkie nail and ran it across her nose to feed her habit. Swiftly jerking her head back to deter her nostrils from running, she heard a knock at her door. "Come in," she yelled and continued to concentrate on her high as she indulged the substance up her nose.

Walking in, Semaj stared at Paris and shook her head disgustingly. Before she started kicking it with Paris extra hard, she knew she was a blow head. But for her to continuously make usage of the drug was beyond her.

Not stopping once even after seeing Semaj, Paris powdered her nose snorting the last line, and leaned back with low watery eyes as she savored the feeling. Her euphoric high had caused her to feel some superwoman abilities. She had sniffed three grams.

"I didn't know you still got down with that shit," Semaj said as she retrieved the remote from the entertainment stand and plopped down on the oversized reclining chair. "That shit crazy. Fuck you be on, Paris, man?"

Adjusting her vision to the dimly lit room, Paris focused on Semaj and she was seeing double. "I've been stressing out here lately. I just started back up," she lied. Paris had never stopped. "I really don't have a choice if I wanna escape my problems."

"What problems?" Semaj asked with an attitude wanting better for her friend. "You know that ain't right, though, P. You better than that shit."

"You know what? I'm getting sick and tired of your holier than thy, bullshit! Fo'real. Last time I checked I was grown as fuck and a bitch can't tell me what's better for me!" Paris snapped.

"Are you serious?" Semaj cocked her head back in astonishment.

"Fuck outta here with that shit. You don't know my mu'fuckin' problems, girl!"

"Last I checked I was covering all of your problems." By now she'd pissed Semaj completely off. "'Cause if my memory serves me correctly, I paid your bills up for the next six months, including the note on that Range outside."

"Girl, a four year old Range and you riding in a Benz that comes out next year. Please! Don't go there with me, Semaj."

"I never knew anybody to complain about a new body Range." Shocked, Semaj stared at Paris and searched for the seriousness of her statement. She just knew she was going to admit that it was a joke…but got nothing. That really made her vexed, but because she was under the influence Semaj decided to leave it alone. "You know what. You high right now so I'm not even going to take it there with you!"

"Oh, but you can take it there though. High or sober, I'm still Paris," she said with an attitude as she leaned forward and glared at Semaj, ready to flip totally out at this point. "'Cause it's just like a bougie Hollywood bitch to say what they've done for the next mu'fucka. Bitch, it was never that before when you was robbing cats like the next mu'fucka trying to keep your head above water. Now bitches wanna change and shit," Paris said as her face frowned in irritation.

"I'm not even going to comment on this shit okay, Paris?" Semaj replied. "You buggin' right now and I'm not gonna entertain you."

"You an entertainer now, right?" Paris laughed with sarcasm in her voice. "So I don't see why not. But oh, I forgot you a different person now, huh? But let me put somethin' in ya ear, ma. Everybody can't change, Semaj. Everyone can't become something else when the streets is all they know. I've had to take care of myself since I was a young head, and survived without you thus far! So you can have all that shit back!"

Semaj heard her story and the same line many times, and to her it was nothing but pathetic excuses. But in all honesty, Semaj didn't want this small issue to bloom into bigger problems. "Paris, I ain't mean it like that. I didn't say it to make you feel low or anything. I'm just saying I don't understand

why you using the drugs 'cause you stressing with problems. What problems
are you referring to?"

"It don't matter what problems. They're not your problems," she piped.
"Bitch think they somethin' 'cause they been in a movie. Beat it, bitch!" She
began laughing like a madwoman. "Fuck outta here with that commercial
shit. You think you something 'cause you gotta boyfriend and a career now!
Bet if that nigga knew you murdered…I mean, your Pops murked his Pops
you wouldn't be sitting here like shit gully. Would you?" she said harshly.

"I can't believe you taking it there!" Her words almost got stuck in her
dried throat.

"Fuck you mean! You took me there and now that we're here might as
well take it all the way. How would Qua feel if I told him that you're not who
you portray to be? You just another grimy bitch from the 'hood with a cute
face. You ain't shit. 'Cause if you were you would've never left me once you
got into the business or put on. You and your daddy act like we never used to
get this money together. I don't know when you forgot where you came from
and how we got down."

"When my dreams became a reality. That's when." Semaj jerked her
head back and furrowed her face with a glare that implied, "Girl is you crazy?"
"But I ain't ever forgotten where I came from."

"So when shit presents itself in a better form, y'all just leave a bitch for
dead?"

"Leave you for dead?" Semaj spewed, beyond exasperated. More than
anything, she was hurt. "Them drugs really got your head fucked up, yo.
You a clown. 'Cause when I'm out shopping, you getting everything I'm
getting and the shit going on my tab! When I'm catching flights out, you
right there tagging along right beside me! Everything I got, you got. I'm
eating and you eating too. Fuck you talkin' about something better and we
leaving you for dead? Clown, if anything we keeping you alive. You ain't gotta
do a mu'fuckin' thang and still live the high life. Popping bottles in the club
and rocking the latest Gucci bag don't come easy, my nigga. A bitch a be
happy to wear your shoes not having to do shit and live this life. But yo' ass
complaining about it! Ungrateful ass muthafucka. Throwing shit up in my
face like that. Shit's fucked up, Paris. I swear that's some played shit." Semaj
was damn near in tears.

"Fuck you!" Paris was expressing the way she really felt about her since
the very beginning. "Just write me a check for fifty Gs and we can end this

fake ass friendship now. You ain't gon' have to lavish me no more!"

"Bitch, you got me fucked up!" Semaj barked, popping up from the chair.

"But if you knew what was good for you, you'd write it!" she stated as if this was nonnegotiable.

"You wouldn't!"

"I wouldn't what? Blackmail that ass? I guess you really don't know me then, fo' real, huh?" she smiled wickedly.

Semaj knew where this was going and at that moment was the first time that she realized she'd broken her number one rule: trust no one, which was her only rule. "What you saying? You trying to extort me or some shit?" Semaj asked, staring her dead in her eyes.

"Trying? No! Its extortion, bitch! So write my check and get the fuck up outta my house!"

Semaj shot daggers through her, but knew what she had to do. Digging inside her purse, she retrieved her checkbook and ballpoint pen and wrote her a check out for fifty thousand. After ripping the check out, she tossed it on the table. "You foul, Paris. After everything we've been through, you foul. But you need that shit so I ain't trippin'." She opened the door and slammed it hard.

"Fuck you! You made it this way! Wannabe Hollywood Bitch!" she shouted behind her.

Semaj walked the streets until she finally flagged down a yellow cab to take her home. It was like the world was matching her every mood, because when she was recently elated the sky was blue as cotton candy with sunny conditions, but now that her mood was dreary, the sky was too. Tears of hurt streamed down her cheeks as the rain began to pour down heavily. The falling water hit the pavement forcefully with raindrops the size of golf balls. She dialed her father's number because she knew he was the only one to fix this situation. He wasn't answering. But she continued to try and reach him her entire ride home.

Chapter **14**

In a windowless Jersey City warehouse, Block sat at the head of a limestone slab table in an oversized, swivel chair. To the left of him was his right-hand man, Drakey, maintaining his usual stony silence. The table that seated twelve was now down to only three. The empty chairs represented his members that were now deceased. One of the three men was his cousin, D-Boy, and the other occupants were the head street lieutenants. The tension in the building was thick. It would be hard for a scalpel to cut through it. It was an uneasiness surrounding the room that Block hadn't witnessed since the assassination of his late uncle.

"D-Boy, you know ever since you told me that Quasim is bagging Mitch's daughter I haven't been able to sleep. The thought of them being on the same team never ran across my mind, but you've connected the dots family. Now it all makes sense. He been plotting against me," he assumed. "Now niggas see ain't no action happening on my blocks so they gettin' bold, feeling they can push their own products." Block shook his head at the thought of his current situation. "My workers that are still living is shook and afraid to ride for the team. I be damn if a bunch of New York niggas run me out my own city and scare me off the streets 'cause it's beef. My peoples worked too hard for me to allow their organization to go into shambles over some niggas with no respect."

"Fuck outta here, B," D-Boy said as he searched his cousin's eyes for the truth, which was revealed from his facial expression. "Damn, fam! I ain't know business was that fucked up."

"Not only has it been a drought and the feds hot on a niggas ass, but mu'fuckas got the audacity to send some niggas to get at my people... a... an... and... my wife." His words got stuck in his throat as he thought of his late wife. "I wanna personally murder Santana and Mitch, but I know I gotta be much smarter than that. I gotta get at those niggas when they least expect it. I been letting it die down and lying low. Gotta be strategic."

"Feel that, fam. Think we should recruit some thoroughbreds and put 'im down though. Build a strong team with some wild ass hungry cats. Hollered at this plug out of DC my man's put me on. So we can get the money back flowing. And then have a solid squad of soldiers that's ready to go to war when the time is right," one of the lieutenants suggested.

"I got an even better idea. I've been chatting with my man Ox since the shit happened. He said whenever I give him the go ahead, he gon' send some of his ruthless shootas down here so we can reign again. Y'all know Ox been connected to my family a very long time. My man very upset. Said it's some fucked up shit that went down. With the loyalty that he has had to my family, he feels that it's his obligation to my uncle that he sends some of his most dominant members up here." Ox was a ruthless Jamaican crime boss out of Kingston and had been running the city for over twenty years. He was connected to many dangerous cartels in different regions all over the world, and his empire was the sister empire to many solidified drug and gang organizations in Jamaica. Having the artillery, this was a great army to have behind him.

"So when is we gon' get the ball rolling, so the beef is dead and we can get back to this money?" the other lieutenant inquired.

Little did they know things were about to be back on. Ox had informed him that business was in motion, and this time they were private jet-setting bricks. But Block had to get this situation dealt with first. This was his personal vendetta. "It's just a matter of time before we get this fool, Santana. We just gotta wait because like they say, revenge is best served cold and it's still warm, baby. Besides, I got somethin' special in store for that nigga. Believe that."

D-Boy nodded, agreeing. "No doubt, baby. I feel you. Get that boy when and where they least expect it."

"Fam, though," Block paused to rub his chin and a wicked grin crossed his face. "Mitch ride solo. It ain't nearly as hard to get at him. He feel he untouchable, but I know where he be. I'ma show this pussy what callous and psychotic really is. Got this li'l shorty at this strip joint in Atlantic City that he frequents willing to set him up. We got this nigga, yo. Let's make it happen, baby."

Ciara treaded sensuously across the stage as the rapper crooned from the state of the art speakers, *"You wanna see some ass I wanna see cash. Keep them dollars coming and that's gon' make me dance,"* the crowd went bananas as she turned around and made her ass clap to Travis Porter. Her five foot eight frame was that of a goddess. She held the patrons captivated as they stared lustfully at her nude body, and the men kept their eyes fixated. Climbing the poll, she performed like she had a degree in stripping. Niggas flooded the stage with dollar bills. Hoisting her body to the top, she slowly pressed her ass cheeks into the cold metal while making sexual facial expressions. Sliding down at a leisurely pace, in a swift gesture she flipped over, and dropped into the splits allowing her voluptuous ass to bounce to the hip-hop tunes. She was a pro at knowing how to make the crowd go crazy and niggas loved when she hit the stage because she would always give them their money's worth. She was by far the baddest at the club and some of the club patrons came from all over the New Jersey area just to see her stage-show performance.

Scooping up all of her money from the floor, she smiled at Murder Mitch and motioned for him to go to the private room.

Murder Mitch made his way through the red curtains and walked into the dimly lit red room. Sitting down on the red sofa, he poured himself a drink of Patrón and sat his gun next to the bucket of ice. He'd paid an extra two hundred to come inside with his ratchet and it was worth it, along with the hour he had rented out the private room.

As he placed the five hundred dollars on the armrest, Ciara emerged. "What's up, daddy?" she whispered seductively as she treaded near him. Murder Mitch was one of Ciara's moneymen and every time he came to town she made sure to show him a good time. For proper compensation, Ciara was down for whatever and had no limitations to what she would do for her customers. Murder Mitch was a club regular and had frequented the place for the past three years she'd been working there. Dude always had a fat daddy knot and came to town at least twice a month.

Turning the lighting down a tad bit more, Ciara went for what she knew and began unbuckling his pants as she dropped to her knees enticingly. Positioning herself, she tugged out his penis and just the sight of his tool made her want to give him the best head of his life. Popping out of its confinement,

Ciara began to fondle him and admired the thickness of his long curved dick. Taking him inside her month, she was giving him some great neck.

He had gotten comfortable and threw his head back in ecstasy. As he closed his eyes and curled his toes unintentionally, he palmed the back of her head for leverage. Bobbing her head, with no hands, Ciara inconspicuously grabbed his gun and placed it under the couch.

"Caught cha slippin' bumbaclot, rude boy!" the voice said in a Jamaican accent. Two shottas had guns pointed at Murder Mitch's head.

The voice startled him and instinctively he reached for his gun; it wasn't there.

"You scandalous, bitch!" Murder Mitch immediately realized that he'd been set up. He shook his head at his own stupidity, knowing to never feel comfortable in any environment. He'd used females to get at niggas all the time. What made him assume that his own dish wouldn't come back in the same form? Karma was a bitch and though he knew she'd catch up to him one day, he never thought it would be under these circumstances.

Block had came down to the club a week earlier and had offered Ciara twenty thousand to set him up. He knew Murder Mitch loved Nude Daddy strip club and Ciara would be the perfect advantage. Craving money, sadly, she loved it more than a human's life. Ciara accepted it without hesitation, and the fact that he possibly would have his life ended didn't cause her to flinch.

She told Block the strategy that would work for her, and he sent his goons in to do the job. Before the two Jamaicans escorted Murder Mitch out the emergency exit door inside the red room, which Ciara had deactivated, one goon had struck him across the face with the gun and threw him over his shoulder. He was knocked out cold. They had to because Murder Mitch was gangster and wasn't willingly going to comply with their request like some sucka.

Before they knocked him out, Murder Mitch had already warned them, "You niggas may as well kill me right here, 'cause I ain't walkin' out this bitch like a pussy ass nigga." Even with death kissing his face, he was still the same G.

Nobody on the outside was aware of what was going down in the red room. The loudness from the blaring tunes was drowning out the commotion. When Ciara turned around to rejoin the live party not feeling an ounce of guilt, the other Jamaican asserted with his gun already aimed.

"We leave behind no witnesses, bloodclot!" Her eyes bugged wide in fear, but he didn't give her enough time to plead. He ended her life with the silencer.

I just hope my daughter be straight, Murder Mitch thought as the numbers on his life had clocked down. He was living in his last moments on earth. Death loomed over him. He knew it was near, but knew his demise wasn't untimely. The life he had led for so long had ultimately determined the cruel way in which he was about to die. He had taken more lives, had destroyed more families, and dismantled more drug cartels than any one man. Most people in his position would be pleading for their life, but Murder Mitch knew this was his fate. The cold-hearted man within wouldn't allow him to beg, because his time had come and he had no regrets.

Although weak, he tried lifting his head to look the grim reaper in his eyes but Murder Mitch knew his legacy would be enough for him. His reign of terror was worth it. An infamous street legend, an assassination machine that murder-for-hire story would be told to every hustler and gangster coming up in the game. Notorious was an understatement for Murder Mitch. He gave the ters ruthless and callous a fresh definition the very day he jumped off the porch headfirst in the murder game. But tonight was his judgment day—payment for all his committed sins. He held no pain or anger.

A gruesome sight, Block's torture was unbelievable and the carnage he used was that of retribution. Naked, Murder Mitch hung from a steel pipe where his hands were chain-shackled and he was severely beaten and bruised. Seeing him this way was poetic for Block, a lovely execution for the hated adversary. The two of them could no longer inhale the same air. They would never be able to co-exist and it was time for Murder Mitch's demise.

The image of Block was blurry, and the blood had flooded his vision. The red fluid slipped into his eyelids and stung an unbearable agony. His eyeballs felt as if a lava flame had been ignited within. Block and his goons had beaten him for two days and two nights, rotating shifts. The old adage of how you kill is how you'd die rang true. During his time, Murder Mitch had tormented people and karma had come around full circle. He hadn't felt any remorseful chill in his ruthless bones. Murder had been his religion, coldblooded had been his creed and as nature's law applies, he was reaping what he had sowed.

His ribs were broken; most of his bones were crushed. His face was badly disfigured, but his mental state was so strong he knew even at his weakest point he had an advantage over Block. They both knew he was there to die, but what Block wanted to see was him cry. Tears would have given him satisfaction, but there was nothing that could possibly be done to Murder Mitch because he was a natural born killer and he didn't fear death.

While in this torturous moment, Murder Mitch was unafraid and in his fleeting moments of life, the only face that popped up in his mind was his daughter's. He hated to leave her behind, but he had created a monster, and he knew that she'd be able to survive. As blood leaked from his body and poured from his mouth, and through sticky vision Murder Mitch managed to smirk meanly at Block.

In exhaustion, Block circled the hanging body of Murder Mitch and stared back up at the dying man. Surrounded by a ruthless crew of dreadlocked Jamaicans, Block could have had one of the efficient workers that had been sent up from Kingston take his man out, but this shit was too personal. Block was tired of bullshitting around too, and it was Murder Mitch's time to go. Orbiting around a man who he had once trusted, the barrel of the sawed-off shotgun screeching across the floor as he dragged it, Block was ready to make the lights go off on Murder Mitch. "Fuck you thought, nigga? I wasn't gon' ever catch up with you? Nigga, huh?" Block spit as he lifted his assault rifle up and aimed it skillfully at Murder Mitch's head. *"CLICK-CLACK!"* He chambered the pump back in an attempt to blow Murder Mitch's face off. "This for you, Kan!"

"BOOM!"

A loud crashing sound interrupted Block before he could kill Murder Mitch. A swarm of twenty plus DEA agents with labeled bulletproof vest on flooded the old factory as the warehouse went into complete pandemonium. "Everybody on the fucking ground!" one of the agents shouted.

"What the fuck!" Block pushed past one of the Jamaican members and dropped to the floor, disappearing out of the back easily and unnoticed while thinking how in the fuck the police discovered his hideout. He had to contact Ox.

Meanwhile, the Jamaicans shot it out with the New Jersey DEA. Gunplay unmatched, their marksmen aim flawlessly had given the officers a shootout that the East Coast hadn't seen since the eighties. Bullets flew for what seemed like forever as bodies from each team dropped motionless.

Ruthlessly and carelessly, the Jamaicans let their deadly devices sound off a flinching tune, but outnumbered, the Rasta boys were nearly defenseless, and each of them went down one by one, leaving a trail of dead bodies on scene. This was an event that would cause a great war between two of the most powerful drug bosses in the twenty-first century.

With an unlit Cigar hanging from the side of his mouth, Gio stood underneath the wrought-shed of his privately owned hospital. Flashing red, white, and yellow lights gleamed as the ambulance approached the front entrance. He had enough pull to send DEA agents in, and as instructed, they had brought Mr. Richardson to him badly beaten, but nevertheless alive. Surrounded by an entourage of twelve Dominican men, one of the henchmen stepped forward with his boss and snatched the rear door open.

A grin of satisfaction stretched across Gio's face as he looked down at Murder Mitch, who had once been his most efficient worker. As fast as that smirk of elation washed upon his face, a cold frown took its place. Although the face that belonged to Murder Mitch was outrageously disfigured, Gio had noticed the teardrop tattoo stained underneath his right eye. Everything else was unrecognizable. His face, body and hands were all gruesomely assaulted.

The sight of Murder Mitch infuriated him completely, and instinctively he withdrew his .357 magnum and slapped it across the injured face. He slipped his pistol back inside his waistband, but that didn't damper the hurting emotions that overcame him. Angrily, Gio clasped his strong hands around his neck in an involuntary clutch to squeeze the rest of the life out of Murder Mitch. He had allowed his anger to get the better of him, although his attempts were useless. He was numb and unconscious. Releasing him from his firm hold, Gio watched as his private doctors unloaded the gurney from the paramedics.

Gio spat as if his saliva was fire that would incite a gasoline blaze. Gio wished the fragile body had been doused in petrol so that he could light a match and watch the flesh burn into char remorselessly. But things weren't that simple. He depended on Murder Mitch to survive. He needed his team of doctors to ensure his survival. He had to live so that he could tell him where to find his grandchild.

The highly paid medical team burst through the double doors as they rushed him in for surgery. *I should have never given you my blessings to marry my daughter,* he thought regretfully as the stretcher disappeared down the narrow hallway.

Many years had passed, but his grandbaby stayed etched to his memory. Gio hadn't seen Semaj since she was a baby her doll face had never left his mental museum. There was a void in his organization that only she would be able to fill. She was an heir. Never had Semaj known it, but she was the granddaughter of Gio Milano. She was more than a princess of the ghetto. She was a Mafia Princess. It was only a matter of time before she encountered the life that her mother, Kasey had been born into: Drugs. Money. Murder. Mayhem. Wars. *Omerta.* A life of *La Cosa Nostra.* A legacy that would live on forever.

Chapter 15

After paying the ninety-dollar tab she ran up, Semaj tipped the cabdriver twenty-dollars and walked inside her home overcome with emotion. The pouring rain had her soaking wet. Exhaustion plagued her, but she knew there was no time for rest. She needed her father. She wanted her father so he could soothe her nerves. She also needed Quasim who she loved and prayed to God that she'd never lose his love.

Semaj stood looking at herself in the bathroom mirror and noticed the stress lines forming on her forehead. Worry filled her face as tired bags rested beneath her eyes. Turning around, Semaj twisted on the nozzles to the shower on full blast.

Undressing out of the wet clothing, she stepped into the spacious walk-in shower hoping the hot water would wash some of her worries away, but instead an eerie feeling passed over her. Choosing to ignore the nagging feeling in her gut, she continued to scrub her skin down and grabbed the towel from the rack before stepping out of the shower. Hearing her phone chiming, she thought it was her father until she noticed Quasim's picture flashing across the screen. "Hello?"

"I'm on my way to swoop you."

"Already home."

"Oh," he paused, thinking nothing of it. "Well, I'm on my way home."

"Okay," Semaj said fixin' to hang up. "Wait!" Semaj called out.

"What's up?"

"Have you talked to my Dad? I can't get in touch with him. I been trying for the last few hours and he still ain't picked up. That's weird because my father always answers for me."

"Nah, I ain't talked to him either. But we'll discuss it once I get there."

Quasim hung up not willing to tell her what was going on over the phone.

As Semaj sat in front of her vanity mirror, she heard Quasim summoning for her to come downstairs. "Here I come," she said, wrapping her black silk robe around her shoulders and slid into the slippers. Wanting to conceal her depressing mood, Semaj forced a smile to cross her face.

"Hey pretty lady," he said sweetly as he leaned against the foyer's brick wall. He hated that he was the one to have to deliver the news about her father being missing. "C'mon here, baby," he commanded and she complied. Quasim pulled her close to his chest and rested his forehead against hers. "I need to speak with you about something, Maj."

"What is it?" she asked.

He sighed heavily. "Don't get scared or start buggin' because I'm not sure what's what. And I don't want us to just start assuming shit."

"Okay, Qua. You scaring me." Semaj placed her hand over her chest. "Would you just tell me what is going on already."

"Maj," he paused, staring down into her beautiful eyes. "Haven't nobody been able to get in touch with Mitch in the last couple of days."

"What are you insinuating, Quasim?" Almost instantly, a migraine overpowered her brain and she felt the room spin underneath her. Sweat formed on her nose as her heartbeat blared loudly in her ears. "You think my Daddy been snatched?" Tears were gushing from her eyes as she sobbed inside Quasim's embrace.

He felt so bad. Only if he could take her pain away he would undoubtedly. "We don't know what is going on, Maj. Baby, stop crying. We don't know yet. Please stop crying," he said, begging. She had brought tears to his eyes and he could hear his heart breaking at her devastation. Not because Murder Mitch was missing because Quasim knew the life, but for the pain she endured.

The doorbell rang loudly throughout the house, jarring them from the intimate moment. Seeing the detective at their door with a look of sympathy across his face was the only confirmation needed. Before the homicide detective could break the news, Semaj wailed and fell to the ground in distress. "Please tell me my father is okay!" she screamed helplessly.

"I'm really sorry about this ma'am," the officer said as Quasim helped

Semaj up from the ground. "We will need a relative to come down to the coroner's office. We found a wallet at a shooting scene and need someone to come down to identify the body." He paused. "And again, I'm truly sorry."

"I'll have someone at the morgue tomorrow morning," Quasim said as he closed the door behind him. At that moment all he wanted to do was comfort Semaj.

It was storming. The loud thunder and heavy downpour were every indication that something bad had happened. Lying underneath the soft sheets, Semaj tossed and turned unable to sleep. Restless, she climbed down from bed and walked over to the bay window. The lightning striking lit up outside, but the blistering winds and severe rainfall caused a blurry view, and the sounds of hail hitting the windowpane had gotten her lost in her thoughts.

She heard the squeak of the hardwood floor and closed her eyes as she felt Quasim's hand interlink hers. "You know I'm here if you need me for anything, baby."

He expected her not to respond, but to his relief she replied. "I just can't believe my father is gone," she whispered. "It's like anything good to me leaves me."

"I promise I'll never leave you. On everything, baby, we're forever."

"Every time something right is going good in my life some bullshit happens. I done cried so much in my lifetime it seems like I'm all cried out. I never knew that one person could lose so many people in a lifetime. But I guess it's different with me." She stared out into the dangerous winds gusting with a tear-stained face. Semaj felt like she had to be cursed to lose her mother, her first love, her auntie and then her father in her short life.

"You still have me and we're going to build something beautiful together. A family one day. If you leave everything up to me you'd never have to cry another day in your life. You're mine, Maj," he said. "Now come back to bed."

"When I'm with you everything in my world seems so right. You make me feel like I have something to look forward to," she whispered.

"Me too. Me too," he spoke into her ear. "You're my happiness."

He led her back over to the bed to lie down. Semaj wrapped herself in his arms. He stayed up half of the night rubbing her back to ease some of her pain. With him next to her she found temporary peace, and was finally able to rest her eyes where her father lived in her dreams.

The next morning when Semaj awoke, she sat up in complete shock. There had to be no space left in the bedroom. From life-size teddy bears to huge balloons to dozens of roses and over twenty gift bags filled up with cards, candy and plaques surrounded the room. Her heart smiled at his generosity. Quasim had showered her with the best of things, but this kind approach during one of the most troubling times in her life reminded her why she loved him so much. The material things he had provided for her wasn't comparable to his thoughtfulness. She crawled out of bed and did her morning regimen before making her way downstairs. "Quasim!" she called out.

"Good morning," he said as he extended his hand to help her down the last step. He kissed her forehead. "I set up some places to visit so that we can go through planning his funeral together. Call Paris and see if she wanna go with us. I know that's your homegirl and you'd love for her to help you though this too." He knew how close the two of them were, but what he didn't know was about their fallout. "I'm going to call her," Quasim pulled out his phone and dialed her number.

"*The Sprint subscriber that you are trying to reach is unavailable please try the number or code again,*" an operator's voice blared through the phone. A look of confusion crossed Quasim's face as he looked at Semaj.

She's really mad to get her number change, she thought, feeling as if Paris was being over the top. Although they'd had a misunderstanding or per se a dispute, Semaj felt that they were way better than that. The money was nothing. Paris could have gotten more if only she had asked in a different way. She knew that she would call and apologize and they'd move on, but it was obvious that Paris was serious. Never in a million years would she have thought that Paris would become her archenemy, but in actuality, she had been the disguised foe from the very beginning.

Murder Mitch's death had drew Semaj even closer to Quasim, and he became her personal escort. Putting his business off, he focused on her and planning a small but beautiful memorial service. Her days were filled with choosing flowers arrangements and picking out caskets. Speaking with preachers, deciding on churches and opting cremation, Semaj wanted her father's remains to be placed in an urn so that he could be with her forever.

As Semaj passed through the days, she blocked out everything and turned off her emotions. Numbed, she withdrew as it got closer to having to say goodbye to her father. Detachment was the only way Semaj knew that she'd be able to get through it and keep her sanity. To avoid the pain, she had to disconnect herself from her feelings. Logically, if she was emotionless, then there wasn't a way she could be devastated. She knew her father wouldn't want her to be sad, and for that reason along with Quasim being her strength, she didn't let her father's death break her. She remained strong in what seemed to be the most trying time of her life.

Chapter 16

Paris walked onto the terrace of the fabulous oceanfront bungalow and watched as the sun set upon Berry Island's beautiful skyline. The island was a part of a district in the Bahamas. She tightened her robe as the chilliness of the island's wind breezed against her mocha skin, gracing her face. She took a deep breath as she surveyed her surroundings, taking in what she would describe as the glamorous life. She and her new friend, Vega had been in the Islands for four days and she was having the best time. *This is how my life is supposed to be.*

It had been weeks since she'd lifted the fifty thousand from Semaj. Paris had heard about her father's death right before she left New York for her hometown Baltimore. But full of hatred, she smiled when learning the news. She knew once her plan was executed, Semaj wouldn't have anybody left and Murder Mitch's demise made everything better. Paris could've easily had her set up to be killed, but that was much too simple. She wanted Semaj alone in this world and that was what she intended to do.

She had befriended Semaj, and she'd betrayed her friendship before she could. *Bitch, gon' try to play me like she was taking care of me. But, I'ma show her the meaning of taking care of somebody. Clown-bitch should've known that I'm the last bitch to be at odds with.* When Paris despised someone, it made her mouth twitch at just the simple thought of their name. She now hated Semaj with a passion and she was determined to bring her down just out of spite and pure evilness.

Paris had decided with the money she had gotten from her that she would return back home and find her a baller to wine and dine her. She hated that Semaj had a man and seeing her happy only made Paris feel the romance she was missing in her own life. But now it was her time to shine and Semaj's time to suffer. Vengeance was her motivation and she wanted to hit Semaj where it hurt, and that meant removing the only person left in the world that she could count on.

Informing Quasim on what she was involved in would leave her with nothing: No love…no man…no career. Without Quasim backing her, Paris knew Semaj wouldn't be able to manage and her downfall would soon ensue. Semaj had opened her mouth and revealed too much information that could and would be used against her in her own court of law.

Paris remembered how much Semaj had talked about her first love and how she'd missed him dearly. Before she didn't recognize him from the picture, because a lot about Vega had changed over the years and he was a grown man now. But just like Paris thought, she'd seen him some place before and he was alive and healthy. She knew exactly who he was. Her identical twin sister, Egypt that attended the University of Maryland had caught the eyes of one of Baltimore's biggest hustler's. Paris urged her to talk to him, and Egypt conceded after awhile. But unable to adapt to his lifestyle, two months later Egypt ended the relationship.

With a conniving mentality, it wasn't hard for Paris to jump into the role of her sister and seamlessly impersonated Egypt. She reentered Vega's life. It wasn't as if she was in business to seek unconditional love. Paris simply didn't believe in love. Only people she ever loved were her twin sister and older brother. Other than that love was forbidden. Though she wanted to enjoy the perks of fucking with a boss, she wanted to hurt Semaj more. She even hoped to send her into a mental state by lying and telling her that Vega had a ticket price on her head. It was going to be enjoyable to see Semaj break and driven to a place of no return.

As the wind continued to dance delicately in the air, Paris' hair fluttered through the balmy breeze and she was startled by the strong hands that wrapped around her waist. She turned around and found Vega's, lean, rich chocolate physique before her. Just the simplicity of him made cream form in her panties.

"This view is beautiful," Vega said as he stared out. He knew this was a far cry from the old days and thought about how far he had come. He was now the made man of his city and had a loyal team behind him.

"I know," Paris ran her hand over Vega's chiseled abdomen. Her hand moved its way down to his hardened tool and she began to fondle him. They'd just came back from parasailing and both were horny as shit. His dick was bulging as if it wanted to escape its confinement. "I want you, daddy," she said with a burning desire. Paris felt since there was no love within the situation, and not personal, there was no dishonor toward her sister.

"Is that so?"

"Yeah," she said while trailing small pecks down his chest. Her pussy was throbbing as she grabbed his arm and led him inside the bedroom. As soon as they reentered the room, his hands roamed her stacked figure and he removed her beach undergarments. Planting kisses all over his body, he watched in amazement as Paris seductively bent down on her knees and removed his pants provocatively. With her mouth watering from anticipation, she took his dark beautiful penis into her warmth. His hands were clasped against her head as he guided himself in and out of her tight jaws. Mami's head game was something vicious and she deep throated him like she'd invented it. He tried holding his semen back but was unsuccessful and came prematurely. The cum fluids shot to the back of her throat and she swallowed and licked him clean.

Her pussy was dripping wet and it didn't take one second for her to jump on top of his manhood with expertise. Contracting her walls around the width, Paris rode his penis like a wild cowgirl. While her perky breast bounced freely, Vega's mouth was drawn to her berry-colored nipples as he licked and softly bit them. Their sexual chemistry was on another planet. In a swift motion, he flipped her onto her stomach and eased in from behind. He observed his instrument as he dug inside her juice box. He couldn't believe that her moistures had his dick leaking creams as the only sound that could be heard were gasps and the noises from him making the bed rock.

"Oh, yes! Right there, daddy! Shit!" she squealed as Vega hit her with the death-stroke, teasing her G-spot each thrust as the motion caused her legs to quiver in ecstasy.

Both being freaks it was nothing when she totted her ass up in the air, welcoming him into her third opening. A sex professional, Paris relaxed her muscles with her eyes closed as he grinded her slow. Once inside of her wetness, he rocked his hips while occasionally smacking her left butt cheek to let her know that her performance was grade A. He felt the semen building at the tip and caused him to pound harder as he began guttural grunting. "Fuckin' shit, ma! I'm finna cum!"

"Me too! I love you," she whispered as she threw her ass back at him.

"Gotdamn!" Vega moaned loudly as they came together and he

141

collapsed on her back. Vega lay there in total shock. Homegirl was the best sex he ever had and again she was proving him right. "You're the best I've ever had," he complimented not able to keep the thought to himself.

"I know," she replied quite surely. "And it's forever yours to keep."

Several weeks passed and the year was ending, Paris had moved a lot of her things over to Vega's and although unspoken she had taken the role as his "Main Bitch". It was known that he had plenty of chicks in the streets but it never seemed to bother Paris. She was in it for other reasons than the typical hood fame that the ghetto girl's wanted to get with Vega for. After all she was "Egypt", and she didn't have her ears plugged to the streets, so there was no way she could confront him about the chicks…as if she cared anyway. With her it was about more…it was about revenge…revenge for Semaj.

As she moved around their bedroom, Paris packed her bags for New York and watched as Vega got dressed for the day. "So how long will you be gone?" his Baltimore accent rolled off smoothly.

"I told you only for a couple days."

"You say you going to kick it wit' some classmates?" Vega questioned as he paused to look at her attentively.

"Yes, Nathan. There's nothing you have to worry about. I'll be back New Year's day," she stated as he looked at her with suspicion in his eyes. "I might stop by to see my ex, but other than that, yeah, I'ma hang out with my girls," she said sarcastically.

"Don't get fucked up, E!" Vega smacked her on the ass, causing her to smile.

She grabbed the small Louis Vuitton overnight bag and draped it over her shoulder. "I love you, daddy. I'll see you in a few days." She kissed him on the lips and headed for the door.

Her heart raced in anticipation as she slid inside her car. She felt this was the beginning of Semaj's downfall. *Yeah, bitch, live good while the living is great because once I drop the dime on your ass, it's over for you,* she thought deviously.

As she turned onto the freeway headed for New York, Paris dialed a number. "What up? Who dis?"

"Hey, what up D-Boy?" Paris put on her sweet voice. "There's something real important I have to tell you."

"What is it?" he asked.

"I think I know who killed Cedes."

"What!" he seethed, hurting from the mention of his sister's nickname. "Who, yo?"

"Word is Semaj and her dad had something to do with it. My people told me that she was handling some business for Dean-Bean when Mitch ran into the spot and killed them both. That's not it though. The majority of the robberies 'round the way been set-ups by Semaj, your baby mama before she passed and Mitch before he got deaded. I'm glad I been stop fuckin' with them," she sighed as if in relief.

D-Boy clenched his jaws tightly together as he bit into his jaw. "Good looking. My man's 'bout to handle that grimy bitch anyway. I knew she was a sheisty bitch. Never liked that bougie hoe. And Ta was always try'na captain save that trife bitch."

"You know its all love bra," Paris hung up the phone as a wicked grin crossed her face. *Bitch won't be able to step foot into New York with D-Boy and his goons on that ass.* She burst into a fit of evil laughter as she turned up the radio on a mission to destroy Semaj once and for all.

Chapter 17

It was New Year's Eve and Quasim had been invited to his drug plug's yacht at the pier. Annually, since he first connected with the prestigious and ingenious Dominican drug plug, Quasim met up with him this precise day to discuss business for the upcoming year. Gio was so meticulous on handling business concerning the drug market that he only conferred the matters yearly. Once agreement was set on quantity, the amount of kilograms weren't to be changed until the following year. It was routine and kept the chances of them popping up on the fed's radar at an ultimate low.

This day in particular was special for Quasim, however. A couple months had passed and calmness surrounded Semaj's and Quasim's world. Life for them couldn't have been better. For the first time ever, Quasim had contemplated his exit from the dope game. He'd lost so much to the game he felt it was only a matter of time before his lucky well ran dry. Not one to prolong his hustler's intuition, He decided that he'd willingly pass the game down to his two most trusted men. He was willing to allow them to have the next decade in New York, knowing they'd assist it with great honor. Besides, it was about that time for them to depart from street spokesmen and graduate to the headmen in charge. Quasim had a nice run in the drug game. Minus the bullshit, the game was good to him, and now it was time to see if it'd continue to be good to his most loyal crewmembers.

Now, he wanted it to be all about Semaj and their future together. It seemed to be that she was the perfect woman for him. She made him want to change and become a better man. He'd been through plenty of women in his short twenty-seven years and none were comparable to Semaj Richardson. She brought him so much joy like no other had ever before. She made him want to be brand new, only for her though. And at her big celebration planned at Club Rich later on that night in front of the people he held dear he was going to ask for her hand in marriage. She was turning twenty-three and he was throwing her a party, and asking her to be his wife would make it that much more of a celebration.

Semaj was everything he wanted in a woman and knowing time was of the essence he was ready for the next chapter in their lives to begin. He couldn't wait to see the look on his people's faces when he broke the news to them. They'd probably consider him a sucka for falling in love, but if he was a sucka for loving Semaj then he was willing to be a bonafide sucka.

Quasim, Semaj, Mike-Mike, Slim and Chi rode down the expressway in the back of the chauffer-driven navy Rolls-Royce. Exiting the highway, the driver pulled up to the pier that wasn't even a mile from their exit.

"This is it," Quasim said as everyone diverted their attention to the impressive yacht. "It goes out for three hours and we'll have dinner first and then enjoy ourselves right before we head to the club tonight." Quasim informed them.

"Dang, that shits beautiful, man!" Semaj cooed as she looked on in awe as dusk fell before their eyes. The light emitting from the cruise ship was beautiful in itself. Little did she know that her grandfather that had unintentionally left her mind as a young child was responsible for the opulence she was about to step into.

"Yeah, Gio be on some presidential shit, yo," Quasim boasted, assuring them that they were in the presence of a mega boss. The driver opened their door as they stepped out all dressed to the nines and headed to board the yacht.

"Follow me. Gio is waiting on you in the dining area," a beautiful Dominican woman said in an English accent as she led the way for Quasim and his entourage to the dinner hall. They climbed the stairs that led to where dinner was to take place. The sounds of sensual Bachata music crooned from the state of the art sound system. Once they reached the shiny hardwood floor, Gio raised his forefinger in the air and signaled for them to come over to where two henchmen stood directly behind him.

Gio was a tall, pear-shaped, clean cut man. His thin, salt-and-pepper hair neatly ringed the bare top of his skull. He was obviously in his mid-sixties. His glowing radiation was as if he hadn't stressed one day of his life, but had been through more than one thousand men had been through in one lifetime. "If it isn't my favorite godson!" Gio said, as he stood to embrace

Quasim who he'd adopted in the drug game many years ago. "And who do we have here?" he asked as he looked at the two ladies. Unfortunately, he had just had surgery on his eyes and his vision was blurry and on top of that the doctor insisted he wear a pair of dimly tinted sunglasses when outdoors. He never knew that he was in the presence of his flesh and blood—the granddaughter he'd been searching for for years.

"This is my lady and Slim's girl. They will be joining us for dinner. Then we'll leave them to enjoy the perks of being on this yacht so we can have privacy," Quasim quickly informed Gio while removing Semaj's waist-length chinchilla and pulling out her chair. Gio had strict rules on discussing business around females and outsiders for that matter, and Quasim respected that. He actually took heed.

Gio barely greeted women. It was his personal creed and when he had it was always simple. Gio was a very serious and reserved man, and distant in most situations. He greeted both ladies respectfully, but when he acknowledged Semaj, he was instantly intrigued and attached to her spiritually. "You look very beautiful," he smiled, taking in her outer appearance to his best ability as he grabbed her hand for a kiss. Everyone looked at Gio in astonishment, including his wife. He never let her hand go as if he was flirting with the young lady, but in actuality, it was a sign of his respect.

Chi turned up her nose seemingly irate that Semaj was once again the center of attention. Semaj couldn't help but blush, taken aback by his compliment.

"You just had surgery on your eyes, Gio. Those glasses aren't helping your sight just yet," his wife said in a sweet voice.

Quasim stared at Gio with a look of confusion. Having been that he never saw this side of his connect, Quasim was shocked. It was never smiles and straight business with no distractions. But Semaj was enlightening the usually stern mood into a comfortable, relaxing atmosphere.

"You probably have seen her in the movie that debuted this past summer. She's the lead actress in "Murderess in DC", the movie your daughter-in-law Jah-Jah wrote for my production company."

"You know I haven't watched a movie since "Scarface" came out, my son. I don't get into all that junk any more, Quasim. I'm getting old son. Pretty much into politics nowadays." He smiled warmly before they all sat down for dinner.

"So you're really sure that you wanna walk away from all of this, son?" Gio asked as he took a toke from the Cuban cigar.

Quasim sat across from him at the table, taking a sip from the vintage champagne as he observed his connect and then his two loyal men. He always told himself that he'd never drink while in the game because he never wanted to be off or distracted, but when he made his exit he'd sit back and enjoy life pleasantly. It had been a long time coming and as he thought about leaving the streets alone a nostalgic feeling overcame him. He was *married to the game* and to lose love from something he'd been in love with for so long was a hard decision to make. Giving up a drug empire willingly was rare in the dope game. Quasim would always have love for the streets, but he had to move on before it ended on a worse note. Nonetheless, he'd outgrown the drug trade. Staring at Semaj from a distance, her smile alone jarred him from his second-guessing and he looked directly at Gio. "Yeah. I'm done. Finished, Poppa."

"Now tell me if your exit is because of them New Jersey fellas, 'cause I'll have them fuckin' motherfuckers killed by sunrise," Gio stated, sternly.

"That's not it, Poppa. I gotta leave this shit alone. My run has been successful minus the bullshit. I'm not willing to stretch my luck," he paused, wondering how he'd known about the beef.

"Son, you've known me for a long time now and I know everything good and bad that involves you," Gio stated in a thick accent as if he'd read Quasim's mind. "Not only that but I know everything that's goes on within this business, son. Everything."

"I feel you. Though that's not the case, Gio. I'm just done with taking chances at life. No more for me. I'm gone from this game. After this last shipment my hands will be clean of drugs. I will no longer be referred to as a kingpin or the dopeman. The game was good to me, but I know what I gotta do. I'm going into the New Year a brand new man. I'm cutting all ties to the streets," he said and looked at his men, taking his time before speaking. He knew with niggas like his he had to be meticulous so each word was clear and understandable. "I know you both are capable of running the business. You niggas was the face of my empire, and I know it was with your loyalty and the fear that y'all instilled in the streets that kept the organization moving smoothly. It's y'all turn now though. But one thing I wanna say is treat it good and with respect, and it'll return the love. Don't overplay your position and don't treat the block boys like shit and they'll prove loyalty to you."

"Mike-Mike, I know you's a coldhearted nigga, son. You don't give a fuck about murking a nigga. Your murder game is flawless and that's one of the things I liked about you since we was li'l niggas, fam. But now y'all are in the lead. Y'all niggas gotta hustle with shrewdness. It's the key to this life, family. And a man in this game must be careful and strategic 'cause we don't want the heat finding the big man." Quasim paused, referring to Gio. "With him, it's only one rule to follow. You take your own heat. You don't rat! It's simple. It's basic rules to this shit, real shit, B."

The hungry look in the two men's eyes was confirmation that they were ready to take the city on and enthusiasm was etched to their faces. Needless to say, Quasim couldn't see himself handing the game down to anyone else.

"Is there anything you would like to add, Poppa?" he asked with confidence.

Gio nodded and raised his glass, indicating that Quasim led the meeting well. "What about y'all?"

"I'm just ready fam," Slim nodded, genuinely appreciative. He had given them the knowledge they had needed and the keys to an empire that only few would ever obtain.

"This is to the made life, my bruthas!" Quasim raised his glass as the two followed suit and held their glasses up for the toast. This was turning into a night of celebration for his retirement and Quasim was optimistic about beginning the next chapter of his life.

Quasim stood near the railing on the bi-level floor overlooking the dense crowd. Semaj stood in front of him as she sipped on a glass of wine and slightly bobbed her head to Yo Gotti's live performance. He was her favorite rapper and it was truly a surprise to have him perform for her birthday party. The entire 'hood had been invited to the white affair. Quasim had rented an elite club for the night and she couldn't have been more appreciative.

Semaj remained silent as she took in the excitement the partygoers were engaging in. She couldn't have been more elated with her life. Getting so much love from the streets had her feeling like she was accomplishing things. Semaj thought about how much Quasim had changed her life for the better. She went from 'hood royalty to queen of the galaxy, and it was all because of the wonderful man she had in her corner. They had the VIP section on lock and all his people were popping bottles and having a good time.

Glancing at his timepiece, Quasim noticed it was thirty minutes until the clock struck twelve. Once it hit, he was scheduled to kneel down on one knee and pop that million-dollar question. As the time approached near, a funny feeling passed over him. Something in the air just didn't feel right, but he couldn't put his finger on it. His dopeman's sixth sense was moving him as he surveyed out at the crowd for anything suspicious.

"Bra, you a'ight?" Mike-Mike walked up and asked his man. He could sense when something was bothering him. "You looking wary, my man."

"Yeah, I'm good." Quasim nodded and shook the feeling off.

"You sure man?"

"Yeah, nigga. Let's make that shit happen," Quasim said turning to Semaj. "Ay, Maj, go down to the bar and get Chi for me so she can be up here before the countdown."

She paused for a minute, suspicious. She knew something was up because Quasim already knew she didn't rock with the chick like that. Not knowing what it was, Semaj searched his eyes for an explanation but came up empty handed.

"C'mon baby. I don't want shorty to miss our celebration. Don't be like that," he said with pleading eyes.

"A'ight. But only 'cause you asked me." Semaj slightly scrunched up her face.

"Thanks," he said as he wrapped his arms around her waist and leaned down to kiss her lips. She grinned and took off with an enticing sway at the hips.

"The world is yours, man. And everything in it," Quasim said after Semaj left out of the room and threw his arm around Mike-Mike's neck. His man returned the gesture brotherly style. "I know you got this shit, homie. I want y'all to have everything I had in this game and more. Live larger than fucking life, fam."

"We got this shit. Fo'real, on some real shit, my nigga I love you, man. Even before this dope game shit, we loved you. I'd die for you nigga and that's word to my mutha."

Quasim knew he was sincere and though the thug intimacy conversation was rare, Quasim was sure he'd lie down and die for him without question. "I love you too, nigga. You my brother."

As if on cue the rap artist exited the stage and the DJ allowed Li'l Boosie's "My Brothers Keeper" to blare. Slim walked up to join his people as the trio slightly rocked to the beat with a bob of the head and chanted along. *"I ride for you nigga… I die for you nigga…and if I get caught I do the time for you nigga…"* The threesome lightly prodded each other and continued to move their heads up and down indicating that they were niggas through life and even death.

"This bitch is packed than a mu'fucka," Slim stated amped as he looked out into the scenery of the nightclub. "Damn, man! Y'all seen them fine bitches in the white trench jackets?" he asked, referring to the beautiful tannish colored Dominican stallions that he saw as if they were stationed to their own areas.

"I was peeping them tall, pretty bitches too. It's like four…five of them hoes."

"I'ma have to teach y'all one of my many cautionary acts too." Quasim smiled slyly as they watched on as the thick energy was up and the partygoers vibed to the hip-hop tunes.

From a distance, perched up on the barstool with a glass of cognac, Paris watched as the established couple mingled together, and she waited for the perfect moment to destroy their happiness. It made her insides burn fumingly that Semaj was shining in all of the glory on both ends of the stick. But Paris knew this day would arrive where chaos would run its course. Like when a person's hand itched when money was imminent, hers itched knowing she was impending Semaj's demise. And that itch was about to get scratched. She grinned pleasingly once she noticed Semaj leaving his side. "That's all I was waiting on, scandalous bitch!" She quickly sat her drink on the table. "Was for you to move for just a sec. Once you return your lovely life will be over." An evil leer crossed her face as she relished in this moment and made her way up to the VIP.

Chapter 18

Taking a glimpse at the time, Semaj realized that it was only fifteen minutes left before her and her love's new day would begin dawning. She was overly excited about his decision to leave the street life behind and build an equal standard of living without life of drugs and crime. After finally grabbing Chi from the bar they headed back upstairs making casual conversation, concealing their dislikes toward one another.

The goon that guarded the door stared at Semaj for what seemed like minutes and then eventually stepped aside, ushering them inside by a sway of the hand. Paris had just delivered a devastating blow to Quasim that had his world crashing down on direct encounter.

Semaj noticed when stepping into the VIP room it seemed to have adopted an atmosphere that definitely wasn't the friendly vibe it held right before she exited. Balloons were scattered across the skylight ceiling, and a tall five-tier cake was centered with an artificial piece, which was a replica of her and Quasim atop the amazing cake, but the beautiful surroundings weren't giving off celebratory energy.

Searching the tension filled room for Quasim, Semaj noticed him standing with his back toward her, seemingly overlooking the club with both hands firmly clenched to the rails. As she made her way over to him, his goons, including the ones she knew very well ice-grilled her, and she couldn't understand the cold stares. *Fuck is they looking at me like that for? What kinda game is Qua playing*, she thought growing annoyed.

Walking up behind him, Semaj wrapped her small arms comfortably around his chiseled abs as a sense of security overcame her. In her zone of solace, she laid her head against his back. She felt his body tense up. "Baby, why everybody looking all weird and shit?" she asked, continuing to rub his abdomen. "They ice-grilling me. And why you all tensed up," Semaj whispered as the soft R&B melody that the DJ played soothed her mind. "You can relax now, baby. This is it. No more stressful, sleepless nights. We good and all we gon' do is sit back and enjoy this life and the days of bad are gone," she said assuredly.

With a smile spread across her face and her eyes shut, her mind was peaceful. Semaj would have never guessed in a million years that her life was once again in shambles. That was until Quasim tightly gripped onto her two wrists, throwing them from around him forcefully. He turned around with an expression etched to his face that scared the shit out of her. Semaj flinched just at the sight of him. She had never experienced him looking at her that way…ever. "Baby, is everything okay?" she asked, her eyes bugged wide in fear.

In a daze, he glanced down at the table that sat beside him, and in a swift motion he snatched the champagne flute glass up and broke it across her face.

"Oh, my, Gooooodddd!" she screamed as she staggered backwards. Instinctively she brought her hands to her face. Blood seeped through the slits and onto her white dress.

Before she stumbled to fall, Quasim snatched her up and went into his waistband for his 9mm as his loyal crew followed suit, aiming straight for her head with no remorse. "Bitch! You's a grimy ass conniving trife hoe!" He yanked her up by a handful of her hair and once again sent her flying to the carpeted floor, causing her carpet burns on contact. He slapped her across the face with his gun and instantly the skin on the other cheek burst opened and blood oozed out. "Bitch, here I'm thinking you this classy ass broad with morals and you as sheisty as the rest of these crab ass bitches!" he spewed, fuming.

"What are you talkin' about, Qua?" she asked in tears as she tried bearing the excruciating pain in her face.

"So you wanna sit here and act and shit! Bitch, this ain't the movie set and that shit ain't riding with me!" he yelled harshly and pulled her back onto her feet and slammed her body repeatedly against the floor as if she were a rag doll. It was like Quasim was a brother that had zoned out completely.

He was so infuriated that he couldn't bring himself to cry, though he felt empty from her betrayal. Pausing, he looked down at his clothes. His white threads were splattered with splotching bloodstains. He looked in her eyes full of bewilderment. They were encompassed with love and confusion despite the fact she was sprawled on the floor cringed in discomfort as she forced herself to scramble backwards in fright.

Quasim looked at her birthday/engagement cake, making him even more irate that he'd taken her in with trust and loved her more than he'd loved himself. She was the only woman he'd ever loved. She was supposed to be his wife, but how could he trust her? She represented everything he detested in a woman. He could never forgive her for being involved with the murder of his father. His dad. His leader.

When Paris first delivered the devastating news, he pulled out his burner on her, screamed she was a lying whore for trying to assassinate his woman's character. He cared about Semaj that much that he would have never believed hearsay over her say. That was up until Slim stepped up. "Bra, 'member when I told you I knew the chick from somewhere?" It had instantly all came back to Slim at that very incident.

"Yeah. Why?"

"Now I know. Ol' girl ain't lying. She was the same chick that Big Pat had me go down to bring up to VIP to celebrate with him. That's her, feisty, sexy with a 'hood flair. I knew I remembered that fly mouth bitch from somewhere. That's her bra. Even Chi can vouch for that because he sent her down there first and they bumped heads."

It all became clear to him then because he could vividly recall when a few niggas had told him there was a bad broad that his father met at their strip club, and she was the last person they had known him to be with the night of his death. He had bragged on bagging her after he took her out for dinner. But her identity was unknown until Paris had just exposed her.

Snapping back to reality, Quasim shook his head. "I should've known you was some bullshit after I met your grimy ass dad!" He shook his head as he began to pace back and forth, tapping the barrel of the gun at his throbbing temple. It was as if he was losing his mind completely and ready to punish himself from her deception.

"Why are you doing this, though?" Semaj asked, in between her cries. For some reason though, she felt that her secret had finally come to the light.

At that moment, Paris came from the corner of the room and Semaj got the confirmation she needed. "Sorry, Maj but the queen's time has run its course," she said in a sinister tone. "Look where thinking you're better than other people got you, Semaj. You get a little fame and wanna look down on everybody that was there before this Hollywood shit. But I got news for you. You and your li'l perfect life is over," she snickered, enjoying the sight of Semaj in a room full of snakes trying to escape like a tiny mouse from its temp tank. "I told him everything and left nothing out. You have nobody left. Nobody can help you. You're now left alone in this world and it's the price you have to pay for being a trifling ass bitch." Paris conjured up a throat full of green phlegm and blew it so it could land dead smack in her face. "Sorry, Miss Movie Star, but after this I know your career is over. You have no one to turn to," she scoffed.

"All because I tried to polish you up, though, and wanted you to be something more than a cokehead, you played me over some jealousy shit? I showed you love!" Semaj squealed as she held herself in pain not even thinking about the mucus on her face.

"Haven't somebody told you that there are no friends in this world. Ain't you smart enough to never tell a mu'fucka your darkest secrets," Paris laughed evilly as she ran her hand across Semaj's cheek. "Only if you would've just worried about your fucking self, you wouldn't be in this fucked up predicament. I bet you'd think twice before thinking you're better than anybody else again," Paris stated coldly as she made an exit in satisfaction.

Focusing her attention on Quasim, Semaj hopelessly watched as he pulled out a box from his pants pocket. Opening it up, he shook his head dismissively as he gazed at the emerald-cut diamond ring. "I loved you, man." A lone tear unintentionally slipped down his cheek. "My pops though! You were out to get me too, huh?"

"No. It was just something that happened in the game I was in. I would never do anything to hurt you. Baby, I'm begging you, can we just start over? Please. On everything, can you just hear me out? Your father was never supposed to die."

Looking at her bloodshot cherry red eyes, he was at a loss for words. But as bad as he wanted to start over with their love he couldn't. He was a man cut from a G-cloth, and to forgive her would only show weakness. Quasim couldn't disrespect the G-code for anyone. "Why, Semaj? Why you have to fuck up a good thing?"

"I'm so sorry! Please forgive me. I never knew that was your father until that night my daddy came into your house. I swear to you, baby. I would never do anything to intentionally hurt you. On my life, I never knew."

"And I never knew someone that I held so dear to my heart would be the one to betray me. It's because of me that you broke into the film business. I introduced you to a life that you would've never experienced. Before me you were conspiring with your father setting niggas up trying to make it." He could barely look at her. It hurt too badly. "All that I've exposed you to and this is the shit that explodes in my face!" his voice roared throughout the room as his anger enhanced from the thought of having his father's killer around him for all that time and never knew it. He pulled the hammer back and pointed it at her head, as he stood over Semaj ready to murder her at point blank range. His finger trembled on the trigger.

Disdain and dismay consumed him as he contemplated taking her life. Her dishonor stung at his heart and it disgusted him to know that she was capable of such treachery. She had committed the unforgivable. Even unconditional love couldn't peel away the hatred that replaced the admiration he once held in his heart for her. He hated her with all of his soul and was ready to end her life with one shot, but Mike-Mike stepped in.

"Qua, this bitch ain't even worth it, son," he tried convincing him. "Fam, it's too many mu'fuckin' witnesses in this bitch. I understand more than anybody that you wanna get her but here ain't the place for that shit. We'll get at her later."

Mike-Mike turned out to be Semaj's lifesaver. "Get the fuck out!" Quasim screamed, dismissing her. "Get your shit outta my house and go, bitch!" he seethed in between clenched jaws as he turned his back on her and walked over to the rails. Watching the live party, his entire being felt like it had died right along with their relationship.

Though Semaj felt as if she had actually died, she mustered up the little strength she had inside her and crawled over to him, and tugged at his legs desperately. "What am I 'pose to do now, Qua? I don't have nobody left," she cried, already feeling lost in the cold world. "You all I have!"

Bearing no more love, having no emotions and showing no sympathy, Quasim didn't even look at her. "Then I guess you better go crawl in a hole somewhere and die, because we're done. Now get the fuck out of my life before I change my mind and take you out."

The threat sent chills running up and down Semaj's spine and she could feel the hatred in the tone of his voice. There was nothing she could say or do that would change his mind. It was over. They were finished. He cut her off from a supply that seemed to be a necessity. Like a person with a breathing condition connected up to an oxygen tank, she too couldn't survive without air… her air…Quasim Santana.

He was disconnecting her from a solace which she hadn't felt since her mother was in her life. But after she got killed at least she had somebody. Now she had nobody. Semaj knew Quasim's word was bond. She was now shut out of his life. The past had finally caught up with the present and she was reaping what she sowed. The door was closed and she had to find a new way to enter into the pleasures of life all over again. It was something that she seemed to never escape…it was her story.

As she made her way through the club, Semaj tried her hardest to walk with balance, but still struggled with each stride that seemed like one million baby steps. Her mind was plagued with thoughts and she was unable to think clearly.

Emotionally drained and physically exhausted, she was defeated. Without an ounce of energy left inside of her bones, she forced herself to her car. Reaching her vehicle, all she heard was, "*Three two…one…* Happy New Year!" and noises went off in the building loudly as her shaky hands struggled to unlock her car door.

After several attempts, it finally popped open and she fell into her seat where the tears began rolling down her face. This was how her New Year began. Fucked up!

Chapter 19

Semaj hurriedly packed her belongings into two large, leather duffel bags, not knowing her next move. Keeping up with Quasim's lifestyle trying to pose as an independent chick, had her pockets damn near on empty. Having access to his funds as wifey made financial limitations nonexistence for her. In the beginning, she carried herself having blood money, but even with the advance from her film contract and endorsement money, Semaj was now broke as an 1891 guitar. The money was long gone being that she used it as leverage to help clean some of the dirty money from Quasim's drug profits. Accounted for money lessened any inquires about the source of unaccounted for funds. At the time it was the perfect power move, but now she was suffering in more ways than one from the unexpected outcome.

I gave him damn near all my money for this house. It's mine too, she thought. *But I deserve everything that's happening to me for my wrongdoings.* With only forty-eight hundred left in her bank account, Semaj didn't know what to do or where to go. Quasim was supposed to be her meal ticket out of the ghetto lifestyle, but from the looks, her ticket to Hollywood had turned out to be a nightmare instead of a fairytale story. *More like a ticket to Hell! How could I go on? Where would I start?* She'd trusted Quasim to the fullest and put him in charge of her business ventures, but now he was a thing of the past.

Al-B and Chris aren't gonna deal with me after Qua put word to their ear, Semaj thought disheartened as she stuffed her bags to the brim. *Qua is a silent partner in that business, so they gon' clip all ties with me, and with their legal connections, it's not even worth fighting a case. Besides, I can't afford a decent attorney if I wanted one.*

With an aching body and a shattered heart it broke Semaj down to know that this was the end of them. After all that they'd been through, she couldn't possibly understand how he could end things so easily knowing she didn't have anybody. Semaj felt it would last forever. He was so good to her. She just wished she could turn back the hands of time.

Her heart cried out loudly, making it feel as if it had been crashed with a deluxe grinder device. She hated that it had to come down to this. Being logical, Semaj knew deep inside her soul that no nigga could forgive someone with so much treachery. Knowing Paris, she probably laid the emphasis on thick too, painting a fictitious picture of her being corrupt with no honor.

Hurt and heartbroken, Semaj scrutinized what was once her room. Tears streamed down her face from the sight of the picture that caught her eyes. It had been taken at her premiere party where they seemed like the happiest couple. She went over to the picture, kissed her two fingers and then kissed the frame. *I'm so so sorry baby,* she mumbled solemnly as she grabbed her bags and left.

Built to be strong, Semaj felt that nothing happened by chance so she had to suck up her fucked up predicament and charge it to the game. She understood that he didn't want to start over with her and rebuilding wasn't even a possibility. With the truth surfacing, Semaj knew that he'd fallen in love with a different person, and he wasn't willing to take her as she was. Their relationship was built on a lie in a sense and now there was no turning back. Quasim was no longer the center of life, and the security he provided had already seemed to be in a past lifetime. All she had now was herself.

They never lied when they said karma was a muthafucka and the bitch would catch up to you, she thought regretfully as she headed down the stairs to a destination unknown. Just as she hit the foyer, Quentin had come through the door. *He must know I had something to do with his brother's death,* Semaj thought as she stood frozen in fear. Not knowing if he was there to end her life, her heartbeat thumped rapidly as her guilt-filled eyes spoke a wordless poem of sorrow.

"What happened to your face, sweetheart? Are you okay? Where is Qua?" Quentin asked in concern as he probed for answers. "You don't look too good. Maybe you need to take a seat. Let me get you some ice for your face."

"Can you get me some ice for my heart, because that's where the worst pain is?" Semaj felt her heart shattering with each passing second and it felt as if it were bleeding profusely.

"Tell me what's troubling you." He grabbed her and pulled her into his consoling embrace.

"Let me go, please. I must go," she choked her tears back.

"You can tell me anything. What did my nephew do?" he wanted to know.

Quentin guided her to the kitchen and motioned for her to sit down. He got a small bowl of warm water and cleaned her face up and then fixed her an ice pack where she held it up to her swollen face. He put some hot chocolate on and sat across from her at the island. "Now, I don't know what's going on between you and Qua, but there are several things that I need to lift off my chest about your life in the past."

"Huh?" her heartbeat quickened.

As Quentin stared into her eyes, even as a man it had hurt him to look at her ever since the moment he'd figured out who she really was. Knowing about her fucked up upbringing had Quentin filled with guilt; he felt like shit. Her mother had been snatched away from her life and then her father, leaving her to be raised by the streets. Quentin knew that she'd been raised in the world with no proper parental guidance. "Do you remember a woman named Sabrina?"

"Sabrina?" she repeated. "No, I don't think I do."

"Well, Sabrina was your mother's best friend."

"My mother? How you know my mother?"

"Listen sweetheart, Sabrina is my deceased sister."

It was as if a light bulb had immediately gone off inside her head, and the night of her mother's murder relived in her current mind state. Tears instantly ran rapidly down her cheeks like a rainstorm had approached, and the water poured endlessly from its confinement. A mental image came to her mind where her mother's body lay slumped over and she screamed begging for her to wake up. But it never happened and the blood poured from her head onto the innocent child's tiny hands. Semaj shut her eyes and squeezed them tightly. The memory had been buried so deep inside her, making the acknowledgment of how the murder had occurred be erased from her recollection; but it was coming to haunt her now. *No…please… no…please… leave…God …make them go away. Please!*

"Are you okay?" Quentin rose from his chair and prodded her leg.

Reopening her eyes, Semaj shook her head wildly as if shaking off the memory. "Yes, I'm okay," she let out a deep sigh. "I do remember her."

"Well, your mother took Brina in and put her underneath her wings and hipped her on to the dope game. She went from absolutely nothing to running blocks and fucking up people that got in the way of the dope business. One day she came up with the idea of murdering your mother so she'd be the HBIC. She promised that me and Qua's father would run the business with her as equal partners. Brina was a jokester back in the day so I thought she was bullshitting, and brushed it off because she and your mother were closer than Thelma and Louise. But when she called and told me it was done, I was shocked and couldn't believe she went through with it."

"So she killed my mother thinking she'd take her place?" Just the thought of it sickened Semaj.

"I'm sorry to say, but yes, Semaj. That was her intention. I'm very sorry for how things turned out for you. I promise, sweetheart, if I would have known that she was serious, I would have talked her out of it."

"How could she think she'd get away with murdering her anyway?"

"It beats me, because your old man killed her." He hated to admit it but there was nothing that he could do because Sabrina called her own hand. "I'm assuming she wasn't expecting you to be with Kasey or even comprehend well enough to let your father know what led up to the murder. Her plan backfired in the end."

My father killed his auntie and his dad. Daddy killed two of his family members, Semaj thought confusingly. She knew with all that mess connected there was definitely no way the two could have ever become one forever. It was too much bad news to carry along with them in a relationship. It couldn't grow with them. Because their kin that weren't here would always be a memory, and there was no way it could be forgotten.

For a second, Semaj debated with herself if she should reveal her secret, and after noticing the kindness in his eyes and a look of sorrow, she decided that it was necessary for her own relief. Whatever the outcome would be she would have to live or even die with the results. It was her turn to confess. "Well there's something that I have to admit, too." She inhaled and wiped away the tears that trickled down her face. "Quasim left me because..." Semaj went on to recount the events with Big Pat and left out no details. She even admitted to the part that she contributed to, and how she treated robbery as her full time occupation.

Quentin took what seemed like an eternity to respond. He was trying to digest Semaj's story. *Damn, this girl has it in her just like her grimy ass father,* he thought knowingly. He was aware that Semaj had lived a life of hardship and knew how living "the life" could affect an innocent child the worst. With a father like Mitch, he couldn't expect anything less. He was a hit man and in a killer's mind there were no exceptions of who got murked. For some reason, he couldn't blame the girl for playing the dirty game with her father. Knowing Murder Mitch's background, Quentin felt that it was only normal for Semaj to lead a life of self-destruction. That was all Murder Mitch knew and all he could teach his daughter.

Semaj looked at him and searched for something in his gestures. But when he reached over and hugged her tightly she felt his care was sincere. "I really understand where you came from. I came from nothing too, and did whatever, whether it was right or wrong to survive. I can understand your hunger and in the game there are no rules," he spoke truthfully. He knew in the dope game came the grimy chicks and the robbers. It came with the territory. "But there's one more thing that I think I should let you know."

"What?" Semaj asked, not knowing what was next.

"Well, you know Gio?" he asked. "My nephew's drug connect?"

"Yes, I met him today."

"Really? He didn't recognize you?" he asked with a perplexed look on his face.

Semaj found the question rather odd. "Why would he recognize me? I don't know him."

"Gio is a huge drug plug. Actually only a few good ones are left in America."

"Okay…" Semaj said, wondering why he was providing her with this information.

"Well, he is your grandfather. That's Kasey's father."

Semaj took a couple of minutes to absorb what Quentin was telling her. "Fuck out of here! No way!" She covered her mouth, astounded. "Excuse my language, I just can't believe it!" But the more she thought about it, the more it all made sense. She started to remember his name…she started to remember him. Giorgio…Gio Milano…Giorgio Milano.

"True story. When your mother had died he put a ticket on your father's head. Any person with information on you or your whereabouts would get a reward."

That's why he said I looked familiar. He's my grand poppa. How ironic can this world be? It's crazy! Semaj was flabbergasted by the fact that her grandfather was the infamous Dominican Mafia boss—the dope king of America. *That's why my Daddy never mentioned my other family and he never wanted to discuss my mother's death.*

"Do you still love my nephew?" Quentin inquired, jarring her from her trance.

"Yes, I love him. But I know we could never be together again. Too many bad crosses invaded what was supposed to be a happy life."

"Sweetie, sometimes destiny comes in a form that we may never be able to understand." He knew that it was more than likely true though. They could never be. It was written and the only true love they would ever share was what it was before this occasion. The past had killed their future. "Quasim never loved before and when he brought you around I knew that it was real because I had never seen him that happy. For you, my nephew decided to leave the game alone. Tonight, on your birthday, he was going to ask for you to be his wife."

"Are you serious?" Semaj's voice cracked as the tears started up again. "He wanted to marry me?" She held onto her chest.

"Yes. And once I tell him everything he'll have a better understanding of your life. And to say that you are the granddaughter of Gio Milano would throw him back. Quasim has a great deal of respect for that man. Trust me, if nothing else, he'll feel at ease since you have a part of a man that he'd lose his own life for in you. Not saying that you will be able to revert back to what y'all were before this incident. I know you won't be on bad terms though."

"You think he'll understand where I came from?" Semaj asked.

"You'll never know if you don't see. I will call him. But you have to go back to the club now and try to make it right."

"You sure this will work?"

"That's what we will see. Now go." Quentin walked her to the door and watched her pull away as he dialed his nephew to let him in on every detail.

Quasim had been standing at the rails since Semaj had left, overlooking the partying crowd. He was in his own world thinking about what had just happened and how he'd lost his only love in the blink of an eye. His thoughts were boggled and an unstoppable pain ached at his heart. *She was*

my everything. This love was real. Outta all the bitches, I would have never knew that she would be the one plotting against me and my family from the beginning, he thought with bitterness.

Before Semaj, his heart had been off limits. But he didn't wear his protective gear when it came to Semaj. He had trusted her and would have killed anybody for her if need be. She had his heart, and bruised it to a place that couldn't be healed. It would forever be scarred.

If Slim had not reflected back on his memory, Quasim would had never believed a thing Paris had told him about Semaj's involvements. He loved her that much. How could she be so coldhearted, staring him in the face every day, after all she'd done? She was grimy like many bitches from the ghetto and held phoniness in her persona that he'd never witnessed in all his days. He deemed her worthy of his love and trust, but she faked it and played him the entire time. He had been sleeping with the enemy from jump-street; he could never forgive her.

But as he continued his deep thoughts somehow a feeling of love crept back into his heart in tiny volumes. Quasim hated that he was allowing himself to still love someone with so much larceny instilled in their heart. It was something that would forever haunt him. He knew that forgetting and forgiving were two totally different things though. To relieve himself from his guilt and his own demons he knew what he had to do and ordering a hit would not be his plan anymore.

Twirling the ring between his forefinger and thumb, Quasim looked at the beautiful piece of jewelry intensely and retrieved the box from his pants pocket to place it back inside. Pulling out his phone, he was preparing himself to say he was sorry for hitting her with his gun, but on second thought, he opted against it for the profound loyalty that he held for his father, even in death.

At that moment, his phone rang. His uncle's picture flashed across the screen and he pressed the icon to answer. "What up, Unc?"

"Qua, Semaj told me everything. But there's something that I must tell you, son." Quentin went on to fill his nephew in on the conversation that he and Semaj had only minutes before.

It was as if the information thrown at him hit him like a ton of bricks. He couldn't believe it. *Gio, is her grandfather? My auntie killed Gio's daughter? What the fuck?* Quasim was tripped out. *If Gio, knew any of this, the mu'fucka would try to wipe out everything ever connected to Auntie Brina.* He shook his head in disappointment. *Gio done cried to me about his daughter's murder.* How could their lives be so intertwined? How could he fall in love with the granddaughter of Gio Milano? How could any of this become one big story? "This shit crazy, yo. Real shit, she Gio's, granddaughter?"

"This is a small world, son. But, Qua that girl has been through so much she didn't know any better. All she knew was the streets until you entered her life and made it better. Things work in mysterious ways and don't ask me how or why because I can't answer that for you. But even if you will always have that memory embedded in your head, you gotta at least understand where that girl came from. I'm not saying you have to be with her because I know how close you and Pat was, and it hurts me to even feel sorry for the poor girl because that was my brother. But I learned over the years that only God can judge and forgiveness is the key for our own sins." It was unusual for Quentin to preach the gospel but he felt compelled to.

For a second, Quasim was at a loss of words but he managed to speak. "Funny thing, I was just thinking the same thing, man."

"I sent her back up there, Qua. You need to hear the truth, and know that girl never meant to hurt you by setting up Patrick."

"A'ight, man. I know we'll never be nothing 'cause that's my father and if it was the other way around, Big Pat would never play me. But out of respect for Gio, she's worth a sit down so we can discuss everything."

"That's all I'm asking you to do, fam. Understand that she never purposely meant to cross you."

"I feel you. I'ma holla at you though," Qua said about to disconnect the call.

"Qua," he heard his uncle call out.

"Yeah?"

"I love you, man."

Quasim stared at his phone and found it weird that his uncle had conveyed those three words. He was always hard on him and never showed affection, but today something was different and Quentin felt it was necessary to express himself. "I love you too, Uncle Quentin," he said, pressing end on the touch screen.

Quasim knew it was through the spirit that he was willing to gain the courage to see this through and it meant everything to him to just hold Semaj in his arms, even if it was just for one last time. Quasim looked at his phone and scrolled down to locate her number. He listened to the ring back tone just for him. It was Monica's song, "Everything to Me."

"Hello," she answered on the fifth ring.

"I'm sorry everything had to come down to this." Quasim's voice was full of sadness.

Semaj immediately burst into a fit of cries as she navigated through the city streets and headed towards the nightclub. Her hands were trembling and she could hardly see through her teary vision, but whipped the ride as if it was a racecar and she was in competition with the NASCAR driver Jeff Gordon. "I know it will probably never be the same, but I just want you to understand me. I'm sorry, and I promise I was never the culprit when it came down to you. I would die for you. I love you more than I love the air I breathe. But I understand if you don't want to be with me. I just have to tell you my reasons for living that life. I'm fifteen minutes away. Will you please wait for me."

"Okay. I love you, Semaj. Hurry up."

"I love you too, Quasim. I'm hurrying. You just don't know how much I love you."

"I love you, believe that." Quasim hung up his phone and a feeling of closure overcame him. He knew they weren't ready for the rebuilding process at this given moment, because there were a lot of things that had transpired. Deep down inside, he hoped once she arrived that he would be able to resist her. Just the mere sight of her smile sent chills down his spine and her natural scent always intoxicated him. But everything between them was a lie, so he had to let her go.

"I'm gonna love you forever though," he muttered as he turned away to a room full of his loyal friends that were silent as if trying to read him. He walked over to Mike-Mike, whispered something in his ear and the two men exited the room.

Chapter 20

Block and his right-hand man, Drakey had been lurking across the street from Club Rich in Block's triple black S550. The club was packed and people poured into the dual glass entrance looking their best. Block promised that he'd get Quasim Santana when shit cooled down and when he would have his guard down. Block had major pull and it just so happened one of his distant homies was the owner of the club that Quasim was renting for the night. He contacted his man, and due to the favor the owner owed him, he allowed him to bring in the club's security for the night. Nonetheless, Block came up with a fabricated story indicating that he needed his own bouncers present for him to attend the party. The owner went for the okey-doke, not knowing that he was welcoming murder on his nightclub's forefront.

The security was a team full of Jamaicans and Block swore that the only way Quasim was leaving out of the club was in a body bag.

"You ready?" Drakey asked, pulling from the cigar-inspired blunt and tried to pass it.

"I'm cool. I gotta be alert and on point with this buster ass nigga. I'ma do this man in. Let's do this shit, son," he said as they made an exit from the vehicle and walked through the entrance strapped-up triple times with protection surrounding the club's entirety.

"Damn, that shit's crazy. All that shit between you and Maj is buggin' me the fuck out," Mike-Mike said as they began walking down the wraparound stairs to meet Semaj before she came inside the overly crowded club.

"That's what I said. Man, my mind so fucked up behind this shit I don't know what the fuck is what."

"I know you love that chick. Fo'real that's why I stopped you 'cause I knew later on you would've regretted that shit."

"Shit wild and crazy and I do still love her," Quasim admitted as they made their way to the exit of the club.

In a million years neither of the friends would have imagined what they were walking smack dead into. It was as if Quasim had seen a ghost as Block made his way through the metal detector, which he figured the dread-headed bouncer had disarmed as an insider had did for him and his entourage through the rear entrance.

Sensing a person staring, Block surveyed his surroundings and about one yard away his eyes fell on Quasim. He and Quasim locked eyes as if a lightning strike had shocked a cable wire. Electrocution energy flowed through both of their veins. Death sat within both of their eyes and they already knew what was coming next, Mike-Mike sneakily pulled out his gun as Block implied through his eyes for his goons nearby to get ready for the gunfight. But to him and the naked eyes, Quasim and Mike-Mike were outnumbered and the people that they did have weren't aware of the current situation. What Block didn't know was that Quasim never felt comfortable in a room full of snakes, making him always well prepared for any situation that was presented to him.

"*BOOM!*"

The sounds of gunfire filled the interior of the club. There was pandemonium in the crowd and innocent bystanders scampered for the exit as others became aware of what was going on. Dozens upon dozens of bullets were flying through the club hitting the innocent, as the assailants took cover scuffling their way behind protective shields. Some even grabbing bystanders using them as human shields.

Block and his crew knew what they were coming for giving them an instant advantage over Quasim's squad, but it didn't take too long for his crew to catch on.

While their advantage was in the beginning having a club full of goons with glocks and nines, Quasim had some goons out of this world that had been hired for circumstances alike. His female shooters were like a sniper at its prey. The crazed murderesses were on point and within a matter of seconds, the Dominican women ripped open their trench coats and went out gun blasting with army assault rifles and machine guns, making this an instant war zone. Quasim's crew up top ran down the wrapped around stairs on cue, and before it was all said and done, both crews were dropping dead with the exchange of bullets.

Everyone was trying to protect the boss, and traded shots with the many Jamaicans that were targeting Quasim. Instead of scuffling for an exit, the many goons that knew Santana went out guns blazing also, and his henchman too were trying to save him, and shoot him out to safety. Everyone in the building was on some straight gangster shit, and the scene looked like something snatched right out of a street mafia movie.

When the shooting finally came to a halt, it was only a few members on each side left and nearly everyone was out of ammunition. Quasim looked around and noticed that the female shooters were all left standing, but his man Mike-Mike wasn't so lucky. He lay dead pooled in his own blood with a chopper in his hand and his eyes staring up to the skylight ceiling.

The main floor was covered with so many bodies it was a horror scene, but Quasim knew he couldn't dwell on it. He had to bounce before the cops showed up. With the Dominican ladies shooting him toward the exit, two in front, guns drawn, and two behind him backpedaling, the five headed for the exit.

But what they didn't know was that Block was hiding behind the booth where the money had been collected for admission. As they made way for the entryway to exit, Block peeked over the booth and watched as they approached. He quickly took out his clip and with the heart of a lion, he knew with the two bullets left in his .357 what option he had to make. He would use his shooter's ability to take Santana out. He didn't care if the women took his life in the process. Many niggas would bitch up in this predicament. But as long as he officially erased Quasim Santana from the map was all his heart longed for. He would be content.

Without warning he fired two shots. They ripped through Quasim's chest and before he dropped, the two men locked eyes. As blood leaked from the side of his mouth, Quasim's body hastily dropped to the ground and violently jerked.

Block pointed his empty gun at the women and made a threat through his eyes. Being that they were trained murderers—born assassins— the ringleader looked at him. She noticed the seemingly obvious also: if any ammo was left he'd undoubtedly pop off without hesitation, as they would have returned the same exchange.

"I give you credit. You won this one, but not for long," she said in a thick accent, and they departed, hating that they weren't able to save Quasim. The murderess knew that Gio was going to be devastated once they reported the news to their head boss who hired the guns to inconspicuously protect him. They had been there to protect his every move and had succeeded until now. Somehow, the contract killers slipped into the fretting crowd and disappeared into the night invisibly.

Semaj was crying tears of joy at the idea of having a second chance with Quasim as she pressed down on the accelerator. She didn't know what was next in her life. She didn't know what this moment would bring, but just to have Quasim understand what her predicament had been was a start in the right direction. It would be hard for her to move on without him as her other half, but as long as they would remain
friends, she couldn't complain.

Her happiness in an instant turned into devastation as she bent the corner and noticed that uniformed cops were everywhere. The glass facade of the club had been shattered and the crime scene had been roped off with yellow crime scene tape. Officers were trying to corral as many witnesses as possible. While paramedics were bringing people out on gurneys, the coroner personnel were bringing fresh corpses out in body bags.

"Oh, God, please, no! Let him be okay!" With a hollow feeling at the pit of her stomach, her heartbeat became erratic. Semaj pulled over. She couldn't drive any further. After parking her car incorrectly, she hopped out and ran full speed toward the crime scene. She felt deep down inside her that Quasim was gone.

To confirm her assumptions, she ran past the tape. The next body bag that had been brought out made vomit escape from her mouth. Semaj sensed that Quasim was inside the black plastic. Having to see for herself, she ran through the yellow tape and begged to see the face. What she discovered would forever haunt her mind. It was Quasim lifeless body, and in total shock, she didn't cry, scream, or act out in mockery of her grief. All she did was move backwards and returned to her car in slow strides.

When Semaj finally slid inside the car, she couldn't stop the tears from flowing. She pulled the gear in reverse, her hands trembling and placed them onto the steering wheel. She gunned it, hitting ninety miles per hour on the expressway to deliver the devastating news to Quentin. It was crazy how a person's whole life could change in a matter of seconds, and now her love was dead, and again she was at square one. She didn't have anybody left. No Tala…No Daddy…No Qua. It pained her heart that she was robbed of the chance of seeing Quasim one last time. Now she'd never know if he'd forgiven her completely. She felt like she'd been cheated. She had been stripped of everyone that she had ever loved. Semaj felt deep down inside this was God's punishment for living life as the devil's advocate.

Semaj was driving through the traffic lights like a bat out of hell, cutting corners at illegal speeds. Finally pulling through the gate, she parked in the front of the house. She got out and bolted to the door. The door was locked so she opened it using her key. When she walked inside a cold chill ran down her spine. Shaking her paranoia off, Semaj proceeded to search the house for Quentin while calling his name.

She found it odd that he wasn't answering since he said he'd be there once she returned. When she walked inside the sunken living room, she screamed frightened at the gruesome sight that lay before her. It was Quentin lying in a puddle of his own blood. "Oh, my God!" Semaj covered her mouth, hoping to prevent the vomit from spilling out. Needing to escape, she quickly turned away, and to her surprise, a hard shove knocked her to the ground.

Suddenly Semaj was yanked up by her hair and tossed to the couch to be met with they eyes of a man that had death etched on his face. She knew she was in deep shit and there was no way of getting around it. Her fate rested in his hands. He didn't care about his child's mother so why would he give a shit about her? She had encouraged Tala to steal his money and as Tala had met her unwanted fate, it was now Semaj's turn.

At that moment, another man's face became visible and his stare was even more menacing. "You thought you got away with taking my money, huh? You thought I'd never guess that it was you. But check, that act you pulled didn't work with me, shorty. I'ma have a ball killing you."

Semaj stared speechless, because she wouldn't have ever guessed that he'd find out that it was her behind the robbery. He looked scary and evil. His face was grossly unshaven and he held revenge within his eyes. But it was him. He finally caught up with her. It was Gabe and he knew everything.

"This can't be real!" Semaj muttered in shock.

"This is definitely real and I'm going to fuckin' make you a believer," D-Boy threatened through clenched teeth. "You're the reason that me and Ta broke up. You're the reason that she stole my money. You're the reason that she's dead." He drew his leg back and forcefully kicked Semaj in the stomach.

She cringed in pain as she spat up blood violently. "No, *you're* the reason. You tried to kill Ta and probably was the one responsible for the shooting at the venue, clown ass nigga!" Semaj knew her life was on countdown so there was no need to bitch up. If she had to die, she was going out like the gangster bitch her father groomed her to be. "Nigga, man up to what the fuck you did."

"And you and your father killed my sister," D-Boy stated matter-of-factly.

"Let me guess. Paris told you that too." A chuckle managed to escape her lips. "But I bet she didn't tell you that it was actually her and my father who killed Mercedes and Dean-Bean. You niggas letting this bitch stretch the truth a bit too long now."

"Just like a coward to lie when their life in the hands of another man," he replied.

"Fuck you and your sister, nigga! I ain't gotta lie for shit. Do what you gon' do, my nigga." Semaj was scared to death, but she would not give him the satisfaction to expose her fear.

"Fuck me and my sister!" D-Boy roared in anger and charged her, hitting her dead in her mouth.

Semaj didn't have much energy in her, but the strength she had left she fought back, and cracked him dead in his eye as hard as she could.

Though the punch indeed hurt, he shook it off and became even more infuriated at her attempt to fight him. He grabbed her neck and battered her face with one blow after another. He taunted and bruised her up badly for the next couple minutes, blaming her for his and Tala's problems, and the murders of his family members. Heaving heavily with bloody knuckles, he never saw what was coming next.

"BOOM! BOOM! BOOM!"

The sound of rapid gunfire filled the living room. Three bullets ripped through D-Boy's head and his brains splattered as his body fell to the ground.

Semaj sat frozen and couldn't believe that Gabe had just squeezed the lever and ended D-Boy forever. She was totally shocked at this point. She didn't quite understand why he killed D-Boy, since it seemed they were both there to extinguish her but Gabe was showing different.

"You just don't know how long I been waiting on this day to come. You were off when that robbery happened at my house. But me being dumb I still didn't think shit of it 'cause I trusted you. Then you turn shade when I get locked up. Imagine how I felt when D-Boy told me that you was a dirty grimy bitch. When he called home and Tala told him that some niggas kicked in the door was the only clarity that I needed. Only to add that Big Pat had gotten killed shortly after I heard he was all up on you in the club. After that there wasn't a doubt in my mind that you bitches were low down and I been out to get you ever since."

"So, it was you responsible for all the shit in my life?" Semaj managed to spew the words out.

"Majority of it. Now the one with your pops was on some mafia shit, and I don't get with all that extra shit. It's only gunplay my way, and I'd leave your body whole with your soul left to burn in hell," he laughed, menacingly. "I must admit, ma, you got alotta love out here in these streets. Muthafucka's protect you to the end and it's very hard to catch you alone. But with me knowing what was going down at the club tonight, if you didn't die there, it was surely going to happen soon after."

"So you had something to do with the club shooting?" Semaj asked slyly trying to buy time.

"Not at all. That was D-Boy's peoples. All I ever wanted was to get back at you. Even when I tried to have Tala tell me where you were, she was so fuckin' high on that shit I couldn't get nothing out of her but she got something from me—that bullet in her head."

"Tala tried to tell me it wasn't D-Boy that shot her but she couldn't remember who. Now I know it was you. So why did you kill your friend?"

"You taught me that there are no friends in this game of life. Besides, if he knew that I had anything to do with Tala's shooting and murder it'd been war anyway. He truly loved that woman."

Semaj was running out of things to prolong this shit any longer so she opted the negotiation route. "There's been so many deaths, Gabe. I can give you the cheese back that was taken and more if you like. We can both just move on with our lives."

"You took it upon yourself to rob me, bitch. With me in debt the Dominicans took it out on my grandparents. You knew that was all I had too, so there's no happy ending to this story. You saying I can move on, but with money on my head, that can't happen, trife bitch. So there's nothing in this world that would make me happier than taking your life."

Semaj stared at him in shock and couldn't believe what he was telling her. He had the connect people at the house on the night that she had decided she wanted to hit his stash, and that left him looking like the villain and in truth, Semaj felt bad. Gabe raised his gun, and a lone shot rang out.

Vega was flabbergasted after seeing a hysterical Semaj flee from the nightclub's crime scene and it was evident that she was badly beaten up. To him, she appeared in distress and he had followed behind her all the way to the suburbs. It was his first time seeing her in years and for some reason he felt that he was connected to her, and instead of watching who he had intended to keep his eye on, he diverted his attention and focused in on Semaj.

He made sure that he kept her car in sight, slyly tailing her, and now that he had seen Semaj, he could no longer repress his feelings for his first love. Guilt overcame him as he felt responsible for abandoning her. But from what he saw in magazines and on TV, she was doing pretty well for herself. Vega felt he should have gotten in contact with her years ago, but he didn't know how she'd respond to a man that was supposed to be dead. As determined as he could ever get, he promised that he'd reclaim her heart no matter what and bring her home with him where she belonged.

Vega had been waiting in the car for ten minutes before the gunfire erupted, and when it did, he reached underneath his seat, grabbed his chrome .45 and darted for the ajar door. Before he entered fully, he noticed a guy standing over Semaj with a gun pointed at her chest. Before he could attempt to get close on the guy, one shot rained just above her head as he taunted her and laughed crazily. Following, he struck her in the head with the cold steel. Utilizing his marksman ability, he wasted no time and aimed his gun and Gabe never saw it coming as Vega emptied a slug into his back.

Rushing over to Semaj, Vega cradled her limp body as Semaj tried focusing in on who was carrying her. Blood was flowing from her head profusely due to the severity of the blow. Whatever strength she had left seemed to be completely deteriorating

"Just hold on, Semaj. I'ma get you to a hospital." Vega carefully laid her across the backseat and headed for the nearest hospital. Though he was far from religious, he asked for God to keep her stable as he took a glance through his rearview mirror every chance he got while bending his SUV at crazy speeds and honking the horn for cars to move out of his way. But as they approached the emergency entrance, she had already slipped into unconsciousness.

Chapter 21

Semaj reopened her eyes two days later. She had been comatose due to the heavy sedation she'd undergone from her intense injuries. Blinking wildly, she was disoriented. She had no clue of where she was, and tried forcefully to adjust her vision to the darkened room. She was enduring so much pain, she felt as if she would die. Her body was aching, throbbing and the intense pain was an indication that the medication had wore off. It caused her to feel every sore in her bones as she lay helplessly in the hospital bed.

Noticing a silhouette to the left of her, she opened her mouth to speak. "Q…Qua…Quasim…" her words came out in a raspy tone, which was barely audible.

Her voice filled Vega's ears and he quickly put down the *New York Post* and rushed to her bedside. With the most concerned look on his face he said, "You're awake? How you feeling?" he questioned, gently rubbing the side of her face.

Semaj looked up and thought she was dreaming again. She remembered Vega carrying her, but then too, she thought she was seeing the light and he was welcoming her to the other side. Then it all came to her. She reflected back on everything. The memory of seeing Quasim's corpse rolling out on the stretcher, and Quentin's body lying in a pool of blood, then Gabe blowing D-Boy's brains out all came to her head. But still, why did this dude look just like Nathan Giles? He was dead and had been for over nine years. How was this so?

"I gotta be dead. Am I at the gates? Where am I?"

Vega chuckled lightly, finding it typical for the twenty questions. "No, you ain't dead, Maj. You at the hospital. And no, you are not buggin'. It's really me. In the flesh. Your man, Vega."

"But how? You are dead and everyone knows this. I was there," Semaj said.

"I know. But I was only shot. My brother was into some deep shit and some niggas came back and tried to kill everyone in the house including me. I flat lined twice, but they brought me back to life. The authorities felt it was necessary to say that I was dead so that the people my brother was dealing with wouldn't come back to kill me thinking I'd rat them out. That's when I had to move out to Baltimore with my aunt and I ain't looked back since then."

Tears came down Semaj's face. She felt guilty and knew it was once again her fault. She had set his brother up and put his life in danger. She had to confess. There was no way that she was holding back this information. She'd already betrayed Quasim. She didn't know how Vega had caught up with her, but she felt that she owed him her life and he deserved the truth. Semaj wanted to begin her new life with a clean slate. "This is some weird shit. But before I allow you to stay here and be by my side I have to tell you something."

"Anything."

"Well, when my father was released from prison, we was all fucked up because we thought our life was gonna revert back how it used to be. But that wasn't the case. Then me, without any persuasion or anything," Semaj wanted to take full responsibility. "I came up with the idea of setting your brother's connect up. I told my Dad where you dropped money off at for Boo. He kicked in the door and robbed the trap. I'm sorry for everything and I can understand if you wanna leave. But I just want you to forgive me. If nothing else comes out of this, I just want your forgiveness."

Her words shocked the hell out of him, because he never took Semaj as ruthless or a do by any means necessary type chick. But then again, baby girl was thorough and he knew it was what the streets had showed her. She was young and hungry for the material world, so how could he blame an immature mind that hadn't actually affected him or his deceased brother? "I forgive you," Vega declared. "Streets be wild like that sometimes. But on some real shit, shorty, Boo was in debt with many niggas so that trap your people hit ain't have shit to do with the shooting that night."

"Are you serious? So he got killed over some other shit?" she asked, surprised.

"Something a lot deeper than that li'l money. But you gotta promise me one thing," he said, ready to get this situation behind them.

"Anything."

"That you will never cross me, ever," he stated as he gazed into her eyes.

"I promise. I won't ever cross you, Vega."

"Then we forever good." he nodded. "And I know you fucked up right now, but the moment I saw you running up to the club all my feelings for you rushed back. I know we were young, but even then I knew you were special. You held a part of my heart since the day I met you. Where I'm going with this is...that I want us to start all over. Brand new."

"You're willing to do that with me?" Semaj asked surprised by his request.

"Why wouldn't I? I've never stopped loving you and a day didn't go by that I didn't think about you, Maj."

"Why didn't you contact me?" Semaj asked sadly. She hated the fact that he could actually move on with his life without at least trying to reach out.

"It was for your own safety, honestly. I wanted to and attempted several times to reach out but couldn't go through with it. I had to leave my life in New York behind. Until the feds were able to get the people responsible for the shootings everybody I loved was in danger including you. By the time it was safe to reach out to you it had been so long and I felt the damage was too deep to repair with you. I doubted you gave a fuck I was alive. You had already mourned my death and moved on with your life. You gotta understand that."

"I do, but I never stopped loving you," she replied.

"Just know I'm never letting you go again. Not neva," he expressed with more sincerity filling his voice with each word. "I'ma be with you forever."

"I wanna tell you everything that has happened since you been away from my life." She filled him in on each detail, not leaving out a robbery or a killing. She even told him about Paris and Quasim. She didn't want to lie to him about a thing.

"Damn, you gangsta for real!" he said, impressed. "You were on your grind and I ain't never knocked a person that hustled no matter their hustle. But I'm just glad you wiser now, shorty, because that robbing shit for the birds. We know how to get to this dough without all that bullshit. I admire you for jumping into a legit place. But we together now. I'ma make sure you forever and a day straight."

"Vega, I'm so happy to have you back in my life because everybody else is dead and I was feeling completely alone. I was beginning to think I had nothing to live for."

"I'm here, Semaj. You don't have to feel alone anymore. We together now."

"And that's a beautiful thing but know my heart is still aching over the loss of Quasim. I believed I was going to spend the rest of my life with him."

"I understand that. And no disrespect because I know you loved that man, but he's dead now. He would want you to move on and find happiness with a nigga that will love you as much if not more than he did."

Semaj thought about what Vega said and a feeling of guilt quickly swept over her. She had just lost a love that she considered to be real, but here she was considering going back to her first love. She couldn't deny it, her feelings for Vega never left. She just repressed them because she thought he was dead. But now he was alive and this was their opportunity for a second chance at love. Semaj did believe in the old adage: If a love leaves and comes back it's destined to be.

At that moment, the news broadcast came on. There it was... Club Rich, still roped off with police cars and uniformed authorities everywhere still doing their work.

"I'm standing behind the nightclub where the brutal massacre occurred two nights ago, leaving thirteen dead and a countless amount wounded and injured. Police officials are still investigating what many sources are saying was a shootout between two rival drug lords. What makes this case so much more complex is that Brandon "Block" Stevens, who has been under federal surveillance for nearly two years, and federal agents labeled as the kingpin of Newark, tried to escape as an innocent bystander. With the details they have through wiretaps on Stevens's phone, agents are saying that the intended victim Quasim Santana has had prior altercations with Stevens, but the police aren't releasing too many details on the wiretaps. But they have released a statement confirming that the suspect Brandon Stevens was found last night in the county jail dead in his cell after being fatally stabbed. Currently there are no suspects. The case is still under investigation

we'll bring you more details as the story develops."

The newscast had brought tears to Semaj's eyes. She just couldn't wrap her mind around how the fuck this shit happened. Quasim was always alert and aware, but now he was dead. Though she didn't know where their relationship would have gone had he not been murdered, the shit broke her heart.

"It'll be a'ight," Vega promised.

"I just can't believe he's gone. I had just talked to him. It's crazy because that was the main reason he wasn't dealing with Block. He knew the feds were watching him, but no, Block wanna take it like Qua was try'na play him. That's that fuck-nigga shit. And all along, police were really onto his ass. Hell, if Qua would've fucked with dude he'd be in jail doing that stupid long time. That's wrong and I feel so bad for what happened. Everybody is dead because of Block's bitch ass."

"Don't feel bad. You couldn't stop what happened. I'm just glad you wasn't there when it went down."

"I know. It's like God keep try'na tell me something. He's always sparing me. I guess it's true, everything does happen for a reason because if Qua wouldn't have never found out, I would have still been at the club partying."

"You special. Believe that," Vega smiled.

"What I can't understand is how Block got murked that quick. I know Quasim got pull even through death, but damn, niggas work quick."

"You know ain't no niggas have shit to do with that. Only folk with mafia ties could get some shit done that fast."

Instantly, she thought back to what Quentin had told her. "Oh, his plug…my…my…grandfather."

"What?" he asked perplexed.

Semaj explained to him how Quentin had told her that she was allegedly the granddaughter of the infamous Gio Milano and how it all made sense. To say he was taken aback would be an understatement. Vega was astonished and couldn't believe what he was hearing. He'd heard a lot about the man, but had never known anybody that was actually kin to him.

Paris grabbed the cordless phone from the end table and dialed Vega's cell number as she had for the past three days. It was going straight to voicemail. When she arrived to his home on New Year's Day, she was worried to death. She called every hospital and jail in all of Maryland, learning that none of the facilities held a Nathan Giles. It wasn't until she pulled down on his block this afternoon that she found out he was more than good. His little man told her that he'd indeed talked to Vega, and he said he'd be back home no later than evening. That information pissed her the fuck off because she wasn't even aware that he was out of town. To add insult to injury, the nigga hadn't even attempted to call her.

What had her fucked up was when his soldier told her that Vega was in New York. It was something extremely fishy about that shit, and Paris was sure to drill his ass to death when he did decide to stumble his black ass through that door.

As each minute passed, she grew even more irritated, assuming that he had taken one of his little hoes to experience the ball drop in Times Square. Though she was aware of the chicks, Paris didn't care, because a fuck was a fuck. But the thought of him lavishing some other chick and he was fucking her naturally bothered her.

What Paris was oblivious to was the girl that she was trying to destroy, the chick that she was supposed to ruin and take everything from was about to erase her out the equation.

Needless to say, trying to wreck Semaj's life caused Vega to run straight into her arms trying to play hero. He was getting a bad vibe about "Egypt." She left him without notice over two years ago after their brief two-month relationship, and one day she popped back in his life wanting to give their relationship another try. Things had been going smoothly but his hustler's intuition was telling him something wasn't quite right. He didn't know if his uneasiness was due to his paranoia for women but deciding not take any chances he had followed her to her destination. It eventually led him to the nightclub. He parked outside waiting on any suspicious activity, and miraculously spotted Semaj. Now "Egypt" was no longer a factor.

Vega had the woman who he felt was made just for him, and with her in his life there was no turning back. Unknowingly, Paris caused the unintentional as she anxiously paced back and forth, waiting for Vega to arrive home so she could curse his ass out for having her stressing, and then fuck the shit out of him. Little did she know that would never happen again, and she was one of the girls left in his rearview mirror.

Still in tremendous pain, Semaj made a great effort to slip out of the issued hospital gown, so that she could get out of the place that held her captive long enough. Her body was weakened and her spirits was even weaker. She was so afraid to turn around and look at her face. She was afraid of what she might see. Her body was drained in every way, so she knew her face had to be fucked up, being that she'd gotten beaten more than once in the same night—with pistols and anything else niggas could grab a hold of.

Her curiosity was getting the best of her. She slowly turned around and saw her reflection. Her face was swollen with black, purple and blue bruises. Cuts and slices appeared on both cheeks. She just wanted to scream and cry. She couldn't fathom how Vega could stand looking at her as if her face was normal.

"This is some ugly shit. How I 'pose to walk around like this?" Semaj thought aloud as she examined her face in the mirror in horror. It was a hideous sight to see and no longer able to take it she turned around to grab the items out of the bag. Vega had left and got her an outfit to go home in. He knew she'd probably have a fit if she had to leave in her hospital gear.

Slipping into the almost too small teal jogging suit, Semaj laughed at his effort. She put on the sneakers he bought her and shielded her face with a pair of oversized designer sunglasses. After she dressed, she felt a little at ease, though she knew she wouldn't be back to her normal self until her face cleared up.

"Damn, ma, ya hips sprouted something crazy. Maybe I should've gotten a medium," Vega commented as soon as Semaj came out of the restroom.

"Don't you think? I'm not fourteen anymore. The kid do have hips and ass for days now," Semaj laughed.

"Oh, it's back to the regular ol' Semaj. That's what I'm talkin' 'bout! That's the sassy chick I 'member. My boo back."

"Oh, shut up. I ain't never went nowhere, nigga."

"Nah, but on some real shit. Did you take what I was saying last night into consideration?"

"You know I did. I want to give us a try but I need you to be patient because I'm still trying to deal with losing Quasim."

"I understand that. But what about you moving to Baltimore with me? 'Cause you here and me there that shit just ain't gon' work"

"Moving to Baltimore isn't exactly us taking our time but then again there ain't nothing left for me here. Everybody that meant something to me in New York is dead. I think starting over in Baltimore is a good idea. But don't you think you need to handle shit with your li'l females before I move there."

"For what? I'ma just tell them what it is. Hell, bitches ain't got no other choice."

"Now is that the way you speak on ladies?" she asked, showing her dislike.

"You still, silly. But real talk, me and chicks," Vega cleared it up respectfully. "Was just kickin' it. It was never anything serious. I was fucking with a couple chicks heavy, but for real, I couldn't love after you. They pretty much know where we stood on a friendship level."

"They better, because I ain't got time to be beefing with no females over you. Been there, done that shit. But I'ma keep it real with you. I ain't going to the house you fucked all kinda hoes in either. We can stay at a hotel until we find something together."

"Already know how you move. You ain't finna sleep nowhere I had another bitch laying up at. I gotta townhouse out the way that don't nobody know about. I go there to clear my head when I don't want to be disturbed. Or just need to relax without having to have my pistol close for real."

"Umm, really?" She put her hand on her hip, and shifted her weight to one side as if trying to read him.

"True story, ma. We gon' stay there until we find something more permanent. Cool?"

"Yeah, Cool!"

After paying the tollbooth Semaj smiled at a breath of fresh air as they cruised the Key Bridge. She welcomed the different city with open arms.

"I can't believe that you actually agreed to move to Baltimore," Vega said.

"I need a fresh start. I need to start all over. I mean, I'm Brooklyn 'ta the heart," Semaj laughed. "But I need something new in my life right now. Back home wouldn't do nothing but remind me of all the tragedies I had in my young life. That's why I left everything. I didn't want nothing to remind me of all the bad shit."

"I feel you. I told you I got you, though," Vega said as he exited the highway and pulled through his 'hood. "You can get out whenever you feel like you ready and get everything you need or I can send somebody out for you. I got a Porsche truck that I barely drive. You can push that until we get you another ride, ma. I got my favorite girl back. A nigga can't be any happier."

Semaj rolled her eyes bashfully and then allowed her head to sink into the expensive suede headrest of the Range Rover. Being with Vega made her feel secure and comfortable because she felt at ease and knew she could be herself around him. She didn't have to try to impress him, because he knew who Semaj Richardson was and where she came from. She was grateful to have had Quasim in her life though. One thing Semaj had learned was money was everything if one makes it that, but Quasim made her grow up. Without self-love that shit was dead, and she thanked God for allowing Quasim to prepare her for real life.

Vega coasted up the strip and pulled down on his little man. Parking directly in front of his loyal solider, who was manning a gainful area, he looked around at the group of hustlers and after grabbing his gun, he popped out and greeted each hustler from his camp while blazing up a blunt of cush for them.

Semaj looked out of the lightly tinted window and watched as he conducted himself. Unlike Quasim, he showed his face in the 'hood. His creed was that any real boss would show his hood love and in return they would show honor. To him, loyalty brings forth royalty and in this case, the paper was why niggas hustled from sunup to sundown. To Vega, this was the only way he operated. He kicked shit with his niggas on the block, and with the respect he showed them had his goons ready to shake anything for him and his concrete jungle was full of vicious animals.

"How shit been since I been away?"

"Everything good money," Micah, his head soldier responded. "Paid off the police district for the month, paid the workers and the two families where you hold that work at. Money is on the rise with that new product we just got in. We gon' have to re-up here in a few days though."

"Damn, work moving like that? We don't 'pose to re-up for another week."

"That's what Pam said. I dropped that cake off to her and she was trippin' at how fast it was moving."

"That's what's up! Shit, everything else cool?"

"No, doubt, baby. But oh, yeah, your shorty rolled through here looking for you and shit. On some ol' stalking shit though."

He laughed. "What you mean on some stalking shit?"

"The bitch was going off on niggas down the way 'cause she thought niggas was lying and shit. Something wrong wit' homegirl fo'real. I told you my mans said his nigga grew up with her and her sister on the east and said her sister killed their parents and made it look like a homicide-suicide. Vega, that chick psyched the fuck out. You need to get rid of that crazy broad on some real shit, I can see darkness in that bitch eyes," Micah stated as he dragged from the piff.

"You scared of females now, nigga?" Vega cracked up dismissively. "Nigga, stop listening to these gossiping ass niggas. Shorty, cool. You know I don't seek out foul bitches. But I got my old boo back so all these hoes getting cut the fuck off anyway," he said adamantly.

"You's a fool, Vega. Let me find out you done fell in love with a New York chick."

"It ain't even shit like that. This my childhood love, li'l nigga."

"That's what's up! I feel that!"

"Yeah, but I'ma catch up with you on a later note, little man," Vega said. "I gotta holla at you about setting up shop in a new area. Shit low-key on that end too, fool."

"Get at me. You know I'm all over the movement, yo."

"Soon as I drop shorty off and holla at the one chick, I'ma come back through and swoop you up. We can talk further then."

"It's on," Micah nodded and turned to continue handling business as Vega pulled away and headed to the suburbs.

Vega pulled into the driveway of the townhome and pressed the button to open the garage. They slid out of the car and walked inside via the garage, and as soon as Semaj stepped in her new home a smile washed upon her face.

"This spot cool enough for you? I know you used to mansions and shit, Miss Hollywood!"

"Please! I done lived in the worst of the worst. I'm from the 'hood and never will I forget where I came from and what I had to go through to get here," she conveyed, laughing but was for real. "I love it, though. It's really beautiful."

The 3,200 square-foot townhouse instantly made her feel at home and it was perfect. Everything looked custom made but still livable like you didn't have to be afraid to touch it. She was surprised at his choice of style. The cream, brown and burnt orange modern décor was exquisite. From the furnishings to the fixtures and stainless steel appliances was beautiful and it seemed to be pulled straight from the pages of *Better Homes and Gardens*.

"Now you sure you gon' be cool while I'm gone? 'Cause I can have my Aunt Pam come and sit with you."

"I'll be good, Vega. Just don't be out there acting a fool. I still remember how you get when I'm not around," Semaj said as she screwed up her face playfully.

"That's the old me. I told you it's me and you, fo'real. The hoes prior don't mean nothing to me, babe. We starting fresh and you better believe I ain't gon' do nothing to mess things up between us. On my heartbeat, Maj."

"Yeah, and on my heartbeat too, you better not!" Semaj teased, but her heart fluttered at his expression. "But go on 'head and do what you gotta do so you can get back to me."

"A'ight." He bent down to kiss her forehead and headed out. "Call me if you need me for anything."

"I will."

"We going down to the Harbor later too, and I'ma show you our hotspots, so be ready. Love you."

"Love you more," Semaj said as she walked him to the front door, and watched him back out the driveway and pulled away from their home.

This was a new beginning and Semaj was trying her best to go into it with a positive outlook. She sat Indian-style on the plush carpet and thought how she had to get her life back on track despite the obstacles thrown at her. She loved acting and she wanted to get back in contact with her agency so they could still keep her relevant in the industry. Though she was building a new life for herself in Baltimore, her dreams of becoming something so much more had never wavered. Even through her troubled times, she had to remain strong. Not willing to allow anything to rob her of her dreams, Semaj pulled out her cell phone and dialed Christopher Cunningham.

"Hello?" he answered on the third ring.

"Hey Chris, this is Semaj. I was just calling to check in with you."

"Are you okay?" The concern in his voice put Semaj at ease. "Al-B and I have been calling your phone nonstop and it went straight to voicemail."

"Yes. I'm fine. Things have been crazy as I assume you are aware of."

"Yes, I am. And I'm sorry for everything that has happened. I can only imagine what you're going through right now. I'm keeping you in my prayers."

"Thank you. But I was calling to tell you that I need some time off but no longer than two months."

"I truly understand. Take as much time as you need. I'll get in contact with your publicist and she'll handle things. Thank you for calling and I'll be checking up on you. Call me if you need anything."

"I will and thanks for everything, Chris." Semaj hung up and a feeling of despair came over her. Chris had been so sympathetic towards her so she knew that he didn't know what had transpired between her and Quasim before his death. She hoped he would never find out but Semaj was learning secrets never stay hidden. She didn't want to deceive anybody but the person she was back then wasn't the person she was today. There was no doubt in Semaj's mind that Quasim deserved credit for that. He believed in her and never thought of her as some useless 'hood chick. He gave her confidence and made her feel that her dreams could actually become a reality.

Even now that he was gone, Semaj knew that he would want her to continue to pursue her aspirations and not just sit around and become another drug dealers wifey. But she was afraid to do it without Quasim in her corner. That's where the feeling of despair was coming from. She didn't want to admit it to herself but deep down inside she knew one of the reasons she was rushing back to her childhood sweetheart Vega was because she felt that was easier than being alone and standing on her own. She also felt like she didn't have the strength to mourn the death of Quasim. So many of her loved ones had been taken away too soon but her strength came from knowing Quasim would never leave her side. But she was wrong and now she prayed that Vega could fill the void that Quasim had left inside of her.

Chapter 22

When Paris heard her phone chiming, she automatically knew it was Vega. She answered and instantly began screaming through the phone. "It's one thing fuckin' bitches, but when you in New York tricking with hoes and shit that's where the muthafuckin' problems come, Vega," she blasted.

"Whoa, shorty! You getting out of line talkin' to me like you done lost your damn mind."

"I'm just saying. Fuck you doing in New York, nigga?" she tried checking him.

"I'ma grown ass man. Calm the fuck down with all that rah-rah shit."

"Nigga, please! You still ain't telling me nothing. Why was my calls going unanswered? Or better yet, fuck was your phone turned off for, nigga?"

Vega sighed heavily. "Egypt" was starting to piss him off, and the woman that he knew was definitely getting out of character. He didn't bother to ponder on it though. He knew he was showing her no respect by ending their relationship over the phone. She was a good girl that didn't deserve the unexplainable closure of their mess-around. But it was something that just had to be done.

"Look, I'ma just be straightforward with you. I followed you to New York because you was acting all weird and shit when you was leaving out," he admitted.

"You followed me?" she blurted out, but instantly felt her ego rising because of his jealousy. "What you thought, I was creeping out on you or some shit?"

"Neva that. I'ma boss so fuckin' another nigga would only make you look stupid. We just cool anyway." He said something that he'd been wanting to say forever. After "Egypt" left and tried coming back into his life, though, he allowed her in, Vega felt she had ulterior motives, and she was just some cool, time-being, in-house pussy. "But you my dawg."

"Yo' dawg? Fuck is you going with this, dude?" she asked, her fury developing. "So why did you follow me all the way to New York then?"

"I'm a very paranoid, nigga. So when you all of a sudden wanna head to the NYC, I had to make sure you wasn't on no grimy shit. Streets wild out here and I be damn if I let a nigga put a bitch on me. I can't let a chick become my downfall, shorty."

She understood his reasons for wanting to be cautious especially since she was one of those grimy chicks that could be his downfall. Paris knew first hand how bitches could be deceitful posing as something they weren't. She had done it plenty of times, and she understood his logic. "I feel you on that."

"But check. When I was up there, I stumbled across my people at that club you were at. Some shit happened where we lost contact and that in itself is a long story. She in a bad situation and need me." He felt that he didn't have to explain anything to her in depth so he kept it simple.

His words spewed at her like tiny volcano balls, causing her face to turn red and the sensation to feel as if a flame had sparked an intense fire internally. She couldn't believe what he'd just conveyed. For some reason, she already knew he was referring to Semaj. What she didn't understand was how her luck was so damn bad that she ran him right into her archenemy. She immediately went in a psychotic rage, because she was trying to ruin Semaj's life. But as the tables had turned, she'd destroyed her plans and it had all boomeranged.

"So what the fuck are you saying, Vega?" she asked incredulously. "A bitch can just come back into your life whenever the fuck she feel like it? What about me? I told you I'm doing this school shit for us," she lied, but should have won an Oscar for her performance.

"E, you know me and you cool. You forever my dawg. And I'm sorry if I gave you the impression that we were something more than we were, shorty. But you and I know it was never going to work. We different kinda people. You'd never understand my life."

"So you can just fuck me all in my ass and tell me how much you love being around me and then just up and leave me like this? What I was your kick-it-with, bitch?"

"You was cool to be around," he replied genuinely. "You cool as fuck, shorty. But on some homie shit."

"So you expose me to making it rain in Norma Jeans on trash, bitches and clubbing 'til the sunrise and now that's just a thing of the past?" she asked furiously.

"I told you, you was cool."

"So that's all it was? What I'm supposed to do? Where I 'pose to go? I done left campus fucking around with you." Paris lied so much it was like the truth to her.

"I'ma real nigga, so I can man up to some shit. For that ma, you can stay there. The rent paid up for the whole year and you won't have to worry about nothing til the lease up. I won't be back there though," he stated surely.

"What about us, Vega?"

"You'll get over it trust. It's plenty niggas out there that can replace me. You cute and cool, so it won't be hard for you to get a nigga."

"Please don't do me like this. You know, I love you. You promised that I was wifey from the beginning. Why you lie?" she screamed into the phone. "If that was the case I would've never came back to your sorry ass!"

"Honestly, shit got real. She my first love and the love never died."

"You gon' regret this shit!" she promised.

"I gotta go, E, and for whatever it's worth, a nigga sorry." He hung up and made the rest of his cut-off calls.

Paris clenched down on her inner jaw line as she went into an uproar. She threw the glass vase, cracking the flat screen TV and turned over the coffee table. In under three minutes, she had destroyed the entire living room. What was once a nice living area was damaged like a tornado had twisted the place out. "This nigga don't know who the fuck he playing with. Maybe he could've got that shit off with E, but I'm the wrong bitch!" Paris yelled as she darted up the stairs to retrieve her phone.

Semaj had just stepped out of the shower when she heard her phone chiming. She wrapped the towel around herself and walked inside the room to answer her nonstop ringing cell. It was a private caller. At first she opted not to answer assuming it was one of the nosy gossip girls back home, but then something allowed her to press the "talk" icon. "Who is dis?"

"Bitch, your worst nightmare!"

"Man, who the fuck is this playin' on my phone?" Semaj asked.

"You think you won again, but bitch the games have just begun. You think I was some shit before, but you ain't seen shit yet. I can promise you that." Paris voice was as cold as ice.

"Paris, you's a clown fo'real. That shit you pulled was foul as fuck. And if I ever see you in the streets bitch, on my Daddy's fresh tombstone, I'ma drag you up and down the block. You better hope I don't see you. Bum ass bitch!" Semaj said sternly. She'd been waiting to get word to her sick-in-the-head-ass.

Paris responded with a ridiculing laugh, then stopped with a quick flip. "Bitch, fight? You may try but there's no beating guns, baby doll. I'm too gangster to be fighting you, corny ass bitch. You already know with me it's gunplay."

"So what you gon' shoot me? You that mad, ma? I mean, you got want you wanted. What more can I do for you?" Semaj asked in confusion.

"This shit has gotten deeper. And only way out of this is if you tell Vega you don't wanna be with him anymore." Paris didn't give a fuck about exposing her hand. She was done disguising her character. They didn't make chicks like her, and she was one of the realest bitches to ever do it. Crazy but there was nothing fake about her.

Is this bitch a stalker? Semaj asked herself as she removed the phone from her ear and stared at it baffled. "I don't know what kinda shit you be on, you insane ass girl, but let me tell you something. What me and my nigga share is something unbreakable. There's nothing you can say or tell him about me that he don't already know. So whatever you thought you were going to do just isn't gonna work, bottom-line," she said fuming. "Sick ass bitch. Quit calling my phone and you stay the fuck away from me and mines, or I will personally kill your ass!"

Paris went into an abundance of laughter. "Everybody know you ain't no killer so fall back, Semaj!"

"Try me and it's gon' be a homicide. Don't let the pretty face and small waist fool you. 'Cause I'ma protect what's mine," Semaj barked honestly.

"Consider yourself dead, bitch."

Semaj's phone indicated that the call had ended. She plopped down on the bed replaying her phone call with Paris. Semaj talked big on the phone but in actuality she knew Paris was demonic and capable of ending a human life and not thinking twice about it. But she knew that Vega could hold his own, and he would never allow anyone to bring her harm. In relief, the words from Tupac came to mind: *"I ain't no killa but don't push me!"* And believe it or not, Semaj had it in her. Being a murderer ran through her bloodline.

Semaj called Vega on the phone and told him everything that had happened. When she mentioned Paris's name, a mental picture came to him. Once they put two and two together, it all became clear to the both of them. "Damn, that bitch that psyched, ma? Should've known, though, because her swag was crazy 'hood and her sister swag was light and way corny." Vega filled her in on their dealings along with her sister's. He told Semaj not to worry about her. His exact words were, "For her own sake she better not move stupidly because just like a nigga, that bitch can be bodied too."

His words were genuine and Semaj was already aware that Vega would go to the end of the world for her. The threats Paris made didn't bother her much. What had her mind boggled was how her life was so damn connected and entwined to way too many people.

"Nathan, come on! Your auntie is gonna kill us! You always late!" Semaj yelled giggly as she stared at her face in the mirror. It had cleared up tremendously, although a thin line above her brow from the impact of the pistol was not going away. Semaj had learned to accept that the scar was a battle wound.

"I'm ready. That's you. Don't game," he replied.

Semaj chuckled as she slipped into her navy Gucci cardigan and clasped the straps together on her flat leather ankle boots.

It was a routine that they did at the end of every month. He, Micah and now Semaj came along and met at his Aunt Pam's house for a catered dinner. It kept the operation in order and their innermost circle aware of what was going on in the streets. Three months had passed since Semaj had moved to Baltimore, and business for Vega couldn't have been better. Semaj brought an incredible balance to his life.

When she came down the steps Vega couldn't help but stare at his woman's intriguing walk and the way her deep denim jeans hugged her ample ass and wrapped around her wide hips, appearing thicker than usual. He loved when she wore her hair bone-straight with the part down the middle. It turned him completely on as if he had never seen her before. He grabbed her jacket from the closet and held it out so that she could ease into it and then they headed out.

Once they arrived at Aunt Pam's, Micah had already arrived and was at the table. They took their seats and after Aunt Pam sat the food out they all dug in. They ate, chatted and drank champagne while discussing business, laughing and joking over the Caribbean cuisine as evening turned into late night. Semaj had fit right into his crew seamlessly and they had all embraced her into their family with open arms.

Before Semaj would have considered herself 'hood rich, but with her royalties coming in she had to admit that it was more to life than just being a ghetto girl from the streets. Life was bigger than the 'hood life, and though her man was a drug dealer and still earning 'hood riches, she promised him that she would help him legitimize his paper. Learning so much from Quasim, Semaj used what he'd taught her and instilled it in Vega. She just wasn't a hustler's woman that all the chicks wanted to become. She was a business-minded woman that brought something to the table this go-around.

Vega had been through many women and none of them had urged him to go legit. Their only concerns were getting money from him. But his Semaj was showing him another side of life, and no one could compare to her. She completed him in a way that no one could fill. She made him whole and made him want to become a better man.

Their feelings were mutual. Initially Semaj believed that she needed Vega to help heal her heart because Quasim had been the love of her life, but now she realized the love she shared with Vega was different but just as strong. Vega was her other half... she was his best half. He brought iridescent to what could have been a black and white world for her, and she thanked God every second she could. They had given each other the best three months of their lives. Instead of being treated like a spoiled child, she was his best friend and sometimes sworn enemy in their harmless bouts. With Vega, Semaj didn't feel obligated to be submissive and would curse him out, and they'd battle like foes and he'd still love her in the next moment. She wasn't a pushover whatsoever, speaking her mind without hesitation, and the bond they had was unique and one transcending the average, boyfriend-girlfriend relationship.

"Man, the new shit you got in Auntie... something crazy," Micah said amped. "Dope fiends sayin' we should start calling that shit Pam's magic," he joked.

"You's a fool nephew," Aunt Pam replied with a chuckle. She knew they did have a potent product. She had been selling cocaine since the late eighties and had an out of state plug that had a direct line connected to a Dominican drug family. When her nephew, Vega came aboard she went from moving ounces to pushing keys of coke a month. Business had been great. It was like Vega was born to hustle and gained them clientele and territory in no time. They hadn't looked back since.

"Oh, nigga, I almost forgot to tell you," Micah said. "This nigga with New York plates came through asking about you."

His street instincts kicked in as he took in the information he was receiving. He didn't like shit like this at all. "Looking for me how?"

"Yeah man. Dude was on some reckless, flashy shit in a 760 joint talking out the side of his neck. Like offering niggas in the 'hood them racks if they show 'im where you be or rest ya head, nigga. Talkin' 'bout he try'na link up with you for some business matters. Li'l goonies wasn't having that shit and about six niggas pulled out that ratchet and start busting at the nigga."

"Word?" Vega asked.

"Nigga got away though. Bet he won't come back around *Bodymore* inquiring though. Nigga better stay in New York wit' that shit."

"I don't know who this nigga is but it sounds serious. We all gotta keep our ear to the streets and see if this nigga still asking around. We need to find out as much as possible. Tell niggas if they see anything funny coming through on the block dead it immediately. It's too much money out here for me to be worried about some hatin' ass jack niggas."

"I feel that. And I'ma make sure we nip this bullshit in the bud asap."

Everyone nodded, signifying that this minor problem had to get deaded before it got out of hand.

"It was nice seeing you guys," Semaj said as she hugged everyone before she and Vega took off and headed home.

As soon as they arrived to their crib, Semaj stripped from her clothes and retired to her cozy bed. She was stuffed from her food intake, and not even a minute later she had fallen asleep.

Removing his clothes, Vega stared at his lady attentively and noticed the slight bulge in her stomach. He noticed that it hadn't been there three months ago. He got excited at the thought of being a father for the first time. He remembered her saying she'd missed her menstrual. Being that her periods had been irregular since her youth, they both brushed off the notion. Sliding in beside her, Vega held her in his arms and he slightly rubbed her stomach in small circles until the comfort of her warm body soothed him into a slumber.

Chapter 23

Semaj looked around the upscale boutique that she and Vega owned and smiled in accomplishment. She promised to legitimize his money and that's exactly what she had been doing for the past several months. And like Vega had assumed, Semaj was pregnant. She was now six months and he couldn't wait for his little man to rock with him. Semaj happily took the news in stride and was elated that she'd have two men around to boss around.

The whole ordeal in New York had seemed like a lifetime ago, and Semaj was on a new level. She was more than comfortable and satisfied. Vega was showing her the sort of happiness she never knew existed. Their personalities were one in the same. They both were outgoing and outspoken. Instead of letting a man change her, Semaj had allowed her and the man to change each other. Although he stayed out a lot, Semaj knew he was out hustling and taking care of business, and she understood that because he was always considerate and made time for her. She loved her Vega and Vega loved his Semaj. Nonetheless, the two complemented each other in a way that only they could.

Receiving her residuals, Semaj was smart with her money, a trait she'd learned from Quasim, and took the money to open up a couple small businesses so the dirty money was washed. Her and Vega were a team and even though he was absent from her life for so long, he was her first in everything so that love never wavered. Semaj felt like the luckiest girl in the world. She was having her first child with her first love, her first kiss, the man she had given herself to first, and their love was one for the history books.

Excited about the grand opening of their new upscale seafood restaurant, Semaj turned to her salesgirl. "I appreciate you depositing the money in the night drop box for me. I really gotta make it over to the grand opening and I'm already late."

"Girl, you're fine," her employee waved her off as she straightened up the store.

Semaj grabbed her keys, oversized handbag and headed out of the building. She pulled her phone from her purse and saw that she'd had text messages from Vega. While fumbling through her belongings, she dialed him up.

"What up, baby? Where you at? It's almost eight and you still ain't here," he said eagerly.

"I'm on my way, baby. Don't start without me, Vega."

"You know I'll never do that. C'mon though. We waiting on you. Love you," he said before ending the call.

Throwing her phone back in her shoulder bag, she pressed the unlock button on her key chain as she walked across the graveled parking lot. She slid into her car and pulled out into Baltimore's night traffic.

Turning her music up a few notches, she allowed Trina to fill the interior of her car as she made it over to the restaurant. The lyrics to the song "Always" seemed to fit her current mood in life. She was blessed to be moving in a positive direction, and although some of the things thrown at her would have made an average chick lose their wits, Semaj was still standing. *This life I live is something crazy. But I guess life wouldn't be life if she wasn't a bitch.*

Her thoughts kept her company the entire ride to her newest endeavor. When she arrived, Semaj was surprised at the amount of people who'd showed up to show them love on that cold winter night. After reading the sign "The Lobster House", Semaj didn't know why but suddenly her stomach began to form jittery butterflies. She shook it off as she hugged a few people who recognized her, and made her way over to Vega who was speaking with one of their investors. Local news stations were on the scene, and after the couple cut the red ribbon, they admitted themselves inside. Everything was in good order and the two couldn't be more pleased.

The soaring dining room was exquisite to say the least. From how the floor-to-ceiling ivory drapes hung, to the massive crystal chandelier and the elaborate fittings made the art deco establishment look amazing. It was like living in a dream.

After eating their first meal at their swanky restaurant, Semaj had found herself getting sick and a migraine hit her that seemed to come out of nowhere. Vega had noticed the ill look on her face, and leaned over to whisper in her ear. "You okay? You don't look too good. Our li'l mans a'ight?"

"Yeah, the baby is good. I'm just getting hot." Semaj picked up a napkin to fan herself. "Maybe I need to go home. It's almost time to go anyway."

"I'ma go with you. I'll just have Aunt Pam and the manager stay back and handle things for us."

Semaj shook her head. "No, you stay, baby. This your place and you worked hard to get it. I want you to enjoy every second of it," she said unselfishly.

"Are you sure? 'Cause I'll bounce if you want me to. This shit ain't going nowhere," he replied concerned about her well-being.

"I'm sure. Stay, Vega. Enjoy your success, baby."

"Okay since you ain't feeling good though, I'ma have my people drive you home." Vega walked Semaj out to the car. He kissed her on the forehead and placed his hand over her stomach. He helped her inside and assured her that he would be home shortly.

Once Semaj arrived home, she was too drained to take a shower and got straight into bed. Getting underneath the crumpled satin sheets, a funny feeling passed over her but she dismissed it and closed her eyes in exhaustion. She was almost asleep when her phone began to buzz. Without looking at her caller ID she answered, assuming it was someone checking to see if she'd made it home.

"Hello?"

"Turn on the local news," the person on the other end demanded.

Instantly she broke out into a clammy sweat. Her heart began to beat erratically while her hands shook uncontrollably. Reaching over to retrieve the remote from the nightstand, Semaj turned on the local news station.

"This is Becky Johnson reporting live at what was supposed to be the grand opening of an upscale restaurant here in downtown Baltimore, but has turned into a disaster. An explosion has possibly taken the lives of at least a dozen people. You see behind me is the building where the fire officials are on the scene trying their best to snuff out the fire. Police have no leads as to what the cause of this was, but fire marshals believe there was a bomb planted inside the building. If anyone has any information on this blaze, please contact the local authorities. We'll keep you updated as this tragic story continues."

Semaj couldn't find the words to speak as if they had gotten lost in her throat. She just sat in dead silence. She was stunned. She couldn't believe what her eyes were witnessing. Vega! He was there! How could this be? She knew he couldn't still be there, but her heart told a story of its own. She dialed Vega's phone to no prevail. She pressed end and dialed his two other phones. Again, she received no answer. She held the phone in her hands and was immobile. Her body couldn't move. The sound of her phone ringing urged her body to answer. She hoped like hell that it was Vega to tell her that he was okay.

That wasn't the case though, because as soon as she pressed the icon to speak, Paris voice burst through. "I must say I wish you were in that burning building, but I guess this is even better because I want you to suffer in this world by yourself." Paris said as her voice kept getting louder. "I told you I was gonna get you bitch. I told you I was the wrong bitch to fuck over and out of all people you should've known that."

"I swear, I put this on everything! I'm going to fucking torture you, bitch! You just better hope for your own sake that Vega is good!" she warned.

"Your threats don't scare me, Semaj! Remember, it's me! Paris! And one thing you know that I know, is the real you! And you ain't gangster at all, mama!"

"Yeah, you right. You ain't seen gangsta yet, bitch. You gon' get that toe tag with your name on it fucking with me and mines though," Semaj promised and disconnected the call as she simultaneously popped up. In a hurry, she threw back on her clothes. *I just should've told him to come home with me*, Semaj chastised herself as she grabbed the chrome .25 that he had insisted she carry. *Please let him be okay God.*

Racing down the stairs, Semaj tripped as she tried her hardest to land on her knees. Instead she'd fallen flat onto her stomach as her purse and car keys flew from her hands. Excruciating pain shot through her abdomen, and she felt like something had burst inside of her. A feeling of something sticky leaked from her vagina. Her mind raced as she held onto her stomach and without warning, panic hit her and she crumpled up where she lay still unable to move.

Semaj knew she had to get up for her baby's sake, causing her motherly instincts to kick in. All she had to do was gain enough strength to call for help. Gathering all the will she had within her, she crawled over to her cell phone. As if her hands were in sync with the buzz of her phone, it started to ring. Semaj was in sheer agony and pissed. She didn't have time for Paris's games when her child's life was at stake. On top of that, she still did not know her man's condition.

"Don't call my fuckin' phone!" Semaj shouted forcefully, and almost hung up until she heard a different voice on the opposite end.

"Is this Semaj Richardson?" a baritone male voice with a distinguished accent asked in concern.

"Hello!"

"Is this Semaj Richardson?"

"Who is this?" she asked in noticeable pain.

"Is everything alright? This is your grandfather…Gio… this is Giorgio Milano."

"Grand… *Poppa!*" Semaj cried out in wails of horror and fear, but for some reason a sense of relief calmed her nerves.

Gio put in a request to one of his most trusted members of the Milano Family to pick up Semaj, and he stared out of the hospital window with eagerness nagging at his inner linings. He could not believe that he had finally located his granddaughter. It had been so long but even during the longest, most hectic times, Gio had never given up on his quest. Many battles had been fought and many wars had been won, but all of that meant nothing when his flesh and blood seemed to have been lost in the cruel world.

But as he had anticipated the day for so many years, Gio couldn't have been any happier, and once he put Murder Mitch out of his misery, his days would be more relaxed and his nights would be well rested. It had been years since he had a good night's sleep, but tonight that would sure change. The bags that had shaped around the skin beneath his eyes and the permanent stress lines that winkled his creased forehead was indication of the fifty plus years Gio had been involved in the streets. Even with the many losses and federal case dismissals surrounding his organization, Gio still wasn't near retirement. He lived by the mob creed: Only way out of the mafia was by his death, and like his grandfather, Marriano Milano who would be turning 101 years old on his next birthday, he was never giving up drugs or illegal gambling.

Jarred from his thoughts, Gio turned around and approached Murder Mitch's bedside. It had been a long time since Murder Mitch had worked for him, and as his henchmen stood to the right of him he knew that he was only seconds from having the worthless man's life ended. He failed to protect his daughter and his men would put Murder Mitch out of his misery with a simple nod of the head. The only reason that he had allowed his heart to still pump mechanically was because of his attempt to get information concerning his granddaughter.

With Semaj found though there was no need for Gio to wait on Murder Mitch to come out of his coma. The shocking phone call he'd received from an associate linked to the drug trade, his granddaughter had turned up. His recovery no longer was a necessity.

Murder Mitch was barely holding on to his life, and with a mere pull of the life support cords, he would meet his maker, Lucifer Satan. There was nothing that he wanted more than to end his life. Gio had trusted him with his daughter's life, and Murder Mitch had failed him terribly as Kasey's protector. Murder Mitch killed many men on his behalf, kidnapped many children on his account and even fed mob wives who husbands had betrayed him to the alligators. But none of that mattered because breaking a promise was considered breaking his loyalty. To a man like Gio, besides being a rat, nothing was worse than a dishonorable man. Gio was from the old school and played by the rules of the mob. Murder Mitch definitely had to go.

As he delighted himself in the idea of Murder Mitch's life coming to an end a look of uncertainty spread across his face. *Allowing him to die peacefully will be too easy,* Gio thought emotionless. He wanted Murder Mitch to see him once he awoke from his comatose state. That way Murder Mitch would know exactly who sent him to hell. Gio didn't want him to die painless. He wanted his death to be painfully cruel, and torturing him to his last breath would give Gio some sort of satisfaction. He had to suffer and if Gio had to wait twenty years for him to come to, he would, and when Murder Mitch's eyes opened the terrorizing and torment would begin instantly. Like it had stormed for forty days and forty nights during the days of Noah, Murder Mitch would thunderously endure the deadly workings of a Mafia Boss. For forty days and forty nights of brutality, he wanted him to die a painful, cruel death in the name of Giorgio Milano himself. He would burn to char and his remains would forever blend in with the dirt. Then, his daughter's soul could finally rest in peace.

Chapter 24

Gio walked inside the workout room with the daily newspaper in hand. Nas and Damian Marley's collaborated album "Distant Relative" was blaring from the speakers while Semaj ran high speed on the treadmill. She loathed running on the exercise equipment. She felt the old-fashioned calisthenics gave off better results. But Gio was extra protective of his granddaughter, and kept her secluded in one of his many vacation homes where she'd been since he contacted her for his personal reasons. She'd been laying low in the opulence of his lakefront estate outside of Connecticut.

Perspiration seeped from Semaj's pores while her ponytail drenched in sweat. Gio knew his granddaughter's intense workout behavior was due to the stress that was weighing down on her. She wanted to get back to work, but in the same breath, she wanted to stay away until they were sure that a doctor could reconstruct Vega's burns. Turns out that he was one of the fortunate that was just exiting the building when the bomb had detonated, and although he had suffered severe third degree burns, he made it out alive.

Gio picked up the remote and turned the surround sound down. He walked over to her with a wide smile. The expression had been there since the first moment his henchman opened the limo doors and reunited him with his granddaughter. Gio stood directly in front of her where their eyes shared in the moment. The last eighteen years had been hard for him because he wasn't able to locate his grandchild, but after all the time that had passed, and all the many attempts, Gio ironically received a phone call from one of his close business associates that informed him his quest in searching for his long lost granddaughter would finally come to an end.

May the Lord rest her soul Semaj silently thanked Aunt Pamela for helping her come in contact with her grandfather. She was one of the ones that hadn't had a chance to make it out of the explosion alive.

"Hey, sweetheart. I have some good and great news. Which do you want to hear first?"

Semaj looked at the aging man and beamed widely as she found him to be so amusing at times when it came to her. For the last five months, he'd been at her every beck and call, and believe it or not, in this short time her G-Poppa was damn near making up for all the years that he was absent from her life. She thought before that she'd been spoiled rotten, but nothing compared to the love a girl receives from her wealthy grandfather. Semaj thought for a moment how her life could've been completely different had her old man not hidden her from Gio. But then again, as he still never forgave Mitch, Semaj totally understood that her father wanted to love and be near his own daughter. She knew her father meant no harm, but she also knew that she would have grown up to be a different woman. She wondered if she would have even been exposed to the street life. "The good news," she laughed as she slowed the treadmill down a bit to jog.

"Well, I've been able to get in contact with one of the best plastic surgeons in the world that specializes in intensified burns. He has done some of the best reconstructive surgeries around and he can start as early as Monday morning."

"Are you serious?" she exclaimed, excitedly. "How much is this going to run us?"

"Serious as can be. And don't worry about the bill, my dear. This is on me. It's already paid in full."

"Thanks, G-Poppa. You're the best!"

"Only for my favorite girl in the world," he winked pleasantly. "Now, are you ready for the great news?"

"What could be better than that news, Grand Poppa?"

He smiled slyly as he held out the newspaper for Semaj to grab. Pressing the downward button on the machine, Semaj brought the treadmill to a complete stop. "Oh my God! Poppa, you didn't!" Semaj screamed in astonishment as she read the newspaper article headline with a huge picture of Paris's face on the front page:

Twenty-four Year Old Girl Found Dead, And The Slain
Appears As A Gory Mafia Hit!

"I told you now that you are under my supervision a person will never be able to harm or touch you, ever. You're not accessible, my darling. Know that you are in the company of great care from now on."

Grabbing the small towel that draped the rail, Semaj wiped the sweat from her face. "Did you share this news with Nathan?"

"No. I thought you should be the one to tell him."

"I don't know how I will ever be able to repay you, grandfather!" Semaj stepped from the treadmill and hugged his neck tightly.

"Just continue to be my sweet granddaughter and that in itself is all the payback I need." He gently cupped her chin and leaned in to kiss her right cheek, repeating the gesture and kissing her left cheek. "We are having a dinner party tonight, here, for your great grandfather, Marriano. It's his birthday. It's time you meet the rest of the family."

"You think, G-Poppa?" She loved to call him that. "I don't know if I'm ready to meet everyone just yet."

"I think the time is perfect, beautiful." His Dominican accent came off in a heavy convincing tone. "They've all been dying to meet you. But if you still don't feel comfortable just yet, I'll postpone it."

"Oh no, G-Poppa. You've convinced me. I do want to get to know them. Tonight it is."

"Wonderful!" he replied.

"I'll be there. But let me go check on Vega and the baby. I'll also fill Vega in on what happened to Paris. " Semaj hugged her grandfather one more time, "Thanks again, for everything," she said with a smile of gratification.

"You are family and there's no need for thanks, Semaj. You are the Mafia Princess, which makes you privileged."

Semaj smiled to herself as she walked down the long corridor. She made her way through the kitchen, and out of the sliding glass door and onto the deck. But in actuality, Semaj still wasn't aware of the massive power and authority that stood behind her family's name. There was a lot that she would have to learn about her heritage.

It was a beautiful, July sundown evening with a windy breeze and an unusual chill for the summer weather. A light draft kissed Semaj's face as she made her way over to her family on the patio. Their newborn baby, Niran squirmed around in his father's arms as Vega patted him back to his peaceful slumber and Semaj sat in the wooden chair beside him. Their son was the reason she smiled every day and with Vega in their lives, Semaj felt that everything that she'd been through was worth what stood before her today, and she'd won at the game of life. Before her child, Semaj never knew a love like this existed, and no feeling in the world could ever compare to the way she felt inside and Vega made it clear that no matter what he'd be there until the end of time.

Semaj felt like this was her payday. Her nemesis had finally been defeated. She felt on top of the world and untouchable. She had it all—her man, their son, and now finally a family. A big family. A Mafia family. Her grandfather treated his great grandchild as if he was his favorite little man in the world. Semaj promised Tala in prayer that she'd allow their sons to grow up together. She was going to make certain of that. She loved what her life represented now. She had never known that she was a part of something so superior. And after all the years of the struggle, at the end of the day, Semaj Richardson was the princess of her own royal family. She was street royalty!

"Vega, I wonder where would I be had you not saved me."

"There's no need to wonder about that. 'Member nothing happens by chance. So if it wasn't that way, trust it would've been another way, baby."

"Great way to put it. We was gon' be back together regardless, somehow, someway!" she blushed, feeling thankful for all she had been given in life.

"No doubt, baby."

"No doubt, huh?" Semaj laughed as they stood watching dusk set upon the gloomy sky where a rainstorm seemed to be approaching. "Let's go get ready for tonight. It looks like rain is coming. It's time to finally meet the prestigious, fam!" Semaj excitedly boasted. "And I gotta tell you all about the good news!"

The sky was pitch black with a dark gray thundercloud amidst the sky, which was distinguishable even through the darkness of the late night, but not even the rain pouring from the darkened sky would will Paris to perch up from sitting Indian-style in front of her sister's tombstone. A stream of tears gushed from her eyes. Her identical twin sister was dead, and it was all because of her. Egypt was a good girl…the good twin that hadn't fallen victim to the streets. She was in college working on her degree and she'd been robbed of her innocent life.

Somehow, Egypt had been identified as her in life and in death, because her death certificate had Paris's government name printed across it and not her sister's. It hurt her like hell that innocent Egypt was a casualty for the life she led in the streets. She was her better half, and the one that was supposed to make something out of herself. Egypt was the only one, besides their big brother that hadn't turned their back on her when the other family said she was responsible for her parents' killing. With the family not taking her in, Egypt still snuck and talked to her every chance she got while Paris went from group home to foster care and back again.

Why did this have to happen to you? Paris continued to cry out as she felt the moisture of the grass from the morning dew. It caused her to slightly shiver from the coldness pressing against her skin.

Her sister was the only human on earth that she cared for more than she cared for herself, and with her gone it had struck a nerve that couldn't be fixed. Nothing could ever take away the pain she was enduring and the obsession she had to make Semaj suffer. Before Paris didn't have all of her marbles, but now the girl was mental patient insane, and the only place for her was the crazy hospital.

"*Beep! Beep!*"

The sounds of the horn snapped her back into reality. Paris hadn't even realized it, but the rain had picked up tremendously and it was now storming and the winds were blustering. With minimum lighting at the cemetery, Paris still managed to see the window rolling down from the Yukon truck. "C'mon, Paris. It's pouring down out here, little sis."

As she rose, Paris ignored her brother who had already made it back to the truck. She leaned forward and kissed her sister's tombstone. She had paid significantly by losing her sister, but one thing for sure and two things for certain, Semaj Richardson would pay for all the pain she brought to her life. "E, on everything, Semaj and her family is gonna pay someday for your death. I won't stop until my heart stops and the casket drops, sis!"

"*Beep! Beep! Beep! Beep! Beep! Beep!*"

"I'm coming, damn!" Paris yelled irritably. Her hair stuck to her face as she jogged to the car, while all she could contemplate was the day that Semaj would see her in the flesh, alive and healthy. She hopped in the car, slammed the door like a crazed madwoman and turned to her brother. "Muthafuck, Gabe! Can a bitch grieve in muthafuckin' peace! Nigga, gotdamn!"

One Year Later

The man stood outside on the balcony of his villa overlooking three miles of white sand and crystal clear water. The sound of the waves crashing against the rocks had become a source of serenity in a world full of chaos. He picked up a magazine that had been sitting on top of the glass table for the last week. Everyday he spent hours looking at one particular image. It was the wedding picture of Nathan "Vega" Giles and Semaj Richardson. The magazine had done a feature on the newlywed couple and the bride dressed in all white was a vision of perfection. The man stared at the photo for a few minutes longer and as if unable to control his disgust any longer he ripped out the picture, balled it up and tossed it into the deep sea. *I'll be back to claim what's mine* he thought before turning around and going back inside his home.

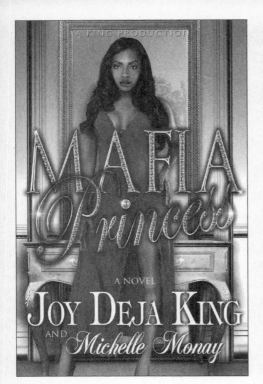

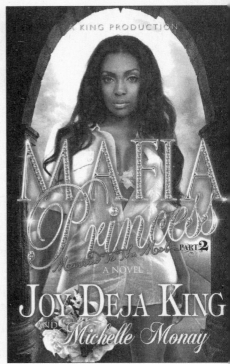

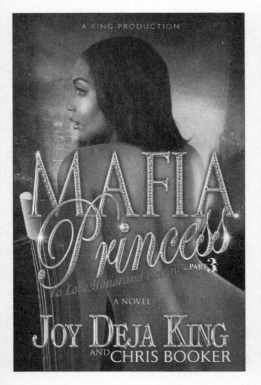

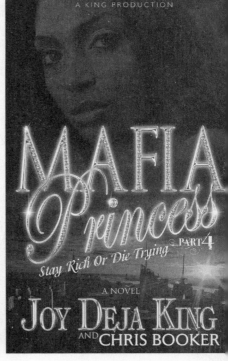

I'm Gettin' That Helicopter Money...

Bad Bitch

JOY DEJA KING

Aaliyah

I came into the world surrounded by wealth and privilege. I could've been anything I wanted to be and I was...I was a Bad Bitch on my way to gettin' that helicopter money and I was loving every minute of it. I chose to walk on the same path as my Grandfather and Father but in different shoes. As I thought about my Grandfather, someone I respected and loved more than just about anybody else in this world, there was one thing I would do differently than him. If I had my way, Maya would've been dead by now, but there was no doubt in my mind that I would accomplish the very thing no one had been able to do, including my Mother. I would make sure Maya took her last breath and was six feet under, sooner rather than later.

I stood in front of the arched window, soaking in the breathtaking views of downtown Miami's skyline from over 250 feet of open bay frontage. Watching as the wind ushered the waves towards the shore, with the sun's golden light shining on the rippling water was the closest I had gotten to serenity in what seemed like many years. My life had me on a nonstop ride of one disaster after another. Starting with being accused of Sway's murder and then sitting in jail until I stood trial. Then my Grandfather being shot and in a coma, my parent's getting separated to breaking up with Amir which was still taking a toll on me emotionally after all these months. So many things in my life had changed, but so many other things stayed the same.

"Are you ready to go?"

"Dale, you startled me," I gasped, when I heard his voice. I turned around and he was standing in the door entrance.

"I apologize. Wherever your mind was, it had to be in deep

thought."

"I guess you could say that."

"Is it anything you want to talk about?"

"No, I'm good."

"You sure? You know you can talk to me about anything. Remember you're my protégé. It's in my best interest to always make sure nothing is keeping you from being at the top of your game."

"I understand that but there's no need to worry. I won't disappoint you or myself. I'm in this game to win and I won't accept anything less than that."

"Then I take it you're ready for our meeting so lets go."

"Of course I am," I grinned, grabbing my purse off the living room table.

We headed outside towards the awaiting car and like always I looked up at the towering palm trees and a smile crept across my face. Miami had become a place that I treasured because everything about it gave me something that New York/New Jersey never could and that was peace.

"Do you feel prepared for the meeting?" Dale questioned, once again taking me away from my private thoughts. I knew he meant well but I was looking forward to having some much needed time alone.

"Yes. We've already gone over this. You're going to lead the conversation. I'm going to sit and listen and when you're ready for me to give additional critical information, you'll casually lean forward and that will be my cue to step in," I stated with an underlying annoyance in my tone.

"No need to get irritated," Dale said, placing his hand on my upper left thigh. "You don't seem quite yourself today so you can't blame me for being concerned. You know how important this meeting is."

"I get that, but have I ever dropped the ball on anything that has to do with business?"

"No and I wanna make sure you keep it that way."

I turned and gazed out the backseat window as the driver made his way to Indian Creek Island for our meeting. I didn't respond to what Dale said because I couldn't deny that I was "off" today. As much stress as the East Coast brought me it was home and I missed my family and more importantly my heart ached for Amir.

"Is it Maya, is that what has your mind someplace else?"

I simply nodded my head yes. I figured that sounded much better than having to confess to Dale I was yearning for my ex.

"I already told you when the time was right Maya would be handled. You need to let that go for now. We have much bigger and significant deals on the table right now that have to be dealt with."

"You're right. I just don't want Maya to slip away. She's been a thorn in my family's lives for far too long and the Peaches situation was the final nail in her coffin. Even the thought of her slipping through my fingers, burns me up inside."

"That's not gonna happen. I got my people keeping track of all her movements. Like I promised you, when the time is right, I will bring Maya to you and you can personally take pleasure in ending her life once and for all. You have to believe that."

"I do. I do believe that," I nodded, looking back out the window. I had learned never to doubt Dale's word. Each thing that he promised me thus far, he delivered it and more. Proof of that was being shown to me once again, as the driver made his way up the long elegant landscaped driveway at 12 Indian Creek Drive. This home was located on Dade County's most prestigious Private Island. I'm talking homes that start at 30 million and go nowhere but up. Juan Alvarez, the head of one of the most profitable and deadliest Mexican Cartels, owned the palatial estate we were now entering. This was the man that would take me to making that helicopter money, purchasing private jets, buying islands and shit like that.

After our ordeal with Peaches and I had to murder that bitch, I became completed fixated on two things: Killing Maya and making money. Dale promised that he would make sure I achieved both. When I realized Maya had set me up to be killed, she was at the top of my list to fall. Dale convinced me to hold back and let that shit settle for a while. At first I resisted his suggestion but I had watched Dale and I respected how he moved in handling his business so I listened to his logic and followed it. He told me to focus my energy on stacking paper because the money would give me all the power I needed, to eliminate Maya and just about anybody else I felt was a threat to me or my family.

After several months of soaking up any and every business move Dale and his brother Emory made, I became the female version of them which made me all the more lethal. I became meticulous with how I handled money, drugs and people we did business with and the more moves I made I wanted to make even bigger ones. Because men dominated the drug business, I had no problem using the female persuasion to my advantage. I dangled it just enough to keep my creditability intact but to also allow our business associates to lower their wall enough for me to get the information I needed to close better deals. It was that calculated maneuvering that put the name Juan Alvarez on my radar. Everyone including Emory swore it would be impossible to get to him. The only person that didn't flinch was Dale. Like me he loved a challenge and like he promised, against all the odds here we were.

When we pulled through the iron gates in every direction you turned there appeared to be armed guards. He had an army watching over him like he was the President of the United States but in the world of drugs I guess you could say Juan Alvarez was.

"This place is unbelievable," I commented, as we got closer to his massive mansion. I had lived and seen many stunning homes in my short lifetime but this place was something completely different. The sprawling European design was beyond breathtaking.

"That it is. But if we play our cards right we'll be able to have one just like it," Dale stated, with unwavering confidence. I couldn't help but smile because like always he made me a believer.

In the brief moment from me glancing over at Dale and smiling at his comment, before our driver could even step out and open the door for us, there was an armed guard on both sides of the car doing that job for him. They immediately began patting us down and I looked over at Dale and he nodded his head letting me know to go with the flow. I planned on doing that anyway. We had come this far I wasn't about to fuck it up now.

"Follow us," the guard that had just finished patting Dale down said, directing us towards the front entrance. A 40 ft. hand-painted ceiling with gold leaf accents in the foyer greeted us. I wanted to gasp as we walked through what had to be over 40,000 square ft. of what I would describe as a grand and majestic masterpiece. After what felt like a never-ending marathon we finally ended up outside. Off in the distance I noticed the dock with a huge yacht and a private lagoon. But it was the over 50-foot long mosaic tiled 24k gold lined pool that truly had me in awe. The water seemed to be calling my name but that feeling didn't last long because once again there were armed guards posted everywhere. Seeing them took all sense of peace or relaxation away but I assumed that was the purpose they were there to serve.

"Mr. Alvarez, your guest have arrived," the guard that had led us in announced. I still couldn't see him because he was sitting down on a high gloss white circular sofa with his back turned to us. I noticed him signaling the guard by putting up one finger. "He's on a call. He'll be with you both shortly," the guard informed us.

I appreciated having a little extra time before we were formally introduced because out of nowhere a burst of nervousness crept up on me. That was so not my style as Dale had taught me how to remain calm even under the most strenuous situations. He warned me that keeping a composed demeanor could be the difference between living and dying in certain predicaments. I quickly closed my eyes and let out a soft breath to center myself and regain control. In that instant I realized where all the anxiety was coming from. I was about to meet the man that would change my life forever.

A King Production presents...

A Novel

JOY DEJA KING

A KING PRODUCTION

Dior Comes Home...

Rich
or
Famous
Part 2

JOY DEJA KING

Lorenzo
Prologue

Lorenzo stepped out of his black Bugatti Coupe and entered the non-descript building in East Harlem. Normally, Lorenzo would have at least one henchman with him, but he wanted complete anonymity. When Lorenzo made his entrance, the man he planned on hiring was patiently waiting.

"I hope you came prepared for what I need."

"I wouldn't have wasted my time if I hadn't," Lorenzo stated, before pulling out two pictures from a manila envelope and tossing it on the table.

"This is her?"

"Yes, her name is Alexus. Study this face very carefully, 'cause this is the woman you're going to bring to me, so I can kill."

"Are you sure you don't want me to handle it? Murder is included in my fee."

"I know, but personally killing this back stabbing snake is a gift to myself"

"Who is the other woman?"

"Her name is Lala."

"Do you want her dead, too?"

"I haven't decided. For now, just find her whereabouts and any other pertinent information. She also has a young daughter. I want you to find out how the little girl is doing. That will determine whether Lala lives or dies."

"Is there anybody else on your hit list?"

"This is it for now, but that might change at any moment. Now, get on your job, because I want results ASAP," Lorenzo demanded, before tossing stacks of money next to the photos.

"I don't think there's a need to count. I'm sure it's all there."

"No doubt and you can make even more, depending on how quickly I see results."

"I appreciate the extra incentive."

"It's not for you, it's for me. Everyone that is responsible for me losing the love of my life will pay in blood. The sooner the better."

Lorenzo didn't say another word and instead made his exit. He came and delivered; the rest was up to the killer he hired. But Lorenzo wasn't worried, he was just one of the many killers on his payroll hired to do the exact same job. He wanted to guarantee that Alexus was delivered to him alive. In his heart, he not only blamed Alexus and Lala for getting him locked up, but held both of them responsible for Dior taking her own life. Lorenzo promised himself, as he sat in his jail cell, that once he got out, if need be, he would spend the rest of his life making sure both women received the ultimate retribution.

A KING PRODUCTION

Baller
Bitches
VOLUME 2
PARTS 4-6
A NOVEL

JOY DEJA KING

A KING PRODUCTION

Young Diamond Books

PRESENTS

A young adult urban tale

Ride Wit' Me

2

JOY DEJA KING

Power

NO ONE MAN SHOULD HAVE ALL THAT POWER...BUT THERE WERE TWO

JOY DEJA KING

A King Production
Order Form

A King Production
P.O. Box 912
Collierville, TN 38027
www.joydejaking.com
www.twitter.com/joydejaking

Name: _____

Address: _____

City/State: _____

Zip: _____

QUANTITY	TITLES	PRICE	TOTAL
_____	Bitch	$15.00	_____
_____	Bitch Reloaded	$15.00	_____
_____	The Bitch Is Back	$15.00	_____
_____	Queen Bitch	$15.00	_____
_____	Last Bitch Standing	$15.00	_____
_____	Superstar	$15.00	_____
_____	Ride Wit' Me	$12.00	_____
_____	Stackin' Paper	$15.00	_____
_____	Trife Life To Lavish	$15.00	_____
_____	Trife Life To Lavish II	$15.00	_____
_____	Stackin' Paper II	$15.00	_____
_____	Rich or Famous	$15.00	_____
_____	Bitch A New Beginning	$15.00	_____
_____	Mafia Princess Part 1	$15.00	_____
_____	Mafia Princess Part 2	$15.00	_____
_____	Mafia Princess Part 3	$15.00	_____
_____	Boss Bitch	$15.00	_____
_____	Baller Bitches Vol. 1	$15.00	_____
_____	Bad Bitch	$15.00	_____
_____	Princess Fever "Birthday Bash"	$9.99	_____

Shipping/Handling (Via Priority Mail) $6.50 1-2 Books, $8.95 3-4 Books add $1.95 for ea. Additional book.

Total: $_____ FORMS OF ACCEPTED PAYMENTS: Certified or government issued checks and money Orders, all mail in orders take 5-7 Business days to be delivered.